$\mathcal{V}$OICES OF THE $\mathcal{S}$OUTH

BIRD OF PARADISE

BIRD
OF
PARADISE

·

Vicki Covington

·

LOUISIANA STATE UNIVERSITY PRESS
BATON ROUGE

08 07 06 05 04 03 02 01 00 99
5 4 3 2 1

Library of Congress Cataloging-in-Publication Data

Covington, Vicki.
    Bird of Paradise / Vicki Covington.
        p.   cm.
    ISBN 0-8071-2386-2 (pbk. : alk. paper)
    I. Title.
    PS3553.0883B5   1999
    813'.54—dc21   98-51108
                                                        CIP

The paper in this book meets the guidelines for permanence and
durability of the Committee on Production Guidelines for Book
Longevity of the Council on Library Resources. ∞

ACKNOWLEDGMENTS

Special thanks to the National Endowment for the Arts for their generous and timely support; to Jack Marsh, Mary Nell Burton, and Jim Marsh for what they remember; to Dennis Covington, Katherine Marsh, and Nancy Nicholas for giving sustenance; to Ashley Covington and Laura Covington for their patience; to Jean Harmon, Sheila Howard, Binky Urban, George Hodgman; and to all the friends of Bill W.

•

FOR

Zelma Huey Marsh

AND IN MEMORY OF

Eva Warren Jennings

AND

Ruby Huey Byrd

•

I will restore to you even the years the locust has eaten.

—JOEL 2:25

BIRD OF PARADISE

·

1

·

THE MORNING DINAH died was cold. I'd gone over to her place early, happy, I suppose you might say, that winter was near. I like the colors of fall, and there's nothing in the world sad in knowing that leaves are dying. Same with people if you're a believer, because you can rightfully say—if you're a believer—that people are like trees: they don't actually die, they just appear to be shedding all color. Of course, this theory breaks down when you're viewing a tree that's sure enough dead, whose leaves don't return even in spring. But I can't trouble myself with exceptions to the rule. Suffice it to say that I have the faith of a child—one that easily surrenders itself to the simple metaphors of nature. I'd hate to be an intellectual. My baby son, Jackie, who's a preacher and also teaches college in west Florida, may be one. I'm not sure. I can say for certain that he asks of himself great, troubling questions. "Doubts are steppingstones to higher faith," I always taught him, but Jackie has taken this to the nth degree. It's all right. His church is interdenominational, and, being Florida and all, they got a right to ask questions. Some are Yankees, too, and it's best to let a Yankee hold on to his or her skeptical fears rather than push for a more lenient and lighthearted faith, says Carmen Dabbs, my best friend, who was married to a handsome and charming Yankee for fifty-three years. Despite the fact he lived in the South all his married life, he remained cautious in his embrace of God. I must say, though, he was one of the most solid men I've ever known, a friend of steadfast love. And you always knew where you stood with him, unlike, I hate to say, a lot of us Southerners who don't speak our mind.

I had no idea Dinah was sick. I knew she was depressed—a hard, cold depression that some widows like Dinah can't shake. It's like when their husbands die they're thrown into a vat of molasses, and the struggle to swim, oh, even to stand, to move, to plain walk through a day, is virtually impossible. The sticky stuff—grief—just glues your arms to your sides so that even the weight of a hairbrush being lifted to your head is painful. I suppose. I've never experienced this. Scotty, my husband, was a drunk, and the death of a drunk makes for another story. But Dinah'd say on some spring mornings, to me, "I just can't lift that brush to my hair."

During her youth, Dinah wore her hair in a sweetheart bob. She looked like Mama, with those sharp features and brown eyes. I was Papa made over, with blue pools for eyes and a less defined face, one that's more easily prone to mold itself to the emotion at hand. Dinah was steady. She didn't marry until she was forty. If Mama hadn't died, maybe Dinah might have married earlier. But she felt, I suppose, responsible for keeping Papa, especially after he lost a leg in the mines and was confined to a wheelchair. It wasn't like today with all the curbs smoothed off for wheelchairs, and houses with ramps. "Wheelchair accessible" was a yet-to-be-invented way of thinking. Oh, the changes I've lived to see, and if you don't believe God works in mysterious ways, witness what George Wallace ultimately did for those crippled and in wheelchairs in Alabama. Why, I bet we got more ramps in this state than anywhere in the country. He poured money galore into rehabilitation, according to my grandbaby, Jackie's daughter, who's a social worker, but that's not to say George is forgiven for his sins, though he is, of course, in God's eyes forgiven if he's humbly asked for it. I had no use for the man, nor did Jackie, but my aforementioned grandbaby, who was born in 1963 and never knew the evil firsthand, caused me to reconsider. To say George Wallace in Maryland was like Saul on the road to Damascus is stretching the point, but you understand what I'm getting at. God's always got something up his sleeve.

So, Dinah was single and lived with Papa in the old homestead after Mama died. She moved with the grace of a devoted daughter, placing the linens just so, dusting the piano daily, displaying Mama's doilies and quilts with no apology rather than considering them old-fashioned and unworthy of show, wheeling Papa to the porch on summer evenings, and wearing that sweetheart bob into middle age, because it was something Papa liked. I was his baby, Dinah was Mama's. That was no secret. But Dinah didn't appear to mind being the one to ultimately nurse him. Indeed, she liked it. And, too, she knew I was busy being married to a drunk—if you don't think that's a full-time occupation, just try it—and raising Jackie. Sometimes it seems like the women are all part of a commune designed to take care of the men, and it really doesn't matter who tends to who. But, granted, I have a distorted view of life in this regard. Carmen, for instance, having been married to a solid Yankee and not a Southern drunk, has no use for this kind of matriarchal view. "That's a little sexist, Honey, don't you think?" Honey isn't my given name, but everyone has called me that since girlhood. It has its pros and cons.

Dinah married a man named Winston Bluet. They'd go skating or stargazing or caroling—those odd little activities so very foreign to a couple like Scotty and me who spent long, arduous evenings fighting over liquor. Who's to say who was more or less happy, Dinah or me? I was married to a drunk man whom I loved with passionate suffering; Dinah married Winston Bluet, a mannered, manicured man who was under psychiatric care for being just too nice for his own good, or that's how I saw it, at least. Dinah loved Winston, though, till death and even more after death. So, she had a blissful marriage, then a brief, wretched widowhood, unreconcilable grief being the stain that love leaves, the legacy of a happy partnership. I, on the other hand, had a tormented marriage and have had, since Scotty's death thirty years ago, an unexpectedly enriching widowhood. Who's to say? Dinah is, according to the believers of which I am one, reunited with Winston. Heaven only knows what my reunion with Scotty will be like. If God has gotten him sober—and only God can do that, I learned in Alanon—then maybe we can have a life together in the afterlife.

I wasn't thinking of any of this the morning of Dinah's death. Though it was a day to honor the dead, I was more concerned with the elements. It was unseasonably cold for November in Alabama. I went to pick her up at seven, early I know, but we had a lot to do. It was Veterans Day, and Dinah wanted to place flowers on Papa's and Winston's graves. Papa wasn't in a war, but that didn't matter to Dinah. She was the kind to send presents even when it wasn't a holiday. Winston Bluet had fought in World War I, and Dinah had paid almost fifty dollars for his graveside arrangement. She was crying, standing on the porch, wearing a red cardigan, when I got there.

"Oh, Dinah," I said as I climbed the steps to the old homestead. Since Winston died she'd given the rockers to charity and let the plants go. The porch was bare. Still, the old place had a singular beauty, a solitary light, despite the wasteland of junkmarts that were creeping like ivy toward it. Papa's five acres contained the home gracefully, though, and from the busy, well-traveled road the old home still had serenity.

Dinah was standing by the black wrought-iron banister.

"What is it, hon?" I asked her. The red cardigan was draped over her, worn like a cape rather than a sweater, buttoned at the very top as if to strangle Dinah's thin neck. The sleeves hung limp. Dinah's hands were clasped as if in prayer. Her hair wasn't combed, but looked like she'd sprayed it. The result was that it had the texture of broomstraw.

"Oh, Cissy," I said and patted her brown strawy hair. I called Dinah this—Cissy—sometimes.

Dinah's nervous fingers flew to her hair.

"I can't get the brush through it," she said.

"Come on in, Cissy. Let me try," I said.

Inside, the old home was immaculate. The piano was dusted, the grandfather clock erect, Mama's rug just where it'd been for ninety years, the china cabinet's glass free from nary a thumb-print. The place held the scent of lavender. We went to the bed-room, and I had Dinah sit on the bench by the vanity. I got her ivory brush, wet it, and gently combed her brown—it was dyed—hair.

"You got some bobby pins?" I asked her, but didn't wait for an answer. Instead, I rummaged through the drawer, which was slightly dusty from loose face powder. I made some pin curls and dabbed them with rosewater. I looked at her chiseled, sweet face in the mirror. I doted on Dinah when we were young. She was the baby.

"Now," I said, "when we get to the cemetery, we'll take these down and you'll have curls."

"Winston likes that," Dinah said.

"What?" I asked.

"Curls."

It got under my skin a bit when she'd refer to Winston in pres-ent tense—"Winston likes that"—but it wasn't grating. And, at that moment, I had no idea Dinah was going to die. Had I known, I might have tossed off my irritation over her lingering involve-ment with Winston. I might have fretted more lovingly over the pin curls, appreciated the smell of her rosewater, or held her tiny hands. But all I knew was that it was Veterans Day, a cold No-vember morning, and we were going to the cemetery. It was some-thing we'd done for years on all the commemorative holidays.

But you know how it is after somebody dies. You play the last scene over and over like an old hymn. Granted, the vanity, ivory brush, and pin curls weren't my last scene with Dinah. It was just the one I replay often because it held the uncaptured moment when I might have held Dinah like a baby and told her the dark secrets of love. I didn't, though. And, naturally, I know it's good I didn't, because what on earth would Dinah have thought—me, Honey, the stoic, falling all over her on Veterans Day morning with a flood of craziness. Why, it would've scared the living day-lights out of her. She was the excitable type.

So, we rode on to the cemetery, Dinah carrying in her lap the fifty-dollar arrangement for Winston's grave. The pitiful spray of daisies for Papa's lay at her feet on the floorboard. I stopped at the florist and bought equal-sized sprays of red, white, and blue carnations made especially for this holiday for Papa and Scotty. I parked by the church, and Dinah commented on the new Family Life Suite we added last spring. Since Winston's death, I'd tried to get her involved with our Saturday-morning quilting or bingo or the senior citizens' choir, but to no avail.

The cemetery is set on a hill, an awkward hill that's hard to maneuver when you're at a funeral, grieving in high heels that sink incessantly into the loose soil. It's so steep on the east side where Carmen's husband is buried that there's some concern over things washing away. I'm truly considering cremation, but Jackie, so far, won't hear of it. Being a preacher, he's attached to gravesides, I reckon.

The reason I carry on so over the steep hill is because I can't help but fear that this was what killed Dinah's heart. We climbed on up to Winston's and Scotty's graves—they're kind of close to each other—and Dinah did fine. Calling forth the grace she inherited from Mama, she placed Winston's fifty-dollar arrangement on his grave with dignity. She didn't cry. We strode on over to Papa's. She knelt to place her spray of daisies, and, just as I was bending over to place, beside hers, my spray of carnations, Dinah shot me a glance I'd like to forget someday. It was the face of a startled, bewildered woman. Death had seized her, and she hadn't yet recognized her captor. All she knew was she'd been grabbed up.

"What is it, Cissy?" I asked her, dropping my carnations. "What *is* it?"

She said one thing to me. She said, "I can't talk to you," as if I were suddenly the alien, and then her eyes lost their fright and she smiled like a woman being seduced. I've seen a lot of people die, but Dinah's dying was the most startling. "Would you call it mystical, Mother?" Jackie asked me when I described it to him. No, it was simply breathtaking and odd. To be honest, I firmly believe she was already on the other side when she said, "I can't talk to you." That's what was so eerie—a test of my faith, because things like this can be either frightening or beautiful, and I chose the beautiful. If it'd been anyone but Dinah speaking to me from heaven, I might have been scared. But, you know, my own sister.

Naturally, I called for help and ran, the best I could in that eroding topsoil, to the Family Life Suite (I was wearing tennis shoes), dialed the paramedics, and ran back to Dinah. I didn't know CPR, but it didn't matter. Dinah was gone. I just took the bobby pins from her hair which we'd forgotten to do upon arriving at the cemetery and smoothed the curls, thinking they were too tight. I shouldn't have used rosewater. It didn't matter, in the long run, because Arlene Faucett, Dinah's beautician, with whom she'd set an appointment for the next day, asked to come over to the funeral home and set Dinah's hair for the burial. You might think this peculiar, but I, frankly, was touched. Anyway, I ran my fingers over Dinah's pin curls, buttoned the red cardigan, and shivered a lot because it was cold and I was holding my sister who'd just spoken to me from heaven. I hummed the first hymn that came to mind, which happened to be the one that goes, "Open my eyes that I may see / Glimpses of truth Thou hast for me. Place in my hand the wonderful key / That may unclasp and set me free. Silently now, I wait for Thee, / Ready, my God, Thy will to see. / Open my eyes, illumine me, Spirit divine." The paramedics got there in no time, and they tried to get a sign from her, but to no avail, of course. I stood nearby. It was like watching somebody knead bread.

2

DINAH AND WINSTON didn't have children, but he'd been married once before. His daughter, Neva Joy, from that marriage, was and still is a devoted member of the community, one prone to take her civic duty seriously. A few years ago, she ran for City Council but lost by a narrow margin to a man named Funsten Jones. I voted for Neva. Dinah didn't raise Neva Joy, and as far as my observations went Dinah only saw her on Christmas morning and during summers occasionally, at least during Neva Joy's childhood. In later years, and especially after Winston's death, Dinah grew to cherish Neva Joy as one might imagine, for they shared a love for Winston, and what on earth is or can be more intense than the love for a dead man? Witness John F. Kennedy. Anyway, it didn't surprise me in the least when Dinah saw fit to leave Neva Joy a quarter of her estate. Jackie, my baby, *was* surprised, but I wasn't. She left me three-quarters, and I must say that an inheritance is a humbling thing. I despise speaking of money. And it's such a peculiar thought, as I've never had any, but Dinah's death thrust me into it. And, as it turned out, the whole ordeal with Neva Joy and the estate was one of those oddities God had up his sleeve for me, because if Neva Joy hadn't first tried to persuade me to rezone the old homestead for commercial, I'd have never met Judson Carmichael, but I'll get to all that directly.

Anyway, on the morning of Dinah's funeral, Carmen Dabbs, my best friend of whom I've already spoken, met me at the old homestead. I was standing in the living room, where I had a sweet and grand view of the lawn which Dinah'd kept up well, thanks to her yardman, Wash—short for Washington. It being November, the lawn had a light cover of amber leaves from all the hickory trees. I felt unspeakably sad. Naturally, I didn't cry. There will come a day when I'll find it in my heart to shed tears over some little thing, but something about Scotty and all that liquor just dried me up. Maybe it's chemical; there's always that remote chance. My grandbaby has taught me that it's all physiological, that even Scotty's love for liquor was a matter of genetics. So, if I like, I can believe that my body isn't constitutionally capable of making tears, just as there are people, Carmen being one, who can go nigh near all day without urinating.

Still, those yellow hickory leaves were awfully sad, and already I missed Dinah. This is a thing of old age: bad news is old hat. *But,* these unceasing deaths begin to come in too fast, so whereas you might have gone into shock over them when you were younger and postponed the sad part, here in this stage of life the sad part happens instantly. Cradling Dinah's body while the paramedics sped over to the graveyard, I was already feeling it. I knew she was dead, and it was sad as Christmas.

The misery of it stayed with me for several days. The sight of Carmen coming along the sidewalk the day of the funeral cheered me, though. She's one of those women who's carried her beauty to old age. She wears bright colors. She has wispy gray tendrils. If someone asked you, "Does Carmen wear her hair in a bun?" you'd probably say, "No," the truth being that she does. It's just you'd never realize it (a bun can be so severe and ordinary) because what you see is the light in Carmen's face, her tendrils, her fine eyes that C.I. Foster, another friend, describes as being brown as homemade fudge.

That morning, I was heartened by Carmen's graceful figure

waltzing forward. She was, best I recall, wearing that long skirt with the big geometric shapes, and it kissed her shins with each step. "Oh, Honey," she said when she walked in and clasped my hands. We faced each other like lovers, and Carmen squeezed my fingers.

"How many times, how many times?" she said. She meant, How many funerals and how many more until it's all over? Kind of like Martin Luther King saying, *"How long, O Lord, how long?"* That's another dead man to love. Naturally, I keep this love a secret. I did tell Jackie once, believing he'd understand, since he's a preacher, too. "How enlightened, Mother," he said. Carmen shares my feelings about Dr. King. Actually, a lot of women our age do, but it's not something the men want to discuss. For instance, I'd never tell C.I. Foster or Dewey, Dinah's next-door neighbor, because it'd be hell to pay. I'd tell Dewey's wife under ordinary circumstances, but here lately she's been taking mood elevators, and I wouldn't want to stop the elevator from coming on up, which might happen if she didn't in fact share my and Carmen's sentiments.

Anyway, Carmen held my fingers. Believe me, Carmen is an angel on earth, and the sight of her makes you believe in heaven. I tried to make Judson Carmichael see how *easy* believing is if you know an angel on earth, but, as I said, I'll get to Judson directly. The business at hand, that morning, was to tidy Dinah's kitchen (which is a joke, as she was the tidiest person ever to inhabit a kitchen) and to get ready for the onslaught of neighborly food.

"Here comes C.I.," Carmen said. "Looks like he's baked a hen."

"Bless his heart," I said.

C.I. stood on the backdoor stoop. I opened the screen. His cigar was drooping between his lips in appropriate sympathy, but when he saw I was all right, when I smiled, the thing sprang to life and he held it gingerly in his amazingly snow-colored teeth. Actually, C.I. could be handsome if he'd get rid of that nasty cigar and lose some weight. His hair is brown as Mr. Reagan's. To tell you the truth, we (meaning me and my neighbors) all look good to be our age. Don't ask me why. I suspect it's got something to do with gardening and our belief in the natural order of things. Faith in God frees you for the most part—I'd say ninety percent free—from the fear of death, and surely that keeps you looking young, not having that old albatross strangling you gently, day by day, all your life. Now the remaining ten percent is something else (no person in human form can be a hundred percent certain), but I'll go into the ten percent later on because it's all related to Judson Carmichael.

C.I. handed Carmen the hen. It was wrapped in foil, but we knew it was a hen.

"Did you bake it, C.I.?" I asked him, sincerely moved. C.I. is a widower.

"Sure did," C.I. said, and his darting little brown eyes shot anxiously all over the place as if spooked. But then C.I. always takes in a place this way like a thief or a paranoid might. "Oh, Miss Dinah," he said sadly. "Miss Dinah."

I took C.I.'s hand.

"She always made me hot tea when I'd come calling," he continued.

Carmen picked up the teapot. "We'll make you a cup, C.I.," she said.

"All right," he said. "All right."

I led C.I. all through the house. I don't know why I did this, exactly. It was an odd gesture. It was like something a real-estate agent might do. But then, when we got to Mama's and Papa's old bedroom, I knew why I was doing it. I wanted somebody to understand, to fathom with me, the vastness of my sorrow. C.I. rose to the occasion, the way friends invariably do. "Your daddy did it all," he said. "Never been a man like that." Papa was a miner, a carpenter, a farmer. "Thing I recall about your mama was those rosebuds. She had one heck of a rose garden," C.I. said. "Best I recall, she grew strawberries, the first ones I ever saw were in her garden."

"Yes," I affirmed. "Asparagus too. And you *know* nobody in this town knew what asparagus was till Mama grew it."

"That's right, that's right," C.I. said.

"*Nobody*," I said.

"That's right. That's it, that's right," he sang.

"Her roses were so sweet, weren't they?"

"That's right, that's right," he went on rhythmically.

"Dinah nor I, neither one, could ever get them going after she died."

"That's right. That's right."

C.I.'s cigar was just agoing.

"Papa'd die if he knew C.I. Foster was smoking a cigar in his bedroom."

C.I. took it from his mouth. "Miss Dinah wouldn't think much of it, either," he said.

I waved that away. "Dinah wouldn't care. You know, C.I., she wasn't really with us after Winston died. She hasn't been here, in this house, ever since then. Sure, her body moved through it, but her spirit was already gone. That's why it wasn't so bad over at the graveside when she died. I held that baby's body and thought, 'Finally, she's free from this.'"

"That's right. That's right."

I stared at Mama's bedspread and quilt stand, then looked at my watch. "Neva Joy'll be here directly. And listen, somebody needs to drive to the airport to pick up Jackie. He's preaching Dinah's funeral, you know."

"How wonderful," C.I. boomed. "And praise God. I haven't heard that boy preach since he was a kid."

"Now he's changed, C.I.," I reminded him. "He's not Baptist anymore."

C.I.'s cigar fell.

"You know that, C.I. I've told you that."

"I know," C.I. said. "I just forgot for a moment. Now, what is he now?"

"Well, he teaches," I hedged.

"Teaches college," C.I. said approvingly.

"Yes. He teaches theology."

"And what is he now?"

"His church is interdenominational. No, that's not right. It's inter*faith*."

C.I. looked at me blankly. His eyes were flat as brown buttons. I stared at his red suspenders, then reached to gently touch his starched collar as if to adjust something. "I don't know what that means, either, C.I., but I do know some members of his church family are Jewish."

C.I. pumped his cigar a few times.

"I have an open mind, Honey," he said.

"Good." I patted his collar. "You keep it that way." I looked down. "C.I.," I said, "would you drive to the airport and pick him up?"

I was only a tad worried about Jackie preaching an intellectual funeral sermon. It's not that we have any of those rabid anti-humanists out this way (that's all more in the fashionable suburbs nearer to Birmingham); it's just that Jackie's very smart and those Floridians like highbrow sermons. In fact, he calls his sermons "messages" or "homilies," and our friends and neighbors probably never heard of a homily, except for Carmen who's heard of everything. Carmen (1) went to college, (2) was married to a Yankee, and (3) worked in an exclusive clothing store in Birmingham for thirty years. All this adds up to a woman who's heard of a homily. Anyway, all my fears were laid to rest when Jackie walked into Dinah's kitchen, because he was so down-to-earth, embracing Neva Joy (who had arrived by then), and just swallowing the whole place up with his presence. Jackie is handsome and tall. He has a fine baritone voice. He looked dressed for a safari, but it only helped us all relax, and I had faith he'd change into a dark suit before the funeral.

"Mother," he said, deeply, and swept me into his arms. He put a hand on C.I.'s shoulder. "Thanks for sending such a grand escort to get me." C.I. had driven Carmen's blue Mercedes to the airport. Then Jackie held Carmen at arm's length as if assessing her beauty. "Carmen," he said and kissed her cheek.

Neva Joy had busied herself with making a fruit salad. She'd brought the ingredients—pineapple, mandarin oranges, raisins, and maraschino cherries. I don't know why she felt obligated to bring food, since she's a family member herself, though I do understand how the preparing of food is terribly soothing and gives one the feeling of being on top of a given situation. This was probably the case. Neva Joy chopped the fruit with gusto at Dinah's counter, like a driven woman. She was hiding behind sunglasses. I say "hiding" because the lenses were pitch-dark. It was like one of those mystery photos where the eyes are blacked out, leaving us only Neva Joy's fretful lips, tiny red nose, and freshly done hair. She calls her beautician "my stylist." He's a Frenchman, according to Carmen. Neva must drive to Birmingham for this, because there are not any Frenchmen out this way, I'm sure. Neva is fifty-something like Jackie, but they are worlds apart.

Jackie put one of his big pastorly hands on Neva Joy's shoulder, and she flinched, then danced aside—carrying her fruit-salad bowl with her. "How are you, Neva?" he asked her in his gentle yet strong voice.

"Just fine, Jackie. You got any mints?"

"No," he said. "Do you need mints?"

"Gum will do," she said. "Got any gum?"

"No," he said.

"Honey, do you have some gum?" she asked me.

I didn't have any. "Dinah's probably got some peppermints somewhere around," I said. "Let me look."

C.I. stuck a pack of Juicy Fruit at Neva as if ready to stab. She jumped back, then touched her French hairdo as if it were going to fall off. Regaining her composure, she took a piece and unwrapped it. "Thank you, C.I."

"You gonna run for City Council again, Miss Neva?" C.I. asked.

Neva Joy readjusted her dress. It was the color of caramel, the same color as the freckles that cover her entire body. "Oh, maybe," she said and brushed something, lint I suppose, from her dress. "Who's going to stay here during the funeral, Honey?" she asked me.

I shrugged, deferring to Jackie, who was looming taller than ever by my side. "Does anyone need to?" I asked him.

Jackie held his big palms up. "That's up to you, Mother."

I eyed his safari outfit and glanced at my watch. "I guess we ought to be getting ready."

"What I was thinking," Neva Joy went on, "is that somebody should be here to accept the food."

I gestured to the casseroles that were threatening to take up all available table, counter, and stovetop space. "Surely, it's all here," I said. One of Dinah's neighbors—the one who had a door key—had let herself in quite early that morning to accept food.

"I know Miss Clara Ruth Sizemore is bringing a lemon ice-box pie," Neva Joy argued, "because she called me for the recipe. Imagine," she said, "calling me, a family member of the deceased, for a recipe." Neva smiled. Neva ought to smile more. It breaks her anxiety into tiny pieces of joy you want to gather up and hand back to her in your palms, as if to say, "See what you can make when you loose the reins."

"And when I gave her the recipe," she continued, "over the phone, mind you, just when I was trying to feed the twins"—Neva Joy has grown twin boys—"she began asking questions, like 'Is cream of tartar really necessary for a stiff meringue?' "

"It's not," Carmen said. Carmen was busying herself with Dinah's china, getting plates ready for after-the-funeral eating. Jackie was backed up against the counter in his safari garb, his right hand against his cheek in reflective, pastoral pose like a man watching an old, quaint movie.

"Well, I told her not to leave it out. There's nothing worse than a flat meringue on the day of a funeral." Neva Joy suddenly stopped chewing her Juicy Fruit and looked at me, then at Jackie, then at Carmen, and C.I. We all kind of looked at one another, then everybody was real quiet. The morning sun fell all over Dinah's tile floor—the same tile as was there when we were growing up; tile holds up well with the passage of time—and all eyes were on the dappled light, broken gently by the remaining hickory leaves. It was one of those moments, you know, you've been there, that occurs during a funeral when everyone's forced to recall what's going on, why this unlikely gathering of certain people is occurring, and who's obviously missing, and why those assembled could never have been threaded together without the death of this particular person. But that's getting into the sacrificial element of my own personal theology, and I won't go into that until later. The pressing problem at hand was to move on away from the orb of light in Dinah's kitchen, gently hint to Jackie—using only subtle eye contact, which is certainly easy enough with your own children who are innately attuned to what your eyes are saying, whether approving or disapproving—that he might want to change into a dark suit, and then persuade Neva Joy it wasn't necessary to linger for food, and proceed to the chapel for the service.

The fact that Jackie did not, in fact, change into a dark suit was soon forgotten, because when we arrived at the funeral home Neva Joy was in a state. She'd gotten there a bit earlier. Neva drives a big van with dark windows.

She stood in one of the funeral home's parlors, amidst florist wreaths, a knuckle pressed to her fretful lips. She wasn't wearing her sunglasses.

"Whatever is it, Neva?" I asked and reached to touch the sleeve of her caramel-colored dress. Naturally, I knew it might be grief. Certainly this was a place to be upset, but Neva didn't look sad; she looked frantic.

"What, Neva? What, hon?"

Jackie and I had ridden over with Carmen, in her blue Mercedes. I felt Jackie's and Carmen's warmth behind me. I knew they were waiting for Neva Joy to say something in the way of an explanation.

"Mother's not coming," she said.

I fingered the cuff of Neva's caramel dress.

"Well, hon, she probably didn't think it appropriate."

"She should have, out of respect for Daddy and me."

Now, mind you, Neva's daddy, Winston Bluet, had been divorced from Neva's mother for nigh onto forty years, and why on earth would she want to come to Dinah's funeral?

"Now, hon, don't let it do you in," I offered, then looked back to Jackie. This called for pastoral intervention, but I knew good and well this kind of funeral-home drama had been one of the reasons he'd left the Baptist Church and moved on to Florida where they have bronze, tight faces and know how to control their emotions. I didn't blame him then, and I still don't. A man of God needs time to study the big questions, and you can't do them proper justice when you're having to devote all energy to figuring out why somebody's crying and what in God's name you're supposed to do about it.

Sensing my dilemma, Jackie motioned me to slip from that particular parlor into the hall. We stood by the water fountain. Jackie put an arm around my waist and drew me to his safari-clad body. "Neva just needs a valid reason to cry."

"What do you mean?"

"She is grieving over Dinah, but she doesn't want to admit it, so she's using this thing with her mother. Anger is easier for her to face than the reality of Dinah's death."

I eyed him warily. "I don't like all that death literature, Jackie. Is that what you're talking about? Stages?"

Jackie threw his head back and laughed heartily. "Oh, Mother," he said and laughed even more heartily. "Tell me," he said and laid a hand on my shoulder, "what bothers you about Kubler-Ross."

"Who?"

He smiled. "What death literature were you referring to?"

"All of it. The very idea that the sweet end result is that you *accept* death, like it's a gift or something."

I realized I'd left Carmen in the parlor with Neva Joy, so I took Jackie's hand and led him back in. Neva and Carmen were admiring an arrangement shaped like a cross that held a Bible and a rosebud in the heart of the cross. Neva Joy wasn't crying. I knew it was Carmen's light-handed influence. Carmen is one of those women who's got an aura of calm. I believe in auras. I can't see them, but I know they exist. Get near Carmen, and you can feel the warm sensation. When artists invented halos they had a good idea. I'd say they were right on track with interpreting God's mystery, and don't be fooled into believing that those Nativity-scene characters and other assorted angels were the only ones who've ever had halos. Carmen wears one, only it hovers near her entire body rather than just her head. Its color is gold. The message isn't intended for the eyes but rather for the hands. It's a tactile reality, and if you think this is all hogwash, you ought to read more about Helen Keller. I met her once. Mama's people were originally from Tuscumbia like Helen's daddy, Captain Keller. Miss Helen, as Mama called her, was the most distinct angel to walk around on the earth since Gabriel flew in to tell Mary she was going to have a baby. But, again, this is all my personal feelings, and Judson Carmichael had a heyday trying to undo all my beliefs. He said to me, "Honey, you're as caught and tangled as an injured bug in a spiderweb." It was one of the more fanciful things Judson ever said early on, though I must say, he's become more fanciful in recent days. But then this happens when one begins to make intellectual surrenders. In fact, intellectuals—the sad kind who've forgotten how to let go—may be the most trapped folks in the world. Mind you, I'm perfectly aware of the fact that I don't know what "intellectual" really means. It's just a term of convenience for me. It's a person who, among other things, has to rely on reason and logic to stay sane, when, in reality, reason and logic will drive you stark raving mad. And anyway, back to Judson. He was *almost* on track, as nonbelievers generally are. He was right by trying to establish a metaphor that involved weaving like the spider's web. Yes, most decidedly, I have woven for myself, as we all do, a colorful and complex design, my view of God's world. It's like a big quilt you pattern for yourself, year upon year, until finally in old age your perception quilt is so luxurious, you can wrap up in it on particularly cold and lonely days, and be warm. And the thing is—I tried to explain this to Judson—there's no right or wrong, because it's *yours*. You made it. It exists. "Honey," he chided, "it's a sham. It's unfounded. Sure, it may be comforting, but it's not real. It's like a drug, it just makes you *think* your pain is gone." Now, if you've reached old age, and you still walk around, like Judson was doing, calling yourself an unbeliever, it's just because nobody's yet opened your cedar chest to show you the quilt you've been unconsciously piecing all these years.

Jackie, bless him, preached an extraordinarily simple and loving tribute to Dinah, calling her "Aunt Dinah" throughout, occasionally gesturing to where she lay in state, moving his body slightly to the pine coffin (it's what Dinah wanted, pine) and directing his words to her. Jackie's service took the form of personal eulogy rather than those uniform funeral services where you read the same old comfortless Scriptures about lofty places in heaven; certain passages cause me to visualize cubicles in the sky, reserved places in a kingdom made up of big safe-deposit boxes full of riches and treasures. Don't get me wrong, I love the Scriptures. I just don't like traditional funeral passages. Anyway, Jackie avoided all the pat responses to death and just talked to and about Dinah. He read the first chapter of Genesis about the earth being formed, which I found reassuring because it was about new beginnings. We buried Dinah up on the hill by Mama and Papa, and Jackie read the Eighth Psalm, "When I consider the heavens, the moon and the stars, what is man?" Only, Jackie added, "and woman."

Later, as we drove from the cemetery, I noted this.

"I always correct the Scriptures in this way, Mother."

I turned to him. Jackie's profile is his daddy made over—handsome, angular, with those blue eyes that look like translucent marbles from the side. Head on, they pierce your soul. They're the kind of eyes—Scotty's were, anyhow—that cause a woman to stay married to a drunk; eyes full of mystery and strange light, and you think to yourself, If I could just ever find a way to fathom those eyes, maybe I could *get the hell* away from this man. But you never do, so you stay and you stay. And then he dies, and you're free from that passionate suffering. And, unless you marry another drunk man, you're free from suffering altogether, because you've become immune due to exposure to such devastating doses. But, you're also free from passion, which is a bit sad.

"Where to now, Mother?" Jackie asked.

We were in Carmen's blue Mercedes. She'd ridden back with C.I. and Dewey. Neva Joy had left alone in her big dark van.

"Back to Dinah's house," I told him. "The food, remember?"

Jackie smiled. "The food," he repeated.

"We'll have casseroles for days," I said and stared out the window. We passed the new Dairy Queen.

"Lot of development," Jackie noted. "It's not the same. I could be anywhere. The town's losing its face. Do you find that disturbing?"

"I reckon so."

"Many houses going down?"

"No." I reflected. "No. Not too many houses. Just a lot of pretty land going to waste for fast-food. C.I. thinks its wonderful. He loves cheeseburgers."

"Have you looked at Dinah's will?" Jackie asked.

"No."

"Do you know where it is?"

"It's in her safe-deposit box at Alabama Home Federal."

"Do you have a key?"

"It's on top of the secretary. If she's told me once, she's told me a thousand times. She was so anxious to die, Jackie, to be reunited with Winston. She's spent her entire widowhood preparing to die. How's Robin?" I asked him. Robin is Jackie's daughter, the grandbaby I mentioned who was born in 1963 and is a social worker.

"Fine, fine," he said.

"Where's she working now?"

"At a hospice."

I stared out the window again. What a dreadful thing to do for a living, I thought, but then I certainly understood being addicted to misery.

"She enjoys her work?" I asked him.

"Yes, very much," he said. "I knew she'd go into a helping profession, didn't you?"

I turned to him. "Why? What made you think so?"

Jackie rolled up the sleeve of his safari shirt, keeping his hand steady on the steering wheel while he did it. "Doesn't it run in the family?"

I shrugged. "You won't find me working in a nursing home."

Jackie smiled. "But you took care of Daddy all those years, didn't you?"

Of course he had a point.

"Do you talk to Ellen these days?" I asked him.

Ellen is Jackie's former wife. Their divorce wasn't pleasant— for me. *They* did fine; I was very distraught. Ellen just got up one morning (as I saw it) and decided she was tired of being a minister's wife. She left and remarried one year later. She married a man who played in a band. "It's a rock band, Honey," Robin had told me over the phone.

"Oh no," I'd said.

"He plays a lot of instruments, Honey," Robin said as if that should make it all better. "He plays a flute, even. He has some class. He plays in an orchestra when he's not on the road."

Robin was seventeen at the time. I worried over her. But, like all worrying, it was wasted time, because Robin became a very serious person, dedicated to her studying and eager to become a part of civilization, to join the healers of the world.

"Robin's happy," Jackie said, avoiding my question about Ellen. It's not a subject easily discussed. Ellen was special to me. I miss her.

I sighed.

Jackie turned on Carmen's car radio.

"I want to drive by the Hollings place," Jackie said. I knew he was going to want to do this, because he wants to do it every time he comes home. The Hollings place means the garage apartment behind L. D. Hollings's home. Jackie was born during the Depression. Scotty and I were living in one of the Hollingses' servant homes. We weren't their servants, of course; we just rented. Back then, you lived wherever you could. After the sixties, we started calling servants' quarters garage apartments. Jackie was born on a terribly cold January morning. Scotty helped deliver him. He wasn't into serious drinking in those days, but he did keep liquor at home. I drank a full cup of whiskey during labor.

Jackie turned into the driveway of the Hollings place. It's a smallish Antebellum-looking home with sprawling porch and nandina bushes which were, there in November, adorned with red winter berries.

"L.D.'s son still live here?" Jackie asked.

"Yes," I replied. "He's probably at work," I said and looked at my watch. It was two o'clock. L.D.'s son is a veterinarian, a kindhearted profession, I've always thought.

Jackie looked long and hard at the Hollings place, and I looked long and hard at him. I suppose he was trying to recall what it felt like, as a boy, to view the big house from our garage apartment out back. Jackie drove on, at a snail's pace, toward the old servants' quarters where we'd lived. I had no interest in the place. My eyes were on Jackie because what on earth is more compelling than the sight of your child, no matter how grown, still trying to assimilate his past? I believe that Jackie leaving the Baptist Church was just Jackie trying to leave this place. For him, I'm sure, it's not a respectable apartment, but a birthplace for servants, and if he was to be bound with the chains of holy servitude (ministers, I understand, can't escape the calling), then he was at least going to west Florida to wear safari clothes and preach to free minds rather than tinkering with small ones.

We got back to Dinah's place at two-thirty. Carmen and C.I. were bustling all over the house, lifting foil from casseroles, answering the phone, and greeting neighbors who were just dropping by momentarily to offer further condolences. By three, all that was left was Jackie, Carmen, C.I., Neva Joy, Dewey, and me.

Dewey had lived next door to Dinah and Winston for nigh onto eighteen years. As I mentioned earlier, Dewey's wife was on mood elevators and therefore wasn't at the funeral, though she'd baked a pineapple upside-down cake, and Dewey was right proud of this fact.

"It's a good sign," he told C.I.

We were all in Dinah's dining room, seated with ivory tablecloth, place settings, and a centerpiece made of fruit, nuts, and sprigs of mahonia holly. It was like a holiday meal.

C.I.'s cigar was in an ashtray by his iced tea. He never lets that thing out of his sight. Carmen had arranged all the casseroles on the buffet, and we'd helped ourselves cafeteria-style. Jackie was being real quiet, and I knew he was still at the Hollings place in his mind, trying to figure out his boyhood.

"Sweet service, Jackie," Carmen said as she picked up her fork and toyed with her sweet-potato casserole. "Very eloquent and inspired," she said.

"Thank you," he said and smiled like a boy.

Jackie was settling in now, forgetting his safari from poverty, just being himself.

"Sara Catherine hasn't baked anything for three months," Dewey said, "until she baked that pineapple upside-down last night. She did it for Miss Dinah," he added with reverence.

"What have y'all been eating, then?" C.I. asked and touched his unlit cigar.

"Sandwiches," Dewey said. He ran his hand over his bald rotund head.

"For three months?" C.I. asked.

"That's right," Dewey said. "Cheese sandwiches. That's it."

Carmen shot me a knowing glance. Dewey was prone to lying.

"Why didn't you get some TV dinners?" Neva Joy asked.

"Couldn't afford them," Dewey lied.

"Not even a chicken pot pie?" Neva pressed.

"Nope."

"They only cost fifty-nine cents," she said. And then, with seriousness, she took off her sunglasses and laid them beside C.I.'s ashtray. She studied Dewey. He was, in fact, shoveling food in like he'd been surviving on cheese sandwiches for three months. "Did you make *grilled* cheese sandwiches or just cold cheese on bread?"

"No grilled cheese. Cost of butter's too high," he said.

Carmen smiled over at me. We'd delivered some government cheese to Dewey a week before—three pounds of it.

"You can grill them in shortening," Neva went on, "if you have to."

Jackie turned to me with a faintly sickened expression. I patted his hand and smiled.

Neva Joy's small freckled hands were clasped in front of her empty plate. "How about some seconds, Neva?" I said.

She looked up at Dinah's grandfather clock. "Actually, I need to get on home and check on the twins," she said.

"How old are they now?" Jackie asked, innocently enough.

Still Neva looked miffed. "Younger than you think," she said and reached up to hold her French hairdo as if it were again threatening to slide off. It was then I noticed her seagull earrings. Like Neva's face alight with a smile, they suggested a lighthearted beauty if she'd only be herself.

"Don't go just yet," I said.

Jackie got up and walked alongside the buffet, selecting seconds. I like to see Jackie eat. It's comforting. He was a scrawny boy, and even though he grew to be a tall and substantial man, I still am heartened when he eats.

"Neva," he said, "do you remember Miss Baker's horses?"

Color flooded Neva's face. Jackie and Neva were in grade school together. "Sure," she said.

"Weren't they magnificent?" he said.

33

He sat back down and buttered a blueberry muffin. Neva Joy turned to the big window behind Dewey and stared at the falling hickory leaves which were turning Dinah's lawn gold. We all continued to eat. Except for the occasional tapping of silverware on plates or ice clinking against tea glasses, the room was quiet.

3

"WHAT HORSES WERE you talking about?" I asked Jackie later as we rode over to Alabama Home Federal to see about Dinah's will. "Why did Neva blush so?"

Jackie adjusted the car's sun visor. "Miss Baker, our second-grade teacher, had some incredibly fine horses."

"So why did Neva blush?"

"I think she probably blushes whenever anybody mentions anything personal or associated with memory, common reference points, that sort of thing."

"I wonder why."

Jackie shrugged. "She just has trouble connecting with people, I guess."

"I reckon," I said.

Our branch of Alabama Home Federal is located in what was once the old Mackin place. Harlan Mackin died back years ago with black lung, and, since he had no heirs, his place was zoned commercial and bought up by the bank. Now I must say it's a sight nicer than Harlan kept it. The bank plants hyacinths along the windowsill in spring, and they've painted the place baby blue (Harlan kept it a mud color, as best I recall). Jackie pulled into the small parking lot which was encased by a rock-and-fern garden. Banks do love to landscape and call themselves things like Home Federal.

Jackie and I were greeted by a girl Robin's age—early twenties. She led us to the designated place and said she was so sorry to hear of Dinah's death. We got the will, went back to the car, and read it—Jackie and me—with the glaring winter sun causing Carmen's Mercedes to fill itself up with solar heat.

I think one reason Jackie was surprised that Dinah had left Neva Joy a piece of inheritance is because Winston Bluet, Neva's daddy, had already left her some money when he died. That's what went to buy her dark van, and rumor had it she invested the rest for the twins to have what C.I. described as "identical lots" on Smith Lake up near Jasper.

"Don't you think we ought to contact Neva when we get back home?" Jackie asked.

I stared ahead, trying to shield my eyes from the wintry glare. The baby-blue bank didn't make sense, neither did the fancy windowsills or the fern-and-rock gardens. This was Harlan Mackin's house, for God's sake. I'd walked into Harlan's place with a key that didn't belong to me, and now here I sat with the contents of Dinah's safe-deposit box. Her will, Mama's cameo and opal ring, and all Dinah's financial affairs had been stored in Harlan Mackin's house and were now dumped in my lap. Time itself suddenly seemed like a crook. I felt I might cry, but naturally I didn't.

Jackie put a hand on my shoulder and turned to face me in Carmen's car. "Are you all right?" he asked.

"I'll be fine, Jackie."

"How're you feeling?"

"I'm feeling like Jell-O that hasn't gelled."

"What are you thinking?"

"All these dead people, making this final deposit into my life. Mama, Papa, and Dinah leaving me all this, all they had on this earth."

Jackie's eyes—Scotty's eyes—pierced me like blue pinpointed lights.

"You look like Scotty," I told him.

"I know."

"Only in appearance. You've got a heart. You're a good man, Jackie."

He popped a knuckle, then put one hand on the steering wheel.

The sky was almost turquoise. It was unmistakably Indian summer—a seasonal disfiguring that I find disturbing because it's not in keeping with the natural order of things. Only three days ago it had been cold.

"Indian summer," I commented.

Jackie glanced up at the sky.

"I don't like Indian summer," I told him.

He turned to me, his eyes warm, searching. "Why's that?"

"It triggers my doubts."

"About?"

"About the orderliness of the world."

"Do you think God is orderly?"

"Well, yes. Don't you?" I looked squarely at him, at his finely chiseled face. His temples were just now beginning to gray. Jackie had already lived past the age where death took his daddy.

"It's an interesting question, don't you think? A student asked me recently if I believed God had a personality."

I waved that away. "I'm talking about the world, not God."

"The creation, not the creator," he said.

I looked at Dinah's will in my lap. I held it up. "This is all that's left of the family. It's all right here in my lap. That is so sad, Jackie." But, even as I said it, even in the moment that I recognized, on the spot, something I'd recall farther down the road as an exquisitely sad instant, I felt myself going all to steel inside rather than melting. Oh, to be able to wilt.

"I can't cry over anything, Jackie," I said.

"I can't, either," he said.

I turned abruptly. "Well, can Robin? Is there something *wrong* with us? Can she? Can Robin cry?"

Jackie laughed and turned Carmen's ignition so that the radio would come on. "Robin can cry, Mother."

"Have you seen her cry? In recent years? Since she's been grown?"

Jackie touched the SCAN button and we began getting five seconds of assorted stations. Jackie had it turned down real low, though, so it wasn't grating.

"Have you?" I pressed.

He put a finger to his lips, then held the finger up as if an enlightening thought had registered. "Yes," he said. "She cried during the Democratic convention."

I sighed, relieved.

"Well," I said and began looking through Dinah's documents.

Jackie then put a hand over mine. "Mother," he said. "Are you aware of the fact that a lot of money may be involved here?" He pointed to a figure on one of the papers. No, naturally, I wasn't aware nor prepared.

Neva Joy took her piece of the inheritance in stride. I reckon this was because it was her second time around, she having received, as I've already mentioned, some of Winston's legacy. But, even days later, when it had all had time to sink in, after Jackie, bless him, had taken me to other banks and lawyers, I still didn't understand where Dinah got all that money.

And so I called Jackie long distance the day after he flew back home to Florida.

"I just don't understand about the money," I told him.

"Well, some of it was Winston's, you know," Jackie said.

"But I thought he left that for Neva when he died."

"Not all of it, Mother," he said. "He wanted to leave some for Dinah to have in case she needed it to live on."

"I don't want Winston Bluet's money," I said. "I don't want anybody's money, Jackie."

Jackie laughed. "It's not *that* much, Mother."

"Well, what are you doing?" I asked him.

"Celia is here," he said.

Celia is Jackie's girlfriend. I've not yet met her, but I've seen pictures. She's Jackie's age, but looks quite youthful. She has natural-blond hair and wears stylish hats—in the photos at least. She's a member of his church. She's an art historian, Jackie says. I believe she's from Savannah or Charleston, one or the other, and I have no idea what she's doing in Florida. Still, I've grown to like the fact that Jackie isn't alone. She's moved in, but we don't acknowledge that fact.

"Well, tell Celia I said hello, and thank her for giving you up to help me bury Dinah and get all this business straightened out, only it's not all straightened out."

"Don't worry about the homestead now. There's plenty of time to decide."

He meant decide whether or not I wanted to move in. He knew, because we'd talked a lot about it before he left. It was already the needler that wouldn't leave me be. Burying Dinah was easy enough. Don't get me wrong, it was and is a hole in my soul, but pretty soon the burying of your family assumes at least the comfort of ritual, and I got an early start burying love, having lost Scotty when I was forty-four.

"Tell Robin I love her," I instructed Jackie. "And keep me posted on her crying. I'm serious, now, let me know every time you see her cry. The thought brings me great joy. Hope," I added.

I've lived in apartments all my grown life—mostly small ones near the old homestead. After Scotty died, I worked as a waitress, and I truly liked this occupation because, as I mentioned earlier, serving up food is a good feeling, akin, I'd say, to nursing a baby. I worked, too, at a dry cleaner's, but didn't find this to be satisfying work.

Money is a foreign object to me. I suppose it was to Dinah too, and that's why she kept hers hid in that safe-deposit box in Harlan Mackin's old bank-house. Read the Book of Proverbs sometime. It's all devoted to rich men, virtuous women and fools. Dinah and I were raised to believe money taints ordinary people, obstructs virtue, and makes a fool out of you. So, the inheritance was like a tiger somebody'd left on the doorstep of my house, and I had to figure out something to do with it. Having never seen a tiger up close, I perceived it as strange, frightful, and yet it pricked my curiosity enough to warrant a peek at its big body. But what to do with it?

The house I rent is painted white. I like the place. I planted gumpo azaleas—you know, those tiny ones that cling to the earth like a baby—along the driveway, and sprigged candytuft by the sidewalk leading to the door. Occasionally, in early spring, I'll try a few peppers and herbs. I have a rectangle of zoysia. I discovered it's the best kind of grass for bare feet like Robin's that padded over it during those fine summers she'd visit as a child. Inside, I have hardwood floors, bluish throw rugs, and some new artwork Jackie had delivered to me by parcel post, compliments of Celia, his art historian.

From my side porch, I have a view of the homestead—in winter, that is, when the leaves are all fallen from trees. Dewey and his wife, as I said, live next door to the homestead. C.I. lives halfway between my place and Dewey's. Carmen lives three doors from me. The neighborhood is flat. We got big trees—white oaks, hickory, sweetgum, maple, you name it. I sat here on my side porch, and these are the things I was seeing when Neva drove up in her big van. I knew she was coming, because she'd called. I knew we needed to talk, but I'd been dilly-dallying around because I didn't want to face the future. This is unlike me, Honey, the stoic.

Neva Joy slid from the front seat of the giant vehicle, and until she did I had no view of her, because, as I said, the van has those dark windows. Neva was wearing a bright-red suit like a swanky businesswoman, along with black leather accessories. I made a mental note of this, to tell Carmen. Carmen can interpret a person's mood or motive based on wardrobe, having worked in the clothing business for nigh onto thirty years.

"Neva," I hailed and wrapped my sweater up tighter to descend the porch steps and meet her in my yard. I kissed her cold freckled cheek. She patted my face with those leathery gloved hands.

"Come on in," I said. "I'll make tea."

"Honey," she said and held my hands in hers. "Why don't we go up to Dinah's to talk."

I felt myself withering a bit. I must admit, I'd not set foot in the place since the day we buried Dinah. I felt very queasy for some reason, knowing nobody lived there anymore. Now, don't get me wrong. I don't believe in ghosts. Angels, yes. Ghosts, no.

"Neva," I hedged.

I tried getting hooked up with her eyes, but her sunglasses hid them.

We stood there. A gentle gust of wind carried some leaves up for a quick dance, then dropped them just as quickly. I bit my lip, staring at the old homestead up the road, in the distance.

"Let me get a wrap," I told her. "It's cold."

I went inside, put on my heavy winter coat, grabbed some tea bags and Dinah's door key.

"We can walk if you'd like," I told Neva Joy.

"I know, but why don't we just ride in the van. It's terribly windy," she said.

The interior of Neva's van was black, naturally. The steering wheel had a leather cover. Neva maneuvered the big thing up the road to Dinah's and parked it with deftness that caused me to respect her as a driver. I kept my hands in my coat pockets, fingering the tea bags.

I don't know where courage is stored in the brain, but I can rightfully say that this part of my brain is plenty big. I bet you I won't hesitate one bit when it's time to leap over the dark abyss (fear) into the Promised Land. For those frightful, excitable types like Dinah, there's the easier form of death where it just grabs you, and, judging from that seduced expression on Dinah's thin face, Winston was johnny-on-the-spot, there to carry her over the abyss. Once you're an angel, you don't have to be weighted with the anchor of gravity. The dark abyss isn't scary, because there's no way to fall into it. Angels can walk on air because they cannot, by their nature, fall into fear. That's what makes heaven heaven— the absence of fear. You've already gone through the big banana, and you're still who you always were. I will probably be a grand angel, because I've had a lot of practice walking off cliffs and making it to the other side on sheer faith. Judson's fear of death is probably his most tender side. Certainly, it caused me to be drawn close. But I'm getting to all that real soon. The pressing issue at hand, at that moment, was to step over the threshold, to enter Dinah's empty house, to walk into the place where I grew up that now belonged to me—and to Neva Joy too, mind you. One-fourth of the house belonged to Neva.

Neva began busying herself in the kitchen just as she'd done the morning of the funeral. She was opening drawers, searching for the teakettle, cups and spoons. "Oh, whatever am I doing, Honey?" she said and pulled off her black leather gloves. "You know where everything is, don't you?"

I patted her spiffy red suit—one padded shoulder of it. "You just sit down, Neva Joy. I'll make tea." I put the kettle on the burner and looked into the pantry. "What should we do with all these canned goods?"

"Well, Thanksgiving is coming up. Why don't we give them to Wash?" Wash, as I've said, was Dinah's yardman.

"Good idea," I agreed.

"Here," Neva said and leaped from the kitchen chair where she'd just then seated herself. "Let me find a box. You think Dinah has some in the garage?"

"Neva, hon," I said and directed her back to her chair. "Just relax, sugar."

Neva Joy put a knuckle to her lips, refusing to sit. "I had miles of boxes in my basement and just last week had one of the twins carry them to the dump."

"Don't worry, hon. We can pick some up at the grocery store. It's no problem."

"No," she said and reached for the wall phone. "Let me call home and see if Ron can check the basement." Neva Joy's twins are named Ron and Don.

There was no stopping her. "Ron?" she said. "Don," she corrected, "is Ron there?" Pause. "What's he doing at the lake? It's cold as a witch's tit."

Neva Joy stood, hand on skinny hip, in those sunglasses, looking forever like a model in all that red getup.

"Go check the basement," she said. "See if there's still some boxes down there."

She waited, surveyed her nails, brushed lint or something from her suit.

The teakettle sang. I poured hot water over the tea bags. I was using Mama's good china—which, of course, belonged to me now, except for every fourth cup, which belonged to Neva. The tediousness of what lay before Neva and me was too astounding to consider.

"Not a single one?" she asked incredulously into the receiver. "OK. I'll be home by three. Take that ground beef from the freezer." Pause. "No, the three-pound package. Ron'll be home by supper, won't he?" Pause. "Well, what did he say?" Neva rolled her eyes at me. "OK, Don. Bye-bye."

She adjusted and readjusted her shoulders, and, finally, she removed her sunglasses, squinting in pain as if she'd been to the optometrist and was still dilated. Neva's eyes are the color of weak tea.

"Now," she said, while she sat down to her tea, sniffed, and rubbed the tip of her perky nose. "Thank you, Honey. This is nice."

I looked at the thermometer, moved the thermostat to 70 degrees, then sat across the table from Neva Joy. The day was gray, and the cloudiness permeated Dinah's kitchen as well, causing me to feel right in the heart of winter—an illusion, since it was still November.

"Thanksgiving," Neva Joy said and sighed. "You cooking a turkey, Honey?" she asked and took a tentative sip of tea.

"No. Carmen's having me over."

"That's sweet. Carmen is a jewel, isn't she?"

"An angel," I said.

Neva Joy nodded.

"A real one," I added.

Neva's eyes traveled to the window. "Mmhmm," she said, and I imagined the words "Old people" trailing facetiously across her mind.

"Honey," she said and began drawing tiny figures and shapes on her napkin with her finger. "Do you want to move in? Do you want to live here?"

I looked down at my hands. They were multicolored with chapped skin, protruding blue veins and yellow calluses. I studied them.

"That's a question I can't answer yet," I said finally.

"What are the pros and cons?" she asked, and I knew from the practical quality of this question that Neva Joy had no idea where I was coming from. I supposed the pros to her might be convenience—that is, not having to go through the pantry or sort the linens, or having more space, or being one block closer to the church; and the cons might include having to pay Wash to keep up the yard, or cleaning the carpets, or worrying over burglars. The fact was, it entailed such a complicated cast of internal characters—Mama, Papa, Dinah, me as a child, me as a young girl dating Scotty, the me that didn't move in to take care of Papa, me as a widow, me on the morning Dinah died. I just wasn't certain I wanted to live the rest of my life with a swarm of memory greeting me like morning sun, day upon day. Unlike Jackie, I felt no need to assimilate my past and gather all the parts of myself together to live integrated under the same roof. I'm certainly not the kind of old person who likes piecing jigsaw puzzles, and, anyway, the past is linear, like a road. I understand the mosaic nature it holds for people like Jackie and his art historian, but I'm Honey, the stoic.

"No," I said abruptly to Neva. "I really don't think I want to live here. I haven't told Jackie that, yet. I haven't told anybody, but since I know we—you and me—have decisions to make, I will say to you, no."

Neva inhaled, then exhaled deeply so that her red suit rose and fell against her chest. "Well," she said and took another less-tentative sip of tea. "Then we come to the question of what to do."

"Yes," I said. "Is it cold in here to you?"

"No," she said. "I'm fine."

I walked over to the stove and poured some more water from the kettle over my tea bag. Scotty always liked cream in his. He was from England. He was born on the ship, crossing the ocean. His parents were tiny people and knew how to dance. Scotty danced, too, with a variety of women, I'm sure, though I never acknowledged this to myself until years later. He knew charm.

Dinah had secured a smallish mirror to the wall over her stove. I glanced up at myself while I poured. As I mentioned earlier, I inherited Papa's eyes that lend themselves to the emotions at hand, which were, at that moment, fear and wistful longing, suddenly, for a man. It was an odd sensation, born, I suppose, from being in a dead woman's kitchen, drinking hot tea with yet another woman who shared with me an inheritance I neither understood nor desired. The longing for a man, as you know, is a grand escape. It can arch your mental process to extremes so that, like a gymnast or a ballerina, you're contorted to such outrageous limits—I'm speaking of passion—that nothing else matters. I wanted this. I desired diversion. I didn't want to sit with a woman and meticulously tend to responsibility. But, since Scotty's death, my life had taken this course. So, this inheritance dilemma wasn't, by any means, a painful, unfamiliar turn in the road. To the contrary, it was suffocating in its predictability. For the past thirty years, I'd been joining hands with other women to take care of business, to bury husbands, bake cakes, deliver government cheese, tend to wills, deeds, documents, and, on Sunday mornings, smooth one another's choir robe and prepare to sing God's praise.

"Well, Neva," I said, turning from the mirror, teacup in hand, "what do you think we ought to do?"

"Rezone," she said, without skipping a beat.

I sat down again, at Dinah's table, and turned my napkin over, then back, then over. Then I searched Neva Joy's face. One might wonder if, as they say, dollar marks were in her eyes. Judson, later on, certainly questioned me in this regard, about Neva. But I'm prone to tune my eyes to a person's innocent side. I didn't exactly see naiveté in Neva's face—though she was chewing gum furiously, rather like a teenager might. Her weak-tea-colored eyes were fixed squarely to mine as if she had nothing to hide, and that red suit lent itself to a composite called "mature woman." If nothing else, I felt a kinship with Neva as a fellow pragmatist.

"Honey," she said and placed a hand on mine. "My best friend is a real-estate agent. You know," she said, as she took the gum from her mouth and wrapped it in a corner of her napkin, "Clare Jenkins, with Jenkins and Major Realty. It's right across the street from your church's Family Life Suite."

I nodded, recalling, in my mind, the tan-colored dollhouse

she was referring to, across from the Family Life Suite, with the Jenkins and Major sign in front.

"I talked this over with Clare. She says if you're not planning to move in, we'd be fools to sell this residential, because whoever buys it will just turn right around, have it rezoned, and sell it commercial for five times the price paid to us. It's worth fifty thousand dollars residential, two hundred fifty thousand commercial."

I considered. "I need to call Jackie," I said.

Neva blinked. She's one of those people who blinks a lot when her thoughts are racing. "That's fine, Honey. See what Jackie says."

Of course, when I called Jackie, he predictably said, "That's up to you, Mother. You should do whatever makes you happy." I found this a funny and sadly peculiar idea. I truly saw no outcome of happiness with the situation. What kind of woman sells her papa's old homestead, built, mind you, by Papa's hands? He was, as I said, a carpenter by trade, though he farmed and mined as well. What kind of civil woman sells her inheritance? Knowingly sells her entire past to a junkmart or fast-food restaurant or parking lot? But then, what kind of pragmatist deliberately gives away $200,000?

4

THE ZONING BOARD met the second week in December. I was already into my holiday armor, so as to not get blasted by the sad, seasonal poignancy. When it was all said and done, there was no choice but to request rezoning and sell commercial because, regardless of how the property was sold, it was destined to be commercial. Neva was right in that whoever bought it residential would simply sell it commercial. The choice was whether to be sad and foolish or sad and reasonable. You may wonder why I didn't just move in, but you've got to understand that I lived independent of Papa, Mama, and Dinah all my life. My self-sufficiency has literally kept me afloat. Pride is a source of strength. Don't believe what the Bible says regarding pride. Pride has given me new life. Time and time again, I've been reborn unto myself because of it. Suffering is a spiritual sport. So, for me to move into the old homestead would be for me, Honey, here in the last leg of the race, to succumb to the cocoon, live in a place that wasn't mine, and, as I said, exist daily in memory's fog. Life is a series of shedding skins, anyhow. The old homestead was simply the last to go. When it was sold, all that'd be left was me. Dying is easier if you're a solitary light with nothing dependent on your rays.

Neva Joy's dark van pulled into my driveway at seven. I grabbed my heavy coat, combed my hair (I wear mine in its natural state—gray with leisurely bodied curls) and put on face powder. I carried a tube of rose lipstick in my pocket. I was wearing a bright-blue dress. I wasn't going to speak. Neva was presenting our case, but I did want to appear commercial, not residential, in my attire.

"Who's gonna be there, Neva?" I asked her on the way.

Neva wasn't wearing sunglasses, since it was night. She wasn't chewing gum either. She was wearing a herringbone suit, and her French hair was in perfect order. She was serious-looking.

"According to Clare, there are ten or twelve people on the Board, all men, of course."

"You should have won that election, Neva."

She held her hands up. *"Que será, será,"* she said.

"Is this the City Council, then?" I asked her. "The twelve people?"

"No," she said. "It's the Zoning Board, but the meeting is held in the City Council Chamber, and the mayor will be there."

"The mayor?"

"Yes." She turned to me. "Is that surprising or something?"

I sighed. "No, no. It just sounds so official, the mayor being there."

Neva waved that away. "Don't worry, Honey. He's in Dewey's league."

"Neva, Dewey's a fine—"

"I know, I know," she interrupted. "What I meant was the mayor's not a mental giant, in the social sense. He's not . . ." she hesitated, searching for the word, ". . . enlightened."

We have a brand-new City Hall building, made of red brick. Let me explain that we are one of those smallish towns near yet ever so distant from Birmingham. We kept our identity. Papa and a handful of others settled here in 1890. Our population has grown modestly, and we're now near twelve thousand. Neighborhoods are marked by and anchored with Baptist churches, a few Methodist, maybe a Presbyterian, but you know what I'm saying. Having lived in a place all your life, you think you know it until you walk into something like a Zoning Board meeting and find not a single familiar face on the commission. It was kind of like a courtroom. The mayor sat in a judge's seat, up real high. Beneath him was a semicircle of Board members; serious-looking men with their hands folded. The jury, no doubt. Neva and I sat in the spectator section, along with Clare Jenkins, the real-estate agent, who shook my hand when we sat down. Clare was Neva's age and also wore a serious, tailored suit. She had on peach-tinted eyeglasses with her initials "CJ" in the corner of the left lens.

The mayor banged the gavel. "The twelfth meeting—this is December, isn't it, gentlemen?—of the Zoning Board of this city is now in order." He coughed a bit and reached for some papers. The mayor is a friend of Carmen's, so I voted for him. I'd never met him until this night. He reminded me of Jack Benny.

"It's my understanding, gentlemen, that we will be discussing the Dinah Bluet estate."

All the men, in seeming unison, reached for their respective papers, and a few put on reading glasses. One got a handkerchief and blew his nose.

"I suppose we'll proceed and give the floor to Neva Joy Bluet Cantrell. Mrs. Cantrell," he said and extended his arm in Neva's direction.

Neva rose. She brushed something from her herringbone suit. "Mr. Mayor," she said. "I'd like to first defer to Clare Jenkins of Jenkins and Major Realty."

The mayor nodded.

The man with the handkerchief blew his nose again.

Clare Jenkins stood. She was one of the tallest women I'd ever beheld. Those monogrammed peach-colored glasses were something else. "Mr. Mayor and members of the commission," she said, holding up a big map. I glanced behind me. Except for two teenage girls, and a black man who was nigh near asleep, the place was empty. "My organization has studied the situation of the Dinah Bluet estate in detail. Due to the pattern and trend of the past five to seven years, it is clear that this land will inevitably be sold to commercial ends. All the property on Mineral Springs Road beginning at the **Y** intersection in town and moving southward to this point—she motioned to the map—has been zoned commercial and most of it developed. The Dinah Bluet estate, which contains 5.4 acres . . ." (Clare then went into a legal description of the property) "is clearly the next bit of land to be sold, with the Dewey Lawler property coming along next. It's just a matter of time. Mr. Lawler is aware of this fact, and he's in understanding of our—Neva Joy Cantrell's and Honey Shugart's—inclination to sell commercial. The other property owners farther down Mineral Springs Road—Carmen Dabbs, Mrs. Shugart's landlord, C.I. Foster, the McWaynes, Hollinses, and Jernigans—are also aware of both the trend, the inevitability, and our request tonight. Clearly, from their absences here, they have no protests."

The mayor took a pencil from behind his ear and tapped his teeth with it. The man with the handkerchief folded it and leaned forward to put it in his back pocket.

Neva Joy tugged on Clare's sleeve, and Clare, as best she could with all that height, leaned down so that Neva could whisper something in her ear. Clare nodded, and assumed her full stand, neck craning upward, not unlike a giraffe.

"Yes," she said. "I can further state that, in my professional opinion, the Dinah Bluet estate would be practically impossible to sell residential due to the commercial endeavors surrounding it on the north side. And, if it did sell, it would clearly be bought by a profiteer, eager only to resell it commercial for profit. Big profit," she added.

Clare then sat down on the bench, and Neva Joy stood. "Mr. Mayor and Board members, due to the testimony just presented by Clare Jenkins, and due to the fact that Honey Shugart and I are legal heirs to the Dinah Bluet estate, we now formally ask the Zoning Board to grant our request that the entire 5.4 acres of the Dinah Bluet estate be rezoned commercial."

Neva Joy sat back down.

"Are there oppositions from the community to this request?" the mayor asked. We all turned. The two teenage girls sat, arms crossed, in matching denim jackets, looking contemporarily bescraggled, their hair slicked straight up, gelled and wild. They smiled. I figured their daddies must be members of the commission seated above us, and they'd been brought along either for educational purposes or just to keep an eye on them on this Tuesday evening. The dozing black man had departed the chamber. So, there were no oppositions.

"I hear none," the mayor said. "Would the members of the Board like to question the petitioners?"

The man with the handkerchief spoke. "Mrs. Cantrell," he said to Neva. "You *could* sell this land residential, couldn't you?"

"That wouldn't be very smart, would it?" Neva snapped pleasantly.

The Board members snickered.

"Honey." I jumped inwardly, first with just the sound of my name and second with the familiarity of being addressed as Honey in this formal arena. The man had white hair—lots of it. I'd noticed him during the proceedings. He was old and handsome. "Are you sure you want to do this? Is this your personal decision as well as Mrs. Cantrell's?"

"Yes," I answered.

The man looked at me. His eyes were strong like Jackie's and Scotty's, only they belonged to a stranger, which added to their eerie force.

I looked down at my hands, resting against the bright-blue material of my dress. I was glad I'd clad myself commercial. I sensed that this man was still staring at me, and I felt myself going cold with armor.

"Well, gentlemen, let's vote, then," the mayor said.

The vote was unanimous. Neva Joy and Clare Jenkins stood and shook hands with one another. Neva hugged me. But, through all this hands-on celebratory rite, I knew the man was coming toward me. My radar told me so.

I felt his hand on my shoulder.

I turned.

"Honey," he said, "I'm Judson Carmichael." He extended those big hands of his, and he cradled mine like they were small, curious animals he'd just discovered.

"Do I know you?" I asked him.

"Probably not."

"You live nearby?"

"Yes," he said. "I was born here, but I lived in Birmingham up until last year, when I decided to move back out in this direction."

"Why did you decide to do that?"

"I wanted to live in the house where I grew up. That's why . . ." he paused, still cradling my hands, ". . . that's why I asked you what I did."

"Oh," I said.

Judson is tall and handsome, but that night all I was truly aware of was his eyes—a frosty gray, but whereas Scotty's had the quality of nailing you against a wall, Judson's were more searching. You have to be leery of a man with those kind of eyes, because he too can be a charmer, only a more sophisticated one who's learned to appear serious. Plus, his white hair was so thick that the word "transplant" crossed my mind.

On the way home, I asked Neva Joy about him.

"Honey, he's that highfalutin lawyer," she said, "from Birmingham," she added disdainfully.

"So you know him?"

"I know *of* him."

"Is he famous or something?"

Neva Joy laughed. "Ask Carmen," she said. "I bet she knows his story."

"What story?" I asked.

Neva waved it all away. "Could you believe the vote was unanimous?" Neva Joy seemed jubilant. I tried to get in the spirit of banter, but I was lost. I felt the way you feel after a car wreck— the whiplashed sensation, like I'd been in forward, then jerked suddenly into reverse, and here I was still unable to achieve homeostasis. This problem with balance was manageable, but later as I lay in my bed with the shades up (I sleep this way), studying the bright star that had been planted in the black sky right over my bedroom window ever since winter had eased in, the unbalance began to arch itself into the distracting longing I mentioned earlier. Still, Judson Carmichael's big, cradling hands were no blessed diversion, but, rather, a reminder that I'd just rezoned my entire past.

5

MINERAL SPRINGS ROAD snakes and bends through our community, a connecting device that eventually reaches the interstate to Birmingham. In the old days, the surface was chert. It was a quiet, ambling country road, lined with water oaks. Dinah's and C.I.'s and Dewey's homes are, as I've said, situated right on Mineral Springs Road. Carmen and I actually live on Magnolia Lane, a tiny dead-end horseshoe that never knew what it wanted to be. It houses my place, built in the late forties, Carmen's fifties ranch-style brick, and in the curve of the U is the old log cabin that some young people from Birmingham rent to their groundskeeper—for behind it are the stables where the young people gather, ride their horses, and grow watermelon.

The morning after the Zoning Board met I went over to Carmen's for breakfast. Now, as I said, Carmen's house is a ranch-style brick, but what keeps it from being ordinary is her sunroom. She and Paul—her husband, the solid and steadfast Yankee I mentioned earlier—had converted screened porch to sunroom. It's the only sunroom in the neighborhood, and, frankly, I can recall the year they did it—1957, the year before Scotty died.

Dewey and C.I. and their wives were all in a stew with the impracticality of a sunroom in the South. "Lord, God, the plants will sizzle and burn in summer." They went on and on, chatting and rattling and clucking as if it were truly a serious matter, and there I was at home, with Scotty drunk as a hoot owl, storming all over me and kingdom come about Jackie being in seminary, how there was nothing on earth sorrier than a preacher. It was hot. And, believe me, one of the most trying circumstances in being married to a drunk man is having to keep those windows closed during Alabama summers—so as to not disturb the neighbors. So, there I'd sit on the loveseat, legs propped on my old brown ottoman, my forty-three-year-old blue eyes staring ahead, "tuned out," as I'd learned to do in Alanon. (I first started going that year, 1957; I had to ride a bus all the way to Birmingham and back every Thursday night.) I'd sit there, planning my life, envisioning myself going to live with Jackie and Ellen—who were married by then—tending to grandchildren while Jackie preached God's word to some fledgling, innocent congregation in south Alabama, an obscure place, a dry county. Naturally, things didn't happen this way. I didn't divorce Scotty, because he died instead.

So, the neighbors went on and on, telephoning one another with one silly insight after another over Carmen and Paul's sunroom, while Scotty raged on, full of whiskey, and I perspired demurely on the loveseat, dreaming of Jackie and Ellen. And the awful part, the part we rarely talked about even in Alanon in those days, was that after Scotty had raged himself out he'd come to me with those eyes, nail my heart, and we'd make love, windows finally, blessedly, open, crickets and cicadas all alive, singing the most normal song in the world.

Anyway, the morning after the zoning meeting was bright and clear, one of those winter mornings where the moon's still visible at eight o'clock and the sky is that cauliflower blue that makes you want to break into song.

"Honey, Honey," Carmen said and drew me into the heart of her household in one swoop, practically carrying me over the threshold of her front door. Inside, she had a fire gently going, and I knew we'd eat grits, blueberry muffins, and cottage cheese. This was our favorite breakfast.

Carmen directed me to the sunroom. It's a splendid sight, a sunken sunny place full of exotic plants and Carmen's parakeet, Melody. We sat at the small glass-top dinette table, and Carmen brought in the aforementioned menu, along with a teapot.

I inhaled.

"Wassail?" I asked.

"Yes, Honey. It's Christmastime, sweetheart."

Carmen was wearing a long, colorful dress that her son brought her from Central America. He's a physician, and he goes on medical-missionary trips down that way every year or so.

I sipped the wassail. "This is good."

Carmen patted my hand, then unfolded her napkin. "I want you to get into the holiday spirit, Honey." She eyed me warily and brushed a gray tendril from her face. Carmen knows I don't like Christmas, which isn't very much of a testimony to my faith, I realize, but there are some things we just can't help, you know.

She spooned some grits onto my plate. "So, tell me how it went."

"It was rezoned," I said. "The vote was unanimous."

"Well, that's not a surprise, is it?"

"No, I guess not."

I buttered a blueberry muffin and took a bite. Carmen's room, being on the west end of the house, allowed a view of Mineral Springs Road, where the traffic moved on, a bit slow since it was still rush hour and many were heading for the interstate to Birmingham.

"I guess Neva Joy was happy," Carmen noted.

"Mmhmm."

"Honey, are you all right about her?"

"What do you mean?"

"About Dinah leaving her part of the estate."

"Do you mean, was I surprised?"

Carmen considered this, holding a muffin up in contemplation. "Well, yes. I guess that is what I mean."

"Carmen, I never considered *any* of this." I put my fork down. "I didn't know Dinah had any money, period."

Carmen smiled. "We never talk about those kinds of things, do we?"

She meant money.

"Did you think she had any?" I asked.

Carmen shrugged. "I guess when Winston was alive . . ."

I nodded. "There *was* that new Buick," I agreed.

I took a bite of grits. Carmen puts Pet milk in her grits. It makes them very outstanding.

"And they did go to Gatlinburg on their anniversary every year," I recalled.

"She didn't wear jewelry, though, did she?" Carmen asked.

"No. All she had was her wedding ring. Mama's cameo and opal ring were in the safe-deposit box." I paused. "Right before they closed the coffin, I noticed she still had on her wedding ring. I didn't take it off. It was a big diamond. Jackie pointed to it right before the funeral-home man closed the lid. I shook my head no, because I knew Dinah treasured it and would want to wear it to heaven. Jackie smiled at me. It was a sweet moment, Carmen."

I felt then, as I was telling Carmen this, as close to crying as is humanly possible and still not be crying. And when I saw that Carmen *was* crying, I felt even more like crying because I wasn't able to cry, and I understood most succinctly how important Carmen's crying was to me and had been over the years. Since we were always together, she could cry at appropriate moments and relieve me of the necessity. And isn't that what most friends do for one another, anyway? Fill up the holes? Complete the picture? And isn't it not so odd at all that we choose people highly unlike us for best friends? And isn't friendship more a miracle than marriage or maybe even children? Or is that just my view of the world?

Anyway, Carmen cried for nigh onto five minutes, and I knew her grits were getting cold. And, as we all know all too well, cold grits are about as bad as cold coffee.

"Do you know Judson Carmichael?" I asked, to change the subject.

"Yes," she said, and, predictably, turned with interest. "Why?"

"He was at the hearing."

Carmen wiped the corner of her mouth with her napkin. We were using those holiday-printed napkins. These had a burgundy-colored goose surrounded by holly. "He lives in his family's old homestead," Carmen said.

"That's what Neva Joy told me. What do you know about him?"

Carmen dabbed her mouth again, then reached up, unclasped her sterling-silver earrings, and laid them on the table. "I really don't know much at all," she said. "He's divorced."

"*Divorced?*"

Carmen smiled and lightly patted my hand. "People get divorces, Honey."

I waved that away. "I know, I know. It just always takes me by surprise . . ."

"Somebody our age," Carmen agreed, nodding.

". . . to have a choice in the matter," I went on.

Carmen continued nodding. "Other than death," she affirmed.

"He was right interested in my estate," I said.

My estate. I heard myself saying this, speaking this foreign language.

Carmen turned, again with interest.

"He wanted to know if I was certain I wanted to do what I was doing. He asked me publicly, during the hearing. It caught me off guard."

Carmen studied her earrings. They reminded me of silver sweetgum balls.

I got up from Carmen's dinette table and peered out the sunroom's glass wall into her lawn. "Is that forsythia blooming already?" I asked, noting the golden dots that were sprinkled randomly along the arched branches.

"Yes," she said.

"They shouldn't bloom till March."

"The cherry trees are budding, too," Carmen said and rose to stand beside me.

"Must be that Indian summer that came through after Dinah's funeral," I said, recalling the warm, blue morning when Jackie and I had gone to Home Federal.

"That wasn't Indian summer, Honey," Carmen said softly. "It's the greenhouse effect."

"I've heard of that," I said.

"It's very serious," she added. "Haven't you been aware that the blue hydrangea hasn't bloomed for several years?"

I turned to her. "Yes, matter of fact, yes, I have. There's one in my yard. I thought maybe it was just my plant was diseased."

"The seasons are confused," Carmen said.

She locked an arm through mine, and we stood there in her sunroom, staring at the confused yellow forsythia who didn't know it was Christmas. And, beyond Carmen's lawn was the string of traffic along Mineral Springs Road, thinning now as rush hour was subsiding. And up the road was the old homestead, zoned commercial, destined, I supposed, to be a bank or a children's-clothing outlet—those were a popular thing now to be housed in old homes, or perhaps an antiques store. "Could be somebody'll just buy it and tear it down," I said.

Carmen nodded as if she knew exactly the train of my thoughts.

"Judson Carmichael was big into the marches," Carmen mused. "He was an activist."

"Did he really march?"

"Best I recall," she said.

Carmen, as I said, worked in a clothing store in Birmingham. She was on hand for the Movement. An eyewitness, as they say. She shook hands with Dr. King once. But she didn't march, of course. Judson Carmichael marching was an agreeable thought, and I was able to recall his searching eyes with a more accepting flavor and was ready to discard the word "transplant" when I visualized his prolific white hair. Still, believing honesty in a man's face wasn't entirely a wise idea, I nestled closer to Carmen.

Neva Joy phoned me three days before Christmas to say Clare Jenkins would be placing a for-sale sign on Dinah's property directly after the holiday. She wanted to inform me so that the sign wouldn't take me by surprise. She also wanted to let me know that all of Dinah's household belongings were respectfully mine.

"But Neva, honey, they're a fourth yours," I argued into the phone.

"By law," she said. "But not by the manner of respectable Southern custom."

"Now, that's right sweet of you, Neva. But don't you think Dinah would've so designated them if she'd intended me to have all her things?"

Neva Joy didn't say anything.

"Neva?"

"Honey," she said, and I imagined her brushing lint or crumbs or something from her dress. "Please don't take this wrong, but I don't think Miss Dinah gave a careful thought to any of this. Otherwise, she wouldn't have placed us in this situation. By law, every fourth china cup is mine, every fourth spoon, fork, towel."

"Yes, I've thought about all that."

"So, you just go up there and pack up what you want. Get Wash to help you."

"Wash," I said. "Wash!" I cried. "What's going to happen to Wash? Dinah paid him nigh near four hundred dollars a month. I bet that was his sole income. Why, I haven't even contacted him. How's he going to live?"

"Didn't he have a pension from the steel mill?" Neva asked.

"Oh. Well, maybe so. But he still needs the extra income, I bet."

"Don't you have some yard work, Honey?"

"You know the size of my yard."

"What about Carmen? She has a nice-sized yard."

I sat on my loveseat and stared out the window at Carmen's forsythia bush. "Everything in Carmen's yard is under the greenhouse effect."

"What?"

"The greenhouse effect."

"What're you talking about, Honey?"

"Did you know there's no such thing as Indian summer anymore?"

"Just a minute," Neva said. "One of the twins is coming in." Neva's voice was barely audible, muffled by what I guessed was her hand over the receiver. "Just put it in the freezer," I heard her say. Then to me she said, "Lord, those boys."

I looked at my hands, heavily veined, but quaint in their old age. "OK," I said to Neva. "I'll go up and pack dishes. I think I'll call Wash if I can find his phone number at Dinah's. Keep me posted on the sale of the property, and have a happy Christmas, Neva."

"You too, Honey."

Naturally, I knew I wasn't going to Dinah's that day, because it was Thursday, our day—mine, Carmen's, Dewey's, and C.I.'s day—to deliver government products and Meals-on-Wheels. Here is my week: Sunday is church. Monday is bingo at the Family Life Suite. Tuesday is nursing-home visits. Wednesday is senior citizens' choir practice, study club, and covered-dish prayer meeting (Wednesday is a big day for Baptists, nigh near busier than Sunday). Thursday is Meals-on-Wheels delivery, Friday is quilting, and Saturday is open.

So, anyway, Carmen generally drives C.I., Dewey, and me to Positive Maturity at the United Way building where we get the big van, the food, and the government cheese, butter, and millet when it's available and begin our delivery route.

Carmen had already gotten Dewey and C.I. when she honked for me. The men, as usual, rode in the backseat. I reached back and squeezed their hands.

"Honey the millionaire," C.I. boomed. Carmen doesn't allow him to smoke in her car, and it always makes him extra boisterous with anxiety.

"Hey, love," Carmen said to me, put her car in reverse to back from my driveway, then headed onto Mineral Springs Road.

"Whatcha gonna buy first?" C.I. said and leaned forward so as to almost brush his bearded face against mine.

"Buckle your seat belt, C.I.," Carmen instructed.

Dewey wasn't speaking. He was staring pensively out the window. "What is it, Dewey?" I asked.

He glanced at me.

"Whatever is it, hon?" I pursued.

"Sara Catherine's got an illness," he said, as if this were news.

I nodded, sympathetically.

"What kind of illness?" C.I. asked and swung an arm over

the back of the seat toward Dewey. C.I. was wearing his red suspenders, navy pants, and white shirt just as he always does when out on business. He'd forgotten to shave that morning, though, and he looked like a dolled-up hobo.

"The doctor says it's agoraphobia," Dewey said.

"Ah, no, Dewey," C.I. said with faint shock. I was certain C.I. had no idea what agoraphobia was, that he was only responding to the length of the word.

"Thank goodness," Carmen said. "Somebody has finally given you an accurate diagnosis, Dewey." Carmen turned to me. "Didn't you think that's what was wrong with her all along? She's not depressed; she's just scared."

"Scared of what?" C.I. asked and leaned forward to Carmen as best he could through the restraint of his seat belt.

Carmen held her elegantly ringed hand up. "Everything," she said.

"Ah, no, Dewey," C.I. repeated and sat back to stare at Dewey.

"It literally means fear of the marketplace," Carmen said and glanced in the rearview mirror. I imagined this idea trying to find a place to plant itself in C.I.'s hard, sweet head.

"The marketplace," he repeated.

Dewey was staring at me. I felt it. I knew I was supposed to say something consoling, because this was my role in our group.

"It's treatable, isn't it?" I asked Carmen.

"Yes." She looked again in the mirror at Dewey and rolled up the sleeve of her bright, tropical-looking blouse. "She needs a good psychotherapist, not a medical doctor."

"Why's that?" Dewey asked. He leaned forward, his rotund, serious face flickering with interest.

"Doctors will only give her drugs. She needs desensitization therapy."

Dewey looked to me for help. "Translate that, Honey," his eyes said.

I turned to Carmen. "What does that mean exactly?"

"Somebody needs to lead her step by step back into the world."

Carmen turned into the Positive Maturity parking lot, and

we all got out of Carmen's Mercedes. C.I. stroked the blue exterior. "I wish my son'd buy me a car like this."

"He's not a doctor," Dewey said.

"What's Paul Junior doing these days, Carmen?" C.I. asked. "Still going on those missionary trips?"

"Yes," Carmen said and brushed a tendril from her face. "He's become quite an armchair expert on liberation theology."

Dewey and C.I. looked at me. "He goes to Central America," I reminded them.

They nodded.

It was a windy day. Carmen's bright, sleek skirt clung to her long, thin legs. Carmen is taller than the rest of us. "Don't worry over Sara Catherine, Dewey. She's going to rise above her problems. I promise. We'll keep praying for her, won't we, C.I.?" Carmen said.

"That's right, that's it, that's right," C.I. sang.

"We'll put her at the top of the list for prayer meeting," Carmen added.

"That's it, that's right," C.I. said.

"We'll find her a good therapist is what we'll do," Carmen muttered to me as we began making our way to the Positive Maturity building.

Inside, the big colorful kitchen was alight with busy, happy cooks—men, mostly, from neighborhood churches who donate time to prepare food. The kitchen there has been renovated, done in crimson and ivory tile, and it's a beauty to behold. First time Carmen saw it, she marveled, swearing she was going to do hers in those same colors. She hasn't gotten around to it, and it's no wonder: she's right busy carting old people all over the place.

"OK, boys," she said and began stacking the Styrofoam plates full of hot food onto the cart to take out to the van. Dewey and C.I. wheeled it down the hall, out to the parking lot, and onto the vehicle. "We've got to find a way to stop using Styrofoam for these meals," she said.

"Why's that?" I asked her.

"It's bad for the environment."

Dewey drove, as is customary. Perched up there high in the

driver's seat, his bald head covered with a tweed hat complete with red feather, he looked almost handsome with importance, and I stared out the window from my seat in the van, recalling what it was like when we were all younger, how Dewey and Sara Catherine liked to travel to Florida each summer with all their children. Dewey and C.I. and Scotty too, for that matter, all worked at the steel plant. Carmen's husband ran the wire mill. That's how he, a Yankee, arrived in Alabama, a transfer from the Pittsburgh plant. During the Depression, the men managed to work one day a week at the plant. Scotty and I ran a gas station, just one pump, mind you. Dewey and Sara Catherine worked at the commissary. C.I. and his wife grew vegetables. Paul and Carmen didn't appear to suffer, and I can't say why this was so. Rumor had it Paul was somewhat independently wealthy, but if that was so why did they live here in this, our very modest neighborhood, all their lives? Jackie, as I said, was born during the Depression, as was Carmen's son, and a couple of Dewey's children. I wonder about these children who missed, because of their age, fighting in a war—too young for World War II or Korea, too old for Vietnam; conceived in poverty, conscious of their humble birth and depressed beginnings; lost in history because, I fear, we measure time by wars, and they came of age *between* wars, not during one. Or maybe it's just Jackie, and not a whole generation, who seems to have a fragile nature, a sense of uprootedness, a need to keep running from home. Jackie's generation isn't as self-absorbed as that baby-booming generation born after the war. But they are more troubled nonetheless, I thought as we drove on toward our delivery route.

"Do you think of Paul Junior as a troubled child?" I asked Carmen, who was sitting across the van's narrow aisle, staring, too, out her window.

"He's fifty-five years old," Carmen said and smiled over at me.

"Still your baby."

"I know, Honey," she said and reached over toward me, her gold bracelets dangling from her thin wrist. She brushed a tendril from her eyes. "In some ways, yes," she said, turning to me with interest. "Why? What did you mean?"

"I was just thinking about Jackie, how I worry he's still trying to make sense of his past. I wish sometimes he'd been born at a different time."

"Maybe it was just life with Scotty he's still trying to figure out," Carmen said.

Though it still jarred me to hear somebody outside the family wall acknowledge Scotty's drunkenness, I was oddly grateful to Carmen for always doing so with such nonchalance.

"Maybe so," I said.

"Dewey," Carmen said, leaning forward to the driver's seat, "when was your oldest born?"

"Pete was born in 1935."

"And what about Kevin?"

" 'Forty-eight."

"Who's the more troubled?"

"Kevin," he said.

"Forget my theory," I said to Carmen.

C.I. leaned forward from the seat behind us. "Kevin went to Vietnam," he reminded us.

I looked at Dewey again, up in the driver's seat, and realized that he was indeed shrouded by an illusion of handsomeness, as I'd noticed earlier. But it wasn't simply because he was driving a big van; it was because he was *old*, because he'd worked fifty years in a steel plant, fathered five children, survived the Depression, lost a daughter to cancer, and still had the heart to deliver hot meals to his less-fortunate peers.

"We've got to get Sara Catherine well," I said to Carmen.

"I know a therapist," she replied.

"An old one?"

"Yes. She's seventy."

"Not quite old enough," I said and smiled at Carmen, "but it'll do."

"They don't come any older," Carmen said. "Did you know that for decades women analysts had to treat only children, because they weren't considered constitutionally capable of being self-actualized and complete enough to treat adults?"

C.I. leaned forward and looked at me for interpretation. I held my palms up and shrugged.

"I mean in an anatomical sense," Carmen elaborated.

"What's she talking about, Honey?" C.I. asked.

Carmen turned to him. "No penis, C.I."

Dewey shifted gears in order to begin the long climb up Nectar Hill. The big van coughed and spit a tad, but Dewey held it in control, and it didn't die. I knew that the hot meals—in the covered Styrofoam plates—held turnip greens, fried chicken, and cornbread. I imagined, from the slant of the uphill-bound van, that the pot likker was oozing from the greens onto the chicken, saturating the crust and making mush out of the cornbread.

"When we get to the top of the Hill, I'll show you where Judson Carmichael lives," Carmen said.

I felt myself start a bit. "He lives on Nectar Hill?"

"Yes," Carmen said. "The old brick place right up on the crest."

She brushed a tendril from her face with the back of her hand as she's a way of doing. "You know where I mean, don't you?"

We'd passed Judson's brick house dozens of times, because right over past the crest of Nectar Hill is our delivery route. It's just I had no earthly idea it was Judson's place. The thing that makes my old homestead so noticeable is that it is surrounded by flimsy frame houses. Judson's is an estate, complete with pastureland, servant quarters, and one of those useless, decorative white fences that goes on for miles as if to say, I own all of what's inside. Now, mind you, this was early on in my dealings with Judson. The fact was I didn't really know him. I suppose, in retrospect, the thing that got to me was ignorance that I hadn't heard of his family, that he'd grown up right there on Nectar Hill in the old brick place I'd innocently passed dozens of times, toting hot meals, and, too, that I didn't know of his distinguished legal career. Then again, I'm a loner by nature, or did life with Scotty make me so? Don't get me wrong. I have plenty of friends, and I associate myself with all aspects of church life. It's just that I prefer to not extend myself to more-urban circles or endeavors. I always marveled at Carmen's ease and grace, waltzing in high heels through that clothing store in Birmingham, lunching with business people, then, at nightfall, returning with equal grace to our outlying town. It took all that was within me to get on that bus in 1957 and travel into Birmingham for Alanon meetings.

"There," Carmen said and leaned over me a bit, her long, lean arm extending toward my window. "Slow down, Dewey," she said. Though, as I say, I'd passed the place many times, I suddenly saw it afresh because I knew it was Judson's, and he was becoming an odd, newly discovered creature on the landscape. I was, naturally, only curious, the way you are when you glimpse a bird you've never seen. Instinctively, if you're a lay ornithologist like Carmen and me, you note its color, build, the shape of the bill; spot it in the guidebook; and, satisfied that you have witnessed and identified it, you can happily watch it take flight, leaving that isolated moment when you beheld it. Now, as we all know, birds *can* stay. If you have provided a feeder overflowing with seeds or have built the proper house, they might decide to nest, and then you can study their habits. Hummingbirds, as you know, require the seduction of a bright-red tubular getup. I reckon they're right passionate in their needs, which is strange, seeing as how they're so tiny and elusive. Anyway, all this is to say that sometimes rare and exotic birds will linger because they sense you've got something they need. Once, a male and a female Indigo Bunting tarried for almost a season in my yard. That teal-and-turquoise coloring was too lovely to bear, so I just tried to concentrate on their habits instead of being carried away with their handsome feathers.

"What am I stopping for, Carmen?" Dewey called from the driver's seat.

"That's Judson Carmichael's place," she said.

"Who's he?"

"He's a retired lawyer who's recently moved back here to his home."

Dewey, I noticed, was tapping the steering wheel and staring ahead like a patient bus driver at a stoplight. That day I was preoccupied with Dewey and his situation with Sara Catherine. I recall studying Judson's place with some degree of interest—the wine color of the brick, the design that vaguely hinted of English Tudor, the sturdy planters on the porch that probably held geraniums in spring, the pair of big oaks whose top branches were tangled in a marriage arranged by whoever planted them so close. The pastureland. The fence. The way the home was situated on the crest of Nectar Hill in a way that allowed a view.

"OK, Dewey, you can drive on," Carmen said, and she settled back in her seat, surveying her nails.

Our delivery route covers the area right on the other side of Nectar Hill, once the outskirts of the mining town that lies on down the road. The homes are bungalows for the most part. Since it was Carmen and C.I.'s day to actually run the plates up to the doors, I had a chance to talk with Dewey. I moved up into the seat opposite his and patted his hand.

"Better days on the horizon," I told him.

He smiled and took off his tweed hat with the red feather. He ran his big hand over his polished head. His forearms were toned. Being a steelworker had kept all these men in fine shape.

"Sara Catherine's just going through a rough time," I offered.

Dewey looked at his hat, then tapped his leg with it. "But why now?" he said. "Why not when Sara Beth died? Or when Kevin was sent off to war in 'sixty-eight? Or when he came home, for that matter, all nutty as a fruitcake?"

"Well, you know, sometimes you fall apart when it's all over."

"She won't even walk out to feed the birds," Dewey said. "She tosses bread crust from the window. She had me take the screen down so she could open the kitchen window and toss bread." He tapped his leg once again with his hat. "I'm hard put to remember last time she went outdoors."

"She was at last year's Christmas party," I remembered.

"Oh, well, sure. It hasn't been a year."

I held a finger up. "She was at the Family Life Suite dedication in August."

"She was, huh?" Dewey looked directly at me. His steel-gray eyes were frightfully keen with life. Maybe that's not a blessing. Maybe those of us who get dazed with old age are luckier. Maybe the sharp blade of mental alertness is the harder way to face heaven. On the other hand, heaven's not a dreamy place, and angels don't fly lightly the way some people imagine. Angels, both on earth and in heaven, have missions. A person with a mission can hardly afford to fly aimlessly. People with dreams may float idly in time, but people with missions are clearheaded and busy. Now, Judson eventually called my hand on this too, but he was, of course, wrong. Anyway, Dewey stared into my face, and I knew that, unlike C.I., Dewey wasn't a man to be coddled into comfort.

6

CHRISTMAS FELL ON a Sunday. Jackie phoned early, which wasn't surprising because he gets up at the crack of dawn on Sunday mornings, he says, to polish his homily for the interfaith congregation. Knowing Jackie, I reckon he probably doesn't compose it until then. You might call this procrastination, but I like to say he's simply a man of spontaneity. God probably speaks to Jackie as the sun rises. More than likely, he hears God's voice in those first peach-colored streaks of sky. Mornings are fresh like babies, uncontaminated by events. I find them sad for this reason. They're too fragile and naive. Being Christmas, this particular day was all the more tragic, heavy with unborn events—sleeping children who would wake eager but would quickly saturate with toys and sugar; men and women who would, by nightfall, have been, at least once during the day, forced to think of dead people; old folks like me who, despite their belief in God and the season, would be seduced into the dark side of the holiday. Scotty, ironically, never drank on Christmas, and without my anchor of misery I'd wander around the apartment, not knowing what to do with myself.

"Merry Christmas, Mother."

"Hi, Jackie."

"How are you feeling?"

"Just fine, hon. You?"

"I'm doing fine, Mother."

"Where's Robin?"

"She's at her place. She's coming to church."

"She cried any, lately?" I asked him.

Jackie chuckled. "No, no. No tears."

I could hear somebody rattling dishes in the background, and I knew this was, undoubtedly, Celia, preparing breakfast. Naturally, I didn't ask who it was, and Jackie didn't offer.

"What are you preaching on this morning?" I asked him.

"I'm going to talk about celebration of life," he said.

"That sounds nice, Jackie."

"Some of my congregation are Jewish," he said.

"Yes, hon, I know. You can't get real specific today in your sermon."

"Homily," he corrected.

"Yes, homily."

"And you, Mother? Your plans?"

"I'm singing a solo this morning."

"That's wonderful," Jackie said, and his baritone voice shifted a key lower. "What song have you selected?"

" 'His Eye Is on the Sparrow.' "

"That's rather vague, too, isn't it, for Christmas?"

"I suppose it is."

"Then what?" he asked. "What'll you do after church?"

"I might run up and put poinsettias on Dinah's grave." My voice caught, and I felt the armor rising in my throat that would keep me from crying. Dinah always cooked Christmas dinner for me.

"Mother?"

"I'm here."

"Are you feeling sad?"

"No, I'm fine, hon."

"Don't deny your feelings."

I smiled. Some of Jackie's ideas are so quaint.

"You give Robin my love," I said. "Tell Celia hello, too."

I wore a scarlet dress. I hated looking so like a cardinal when I was going to sing a song about sparrows, but I knew the choir robe would hide my attire, so it didn't matter. I liked the way I looked in this dress. I studied myself in the mirror. The scarlet material against my ivory complexion was pleasing. I brushed my natural curls, debating whether to wear the baby-blue eye shadow Carmen gave me. I decided against. Blessed with Papa's eyes, I didn't need any further highlights. I got my purse and keys, and drove myself to church in the old Plymouth.

Pulling up in the parking lot, I spotted C.I. in the doorway to the sanctuary, dressed in a dark-blue suit, handing out programs. He held a hand up, hailing my arrival.

"Honey, you really ought to buy a new car now that you're rich," he said when I got to the church door. I waved that away and walked into the choir room, which was swarming with people of all ages since the combined choirs were singing.

Carmen flagged me. "What are you singing, Honey?"

" 'His Eye Is on the Sparrow.' "

Carmen's brow flinched slightly.

"I know it's not a Christmas carol," I said.

Carmen patted my cheek. "It doesn't matter, does it?"

She held my robe up, like a mother might, for me to slip my arms in, then she fastened it at the neck, smoothed the folds and adjusted the purple sash. "Regal," she said with pride.

Don't ask me why God blessed me with this voice right up into old age. People say it just gets sweeter, and I know it's true that I haven't gone flat. Song has been the easiest thing in the world for me to retain, so I know I can't quit soloing. Wasting talent is a sin. I'm not big on sin, but I know a sin when I see one staring me in the face. It's just not courteous to not use or wear something that somebody's given you as a well-meaning gift. It goes against Southern ways, not that God is Southern by any stretch of the imagination, but I do think He expects us to be an example for the rest of the country, as far as manners go. Once, Mama made Dinah and me wear the most awful mustard-yellow pinafores because Clara Ruth Sizemore's mother-in-law, who was visiting from Savannah, made them for us. She was supposedly one of the best seamstresses in east Georgia, but she sure didn't have an eye for color.

Anyway, the organ chimed eleven notes, and we marched down the aisle in our purple-sashed robes, singing "O Come All Ye Faithful" or some such. All those carols sound alike to me. Brother Earl gave the invocation and greeting, we said the Lord's Prayer, and did the Doxology. The new minister to youth who looks nary a day over eighteen read the Christmas story, only he should have started earlier in Luke when Gabriel flies in to tell Mary she's pregnant and she acts like there's nothing odd atall over seeing an angel and learning she's pregnant which is remarkable and ought to be talked about more but won't be talked about in most older Southern Baptist congregations because it's too Catholic. The deacons collected the offering and we sang another carol. Then we sat down, and it wasn't until I rose, surveyed the congregation as I've a way of doing, so as to establish eye contact with certain friends—it wasn't until I took in the left side of the sanctuary that I saw Judson Carmichael.

Now. You might wonder if that caught me off guard, which it did; or if it threw me, which it did not. God puts people in particular places at predestined times (I know that only Presbyterians are supposed to believe in predestination, but that's neither here nor there). Anyway, I just incorporated Judson into my sprinkling of eye contacts, and when I got to the chorus, "I sing because I'm happy, I sing because I'm free / For his eye is on the sparrow, and I know he watches me," I looked at Dewey when I sang "happy," and I looked at Judson when I sang "free." When it was over, I sat back down. Carmen patted my hand, and I knew from her damp mint-colored handkerchief that she'd been crying. She sniffed and wrapped the tiny cloth, somewhat nervously, around the finger that wore her ruby ring. Ruby's her birthstone. July, you know.

In the choir room, after the service, I hung my robe on its designated hanger. We initial ours so as to retain order. Everybody was chirping, "Merry Christmas." Half-crazed children gone mad with sugar were flying around the legs of their parents like tikes circling a Maypole.

"What's on tap, Honey?" Carmen asked as she hung her robe and sash next to mine.

"Getting out of here," I said.

"OK, sweetheart." She hooked an arm through mine, grabbed both our purses, and led me to the parking lot.

"Ah," I said, "it's gotten cloudy." The sky was the color of pewter, and there was a sensation of fog, smoke, and uncertainty of bearings. What I mean is there was no blue, distinct ceiling of sky. The day had lost its form. The holiday wasn't defined anymore. Plus, it was real cold. "What if it snows, Carmen?" I cried, suddenly all lighthearted with joy.

Carmen put on her jet-black kid gloves.

"Are you going on home?" she asked.

"I'm going up to the cemetery," I replied. "I've got some poinsettias for Dinah's grave."

"Well, now, listen. Paul Junior and his crew are coming over at threeish. I've got a turkey and some cranberry relish—"

I waved it away. "Thanks, hon, but I'm just heading on home after the cemetery." Actually, I knew I was going up to the old homestead to begin the process of discarding Dinah's belongings, but I knew Carmen would think this a morbid and odd thing to do on Christmas, and I didn't want to hear her fret over it.

Now, as I've already said, I have radar or a sixth sense or whatever you want to call it, and I knew, because of the prickly sensation along my spine, that Judson Carmichael was, at that moment, shaking hands with Brother Earl at the church door and proceeding to his destination, which was Carmen and me. It is a fact, not a mere cliché, that I have eyes in the back of my head.

"Carmen, here comes Judson Carmichael," I said.

Carmen didn't flinch or act funny. She's known for years that I have this special quality, so she just adjusted her black kid gloves a bit and brushed a tendril from her face. "I noticed he was in the congregation," she said. Carmen studied my face. "You're one radiant cardinal this morning, Honey. I like you in red."

"So do I," I said.

"You ought to try that eye shadow, though."

"My eyes are blue enough. I don't need any shadows."

Carmen and I, in unison, let our eyes fall to the pavement. She was wearing fashionable boots. Judson was right behind us.

"Carmen Dabbs," he said.

Carmen turned and smiled sweetly. "Hello, Judson," she said, turning her face up with sophisticated pride as she's a way of doing.

"Honey Shugart," he said and cradled my hands, just as he'd done at the Zoning Board hearing. Again, he studied them with odd curiosity as if holding strange tiny animals.

"That song," he began and held a finger up.

" 'His Eye Is on the Sparrow,' " Carmen clarified.

"Yes. I've never heard it. I like your voice. It's very exquisite," he said to me.

"Where do you usually go to church?" I asked him.

"I usually don't," he replied.

All right. Good, I thought. An honest answer. I decided to warm up a bit. "Well, we're happy you came. You ought to join us."

Judson held a hand up. "No joining," he said.

"Oh, get on," I said. "I didn't mean join as in 'join.' I just meant come back sometime."

"So however have you been, Judson?" Carmen asked.

"Fine. You know I've moved back on the Hill," he said.

"Yes, yes," Carmen said. "So I hear."

"I'm retired now." He kicked some imaginary pebbles with his foot, a bit uncomfortable, I felt, with the word "retired." He was, I noted, wearing fancy wine-colored shoes like you'd expect on a lawyer from Birmingham.

"I'm retired, too," Carmen said. " 'Cept Honey and I stay busy as bees."

"What do you do?" he asked, directing the question to me.

"Bingo on Monday, nursing home on Tuesday, choir, study club, and covered-dish prayer meeting on Wednesday, Meals-on-Wheels on Thursday, quilting Friday."

"A nice life," he said. "I'm serious as I can be, it's a nice life, isn't it?"

"Yes, it is," I agreed and let my eyes travel up to meet his, though I was still light-years away from admitting the full degree of his handsome face. I'm a master at holding objects at a distance. I recall rocking Robin when she was an infant, loving her with all my heart, yet, at the same moment, keeping my heart entirely from her grasp. I confided this once to Carmen, and she told me that this kind of dissonance wasn't, in the long haul, a desirable thing, and that someday I'd probably die from a bleeding ulcer or some stress-related disease. I'm perfectly aware of where I developed this "dissonance" and why, but it's not all Scotty's fault—my problems. And, anyway, some very fine and stately music abounds with dissonant chords, don't you think?

Carmen and Judson reminisced a bit about their career days in Birmingham, and I was on the verge of breaking loose from the situation, was, in fact, inching away from Carmen's car and preparing to cross the alley to my own car in the adjoining parking lot, when Judson abruptly took my elbow in his hand and gracefully concluded the conversation with Carmen. "Is that your Plymouth?" he asked.

"Yes."

"That's my Chevrolet," he said. He was parked near me.

"Bye, Honey," Carmen said. "Remember, the turkey's cooked," she said. "Goodbye, Judson. Good to have you home again."

He waved to her. "I like the sound of that," he said to me.

"What?"

" 'Home.' "

"Yes," I said. "It has a ring."

"Do you do anything on Christmas?" he asked.

"No."

"I don't, either."

"I prefer to keep it an ordinary day," I said.

"So you're not a believer either, then?"

I turned to him. "Of course I'm a believer," I said.

"Then why don't you celebrate?"

"You can be a believer and still not like holidays."

He considered this, ran a hand through that thick mess of white hair. "Yes," he said. "Sure. You're right."

"What do you mean when you say 'believe'?" I asked him.

"What do *you* mean?" he asked. "You're the one who is one."

"I am absolutely certain that God exists," I said.

He smiled, obviously amused. "Certain," he verified.

"Yes. He speaks to me on occasion."

Judson raised an eyebrow. He has bushy, animal-fur eyebrows. "What does he say when he speaks to you?"

"It's not an auditory experience."

Judson crossed his arms and leaned against my Plymouth. I glanced over to his Chevrolet. Though I'm no expert on cars, I knew it wasn't a late model. It was a bit rusty and ill-kept. A point in his favor.

"What sort of experience is it, then?" he asked.

"Mystical," I replied, knowing how pleased Jackie would be with this response.

"Mystical," he repeated.

I feel so for people like Judson who've clearly never had a mystical moment in their lives. Well, sure they've had them, or at least the beginnings of such moments. It's just that, at the precise instant the unfolding begins, they tense, turn their hearts in another direction or get distracted by some convenient concrete object. I understand all too well their predicament. I have the same problem when it comes to people. I never allow this kind of intimacy to reveal itself with another human being. It's just that God is another matter. When he begins to show his face, I'm perfectly at ease, delighted, downright humbly grateful for the moment. I wouldn't think of fleeing.

"I'll bet I know what your problem is," I said to Judson. "You're afraid that if you really believe God is nearby, he'll vanish."

I waited. He put chin in hand as if considering. "You know," he said thoughtfully, "that is some extraordinary elephant shit." He kept his eyes on the pavement, chin in hand. "Now what about Jesus? How does he fit into all this?"

"What do you mean?"

"Does he talk to you, too?"

"No," I said. "Never."

He looked up with interest. "Why not?"

I got up close to Judson's face. "Hell if I know."

He smiled. His teeth were perfect. Dentures, surely. I unabashedly studied the white stubbles from where his morning shave was already wearing thin. His skin was bronze, perfectly toned. He wasn't a drunk.

"Well, isn't Jesus part of the big picture?" he asked.

"What picture?"

He held a palm up. "The Trinity."

"I've never fully grasped the Trinity," I said.

"Do you believe in the Resurrection?"

"Certainly."

"Virgin Birth?"

"Of course."

"Then you believe the whole Christian theme?"

"I don't believe Jews are going to hell."

"Well, that's real big of you."

"Yes, it is. Not damning people to hell is the Christian way to think."

"But didn't Jesus say, 'No man comes to the Father but by me'?"

"Yes, but he was quite a young man when he said it. He would have gotten all the bugs out of his thinking if he'd lived longer. My son feels like I do about other faiths. He has an interfaith church."

Judson nodded. "You have a son. Any other children?"

"No," I said. "You?"

"A daughter, Laramie."

"What a fanciful name," I said and reached for my car door. "Would you care to ride with me over there to the cemetery?" I pointed. The cemetery was, as I've said, right near the church, over a bit from the pastureland that we've kept as is for sentimental reasons—to have dinner-on-the-grounds and whatnot. "I'm going to put some poinsettias on my sister's grave."

Judson opened my side first, and I slid in. Then he went around and got in the passenger's side. I cranked the car.

"My wife named her Laramie," he said, "but we call her Mimi. My wife was an artist."

"What kind?"

"A painter."

I drove over to the cemetery and parked, trying to imagine what Judson's artist wife might look like and wondering who decided on the divorce and why.

"How long were you married?" I asked him.

"Forty-five years. You?"

"Thirty-something."

"Widowed?"

"Yes," I replied.

We climbed the steep hill to Dinah's grave. Judson offered to carry the poinsettias, but I wanted to do this myself.

The ground, of course, was still loosely packed, because it hadn't been that long since the burial. I placed the poinsettias by Dinah's marker and drew my coat collar up higher so as to shield my face from the cold wind, still, mind you, eternally grateful the holiday was overcast.

"You got family buried here?" I asked him.

"No. We're all up on the Hill," he said, meaning, of course, Nectar Hill.

"I didn't realize there was a graveyard up there," I said.

"It's small," he replied.

"You want to be buried there?"

Judson put his hands in his pants pocket and shivered, though he was wearing a right warm-looking camel-colored overcoat. "Yes, I believe I do. When I was working in Birmingham, I thought I wanted to be buried at Elmwood, but I've decided against that. Getting back out here in the country seems to be affecting me."

"Affecting you," I repeated.

"Changing my mind about things like the choice of cemeteries. You? You want to be buried here?"

I knelt and kissed Dinah's marker and said to myself, Merry Christmas, Cissy. "Yes, I'll be buried here. Let me show you." I took him over to Scotty's place and showed him my marker set next to Scotty's.

"That's such a quaint practice," he said, "putting those markers down by your deceased before you even die."

"It is silly, isn't it? Especially in my case. Scotty's been dead for years, as you see." I pointed to Scotty's marker.

"What did he do for a living?"

"He drank whiskey."

The sky was remarkably dense with balls of fog and moisture. I kept thinking, The sky is falling, the sky is falling, and it was a strangely blessed idea—like heaven was coming to earth.

"Let me show you Mama and Papa, then we'll go," I said. I led Judson over to their graves, and I knelt and put my hand on their markers and said the word "Christmas" to myself. They were too far into angelhood to hear me talk or to be able to interpret the words "Merry Christmas," as I'd said to Dinah.

"What about your Mama and Papa?" Judson asked.

"Papa was a miner, carpenter, and farmer. Mama gardened and was a real quiet woman. I was Papa made over. You know, the blue eyes and this face I have. Dinah had Mama's brown eyes and sharp features. Did you know Dinah?" I turned to Judson.

"No. I never heard the name Dinah Bluet until the night of the hearing. You don't regret your decision, do you?"

"No."

"Neva Cantrell is an interesting woman, isn't she?"

"Neva Joy is a card," I agreed.

"High-strung, I take it."

"Yes, but those kind of women get things done. Where is your daughter, Laramie?"

"She lives in New Orleans. She's a history teacher at Tulane. She's married. I have two grandsons. They'll all be coming to see me late tonight."

"How nice," I said.

"What about your son? Where is he?"

"West Florida."

"You say he's a minister?"

"Yes."

"Married?"

"Divorced. He has an art historian, though."

"Beg your pardon?"

"He has an art historian named Celia. You know, a girl-friend."

"Oh, I see," Judson said. "Grandchildren?"

"One. A girl. Her name is Robin. She's a social worker. She was born in 1963."

"A wrenching year," Judson noted.

"She was born on November twenty-second."

Judson turned. "You must be kidding."

"That wouldn't be very mannerly, to kid about something like that."

"It's just that I never thought about the fact that there were babies born that day," he said and put a hand to his cheek. "It's a comforting thought."

"Yes. I was at the hospital when we heard Kennedy was shot. Robin was born that night. Ellen—that was Jackie's wife—was in labor so long, and the obstetrician came through the waiting room crying at midday, and I thought Ellen had lost the baby. Then we heard the President had been shot. One of the nurses felt like she had to go on and tell Ellen. Can you imagine? Can you imagine that your answer to the question 'Where were you when you heard that Kennedy had been shot?'—your answer being 'I was in labor'?" I shook my head. "I loved Ellen very much. I hated it when they divorced. She married a musician."

"So, were you a Kennedy admirer?" he asked.

"Of course."

"Before he died?"

"I voted for him," I said.

Judson adjusted his collar up so that the camel color framed his face.

I looked down at Mama's grave, then knelt beside the marker, ran my hand over the ground, and brushed away the leaves. "Mercy," I said. "Would you look-a-here?"

Judson knelt on one knee.

"What?" he said.

"The daffodils are breaking through."

Judson's face was quite near mine, and his ice-colored eyes held the empty ignorance of a city man who doesn't know when daffodils are supposed to break the ground.

"It's way too early," I explained.

He searched my face with an intensity that caused me to back up—like he was trying to understand more than the seasonal ways of daffodils. I stood up and brushed my cardinal-red dress in the way Neva Joy might, as if something were clinging that oughtn't be. "Well," I said. "Carmen must be right."

Judson didn't say anything. He just stood up, then stared at his wine-colored, polished lawyer shoes, the camel coat collar framing his sober face.

"I'm speaking of the greenhouse effect."

He nodded.

"The seasons are confused," I went on.

Judson glanced up at the sky, then at me, but he was silent. He squinted as if sunlight were a problem, which it wasn't. Later, I learned that this pattern of glancing upward, then at me, then squinting was only Judson's way of assimilating, trying to make sense and reestablish order to his thoughts, but that day it was all a kind of odd gesturing I didn't quite grasp.

"Well?" I said.

He didn't say anything.

"Are you familiar with the greenhouse effect?"

He nodded, still mute, and I had a brief, ever-so-fleeting notion that he was having one of those ministrokes that have become so fashionable an explanation for all kinds of strange behavior. I have my own ideas about this that I've shared with Carmen alone. I believe that those of us up in years have lapses that are only small intervals in time during which we glimpse heaven. Now, this differs from mystical moments which can and do occur at any age, and, as a matter of fact, are quite prevalent among children. You certainly recall beholding a butterfly, staring at blue sky, or chasing a gust of blowing autumn leaves. Unless, of course, you happen to be at that awful juncture of midlife when your childhood is only a sad watercolor of images that has escaped you. But then, as we all know, old age breeds the miracle of recall. You have no short-term memory atall; you can't remember what you did minutes ago, but you can recall with exquisite clarity what you did on your fifth birthday and how it all felt. And, you retain the ability to capture new mystical moments. But I was speaking of the other kind of "spell" peculiar to old people, where we leave this earth for a moment or two, and these spells oughtn't to always be viewed in clinical terms, because it's just as likely to be spiritual as medical.

"Have you ever known a Christian Scientist?" I asked Judson.

"No," he said with a start—this radical departure from the greenhouse effect seeming to startle him out of his silence. "Not personally," he added. "Have you?"

"No, but I think I might be one."

"What makes you think so?"

"I don't believe there's anything magic about medicine."

He chuckled and thrust his hands into his camel coat pockets. "Well, I don't think the people who practice it believe it's *magical,* either, do you?" He studied me skeptically. "Your church isn't charismatic, is it?"

"Hardly," I said.

"Are you some kind of faith healer, then?" he asked, and I saw a flicker of merriment cross his otherwise serious, icy eyes.

"Explain to me, if you will, why alcoholism is a disease but can only be treated by attending little spiritual meetings in basements."

He held his hands up. "This isn't an argument. I only asked if you're a faith healer. It was an honest question."

I smiled, sighed, and let my shoulders fall. "No, I'm not one," I said. I heard a bird squawking and looked around for it in vain. The visibility was nil. "Was that a crow?" I asked.

Judson searched the gray sky, too, in vain. I looked at my watch. It was one o'clock. "Well," I said.

"What happens next?" he asked.

"Well, I was going to call Wash, then go up to Cissy's and pack dishes."

"Beg your pardon?"

"Sometimes I call Dinah 'Cissy.' I mean, sometimes I *called* her that when she was still here, alive." I felt the armor rising in my throat, reliable as metal.

"I still didn't catch what you said."

"Oh. Well, see, Neva Joy—Neva Cantrell—called me and said I could have all of Dinah's belongings even though they're a fourth hers." I stopped. "Is that legal?"

He held his palms up and shrugged. "I'm retired," he said.

I smiled. "So, I was going to call Wash—he was Dinah's yard-man—to see if he could help me haul boxes once I got things packed." I paused again and reached to touch Judson's sleeve. "To tell you the truth, I just wanted to get in touch with Wash today, period. I haven't talked to him since Dinah died, and I feel awful about it."

"Well, can I go with you to call Wash?" he asked.

"Sure, I reckon so."

Judson took my elbow, and we proceeded down the hill, past the collection of buried family and friends, names I knew like the back of my hand, a bed of memory and grace.

7

THERE WAS, FIRST, the problem with lunch. We stood in the church parking lot, considering our very limited options, since it was Christmas Day. Naturally, I didn't have a thing prepared, as I had no intentions of festivity for the day. I told Judson I had some pimiento cheese—homemade, mind you—in my refrigerator, along with some salad mixings: lettuce, red cabbage, black olives, bell peppers, and whatnot. He said he'd made some ambrosia because his daughter, Laramie or "Mimi" as he called her, loved it so, and she was, as I'd learned earlier, coming to his place later that night with her family. When he said the word "ambrosia," the armor rose in my throat so hard I thought I'd choke, because Dinah made ambrosia on Christmas morning and we ate it for dessert along with lane cake following the noon meal.

"Go get the ambrosia," I said, regaining my composure, getting back on top of the situation. "I'll get the pimiento cheese and salad things from my refrigerator. Do you have any bread?" I asked.

"I have more bread than you can imagine," he said, crossing his camel-colored coated arms and leaning up against his old Chevrolet. It was a salmon color. "I have plenty of roast beef and pastrami too," he said.

I waved the pastrami away. "Just bring the ambrosia and bread. You do like pimiento cheese, don't you?"

"Sure."

"Meet me up at Dinah's. You know where Dinah's place is, I presume."

He allowed as how he did, so we parted ways, and I went by my place to get the food from the refrigerator. I considered changing, but decided to keep on the red dress, since it was right comfortable anyway. I did slip off my black high heels and put on the old flats that look like they were made by a basket weaver.

When I drove up at Dinah's place, I left the things in the car for a moment so as to allow myself a short ambling over the property. The front lawn is flat as a pancake, with so many pecan trees that it could almost be called an orchard. Through the trees stands the old homestead, solitary and alive with dignity despite the junkmarts that are, as I say, creeping up on it like fast-growing ivy. The wind was blowing hard, causing me to feel forced into wearing a coat, though I'm the type who will resist one like a stubborn old mule. I like cold weather, but then it never gets raw here in Alabama. Carmen believes I'm a bit nutty over this disdain for wearing a wrap and says I'd never make it a day up North where bundling is a winter necessity. I sighed and allowed myself a blessed gaze into the gray sky balls that had decided to travel in a northeast direction. Whereas at the cemetery the gray globs were draped low to the earth, causing that sky-is-falling sensation, they had now risen high into the atmosphere, had transformed themselves into fast-moving clouds, carrying the angels northeasterly, which caused me to believe the spirits were on a mission to Fort Payne or perhaps east Georgia or Chattanooga maybe. Now, a reasonable person like Judson would simply interpret this as a typical weather pattern, a possible storm brewing up Tornado Alley, originating in the Gulf, sweeping New Orleans, then Laurel, Mississippi, then on to Tuscaloosa, and into Birmingham. When I say a reasonable person might call it this way, I feel the need to reiterate that I am Honey, the pragmatist, when it comes to people, but in all aspects of nature I'm a radical mystic. It isn't a choice I make. It's a gift.

Anyway, I knew I best hurry on inside and prepare the salad. I had full intentions of making it a combination salad, one tossed (nigh near saturated) with mayonnaise, though I felt reasonably certain that Judson was probably of the vinaigrette set, having lived so long in the city.

However, when he did arrive, he'd changed into more casual attire and was wearing the kind of plaid flannel shirt you'd see on a bona-fide outdoorsman. I was heartened.

"Do you fish?" I asked him after I'd taken his big furry coat and tossed it across Dinah's bed.

"Yes, I do," he said. We were standing in the parlor, and I realized Judson was probably right uncomfortable, standing in this strange household where nobody lived but angels. I, on the other hand, was feeling remarkably at ease. It was odd, seeing as how, ever since Dinah's death, I'd been absolutely spooked of the place, reluctant to even grace the door. For some reason—and I'd been conscious of it as I prepared the salad, using Dinah's old green bowl—I'd realized that I was carrying on a holiday tradition, that I was Mama, Dinah, and me all rolled up into one, and I had an inkling of what it had been like, in my youth, to be charmed rather than annoyed by Christmas. Things, I suppose, take their toll on you—whatever happens to be your particular toll-taker in life—and you just forget that there were parts of you that existed prior to the struggle with the old animal. Now, this was still early on in my dealings with Judson, and I wasn't anywhere near peering into the past—Scotty and all. Still, I must say I mark that day, Christmas, as the beginning of a story that goes both forward and backward. When I was quite young, Mama started me in piano lessons. One of the things my teacher had me do was an exercise that began with both thumbs on middle C. The right hand moved up the keyboard, the left hand moved down the keyboard, in simultaneous scales that, because of their opposing directions, created a discordant but satisfying sound.

Anyway, Judson was standing there in his tan-and-navy plaid flannel shirt, and I'd just asked him that odd question about fishing, and I knew it was my bequeathed and rightful duty to make him feel at home. I led him by the elbow, just as he'd led me through the parking lot and the cemetery, to the kitchen.

"Now, what pleases you?" I asked. "Coffee or tea?"

He considered this, tilting his tanned (even in winter), sober face to one side. "Tea would be nice," he said. "I usually don't drink it, but it's that kind of day, I suppose."

I was right relieved when he said "tea" because there wasn't a speck of coffee in the house, I realized, not even instant. Dinah had high blood pressure, and she felt that coffee aggravated it.

I heated water and put a couple of tea bags into our cups— Mama's best china. Judson laid a loaf of pumpernickel bread on the countertop. I wasn't surprised; I knew it'd be something along those lines, rye or whatnot. I took the Tupperware of ambrosia and set it in the refrigerator that was empty except for a big bottle of ginger ale that Neva Joy had left. I was glad to see it. It solved the problem of what to drink with the pimiento-cheese sandwiches and the salad.

"Watched pot never boils," I said of the tea water.

"Beg your pardon?"

"Let me show you the place while the water heats."

Again, I lightly touched his elbow to gesture my hospitality, and I maneuvered us to the dining room.

Judson ran a hand over the secretary and the china cabinet. "These are lovely, Honey," he said with what I knew was earnestness.

"Thank you. They're Mama's."

"They're yours now," he reminded.

I shrugged. "Whatever."

He walked over to the window that looked into the side yard where privet lined the sidewalk, leading to the back door.

"Butterflies love that hedge," I said. "Wash's grandbaby girl plays up here sometimes while he cuts grass. Wash!" I said. "I've got to look for Wash's number."

"Go right ahead," he said. "I'll just make myself at home."

"No," I said. "I'll do it directly. Let's go into the parlor."

We walked under the archway that connects dining room to

parlor. "Dinah just had the furniture recovered," I said, running my hand over the satiny pale-rose material.

"Flame stitch is a nice design, isn't it," Judson remarked. "Though it's popular, I don't think it trendy. It'll stand over time."

Where on earth did he get this kind of information? It hit me somewhat abruptly, like an arrow, that Judson probably had girlfriends, and perhaps one was an interior designer or some such. Then a second arrow hit me, that perhaps she was young. These thoughts caused me to want to mix the mayonnaise into the salad, because, as I said earlier, there's nothing quite like the preparation of food to make one feel on top of a given situation. Still, I knew it best to carry on and gracefully conclude the showing of the house, so I pointed out Mama's hooked rug, the grandfather clock that belonged to Papa's mother, and the bluebirds on the wall. "Cissy belonged to the Audubon Society," I commented. We went through Dinah's bedroom, and I told Judson about the rosewater and the pin curls I'd set here, at this vanity, the morning Dinah died. Judson noted the quilts, calling the double-wedding-ring design by its right name, and the arrows came through the air again, only this time I deflected them with the same armor that keeps me from crying. I led Judson into the cubbyhole of a dark den where Dinah'd sit for hours on end after Winston died, staring at the magazine rack that held Winston's old copies of *Field and Stream*, her needlepoint lying idly in her lap, her tiny hands clasped as if in prayer. Then we went onto the sleeping porch. "Cissy and I slept here when we were girls," I told him.

He nodded.

We went back to the kitchen, and I poured hot water over the bags. "You just sit over there, and I'll finish the salad," I said. I got the jar of mayonnaise that I'd brought from home and spooned some into the tossed lettuce, red cabbage, black olives, and bell peppers. Judson sipped his tea. It was almost touching, seeing this big man doing something demure like sipping tea. His long legs were kind of cramped-looking under the confines of Dinah's smallish dinette table.

"Pour on that mayonnaise," he said. "That's just the way I like it."

Another point in his favor, along with the rusty Chevrolet and the fisherman attire.

I put the pimiento cheese and the pumpernickel bread on the table along with two knives so we could do our own spreading. "Would you like some ginger ale with lunch?" I asked. "It's sugar-free."

"Sure," he said.

When everything was all set up, I sat down opposite Judson. "Would you like to return thanks, or shall I?"

Judson looked at me incredulously.

Without further ado, I closed my eyes and thanked God for farmers. Then I thanked him for the pecan trees out front—a living testimony to the fact that life goes on. Then I thanked him for the angel-clouds that were blowing northeasterly, up to Fort Payne, I reckoned, on their special mission.

I said, "Amen," unfolded my napkin, and passed Judson the salad.

He smiled at me peculiarly. "What are angel-clouds?" he asked with the politeness of a mannered man void of imagination.

I glanced out the window and, though I hated to do something so disapproving as make a guest rise from a table of uneaten food, I truly wanted him to share in the splendor of that sky. I led him to the sleeping porch and opened the screen door.

"Look," I said. "See how they're moving so purposefully toward the northeast?"

"Yes," he said. "Yes, I see that."

"Well, don't you suspect they're going toward Fort Payne or maybe even Chattanooga?"

He glanced upward, then to the ground, then at me, in that way of his when he's assimilating.

"It's the angel part, isn't it?" I asked him, suddenly sorry I'd let spontaneity of prayer get the best of me. I shouldn't have mentioned the angels. I touched his elbow so as to guide him back to the table. "It's just spirits," I said. "I just call spirits angels. So does Carmen," I added, to lend city-folk credibility to the idea. "You believe in spirits, don't you?"

Judson spread some pimiento cheese onto a slice of pumpernickel, and leaned forward, his face suddenly alight with intensity. "It's up for debate, but I don't think you're crazy," he said.

"Well, that's right big of you," I said, repeating what he'd said to me earlier about my idea of letting Jews into heaven.

He took a hearty bite of his sandwich and spooned some salad onto his plate. "But I do believe," he continued, "that you've lulled yourself into a particularly quaint and amusing bed of intellectual complacency in these matters—which is surprising considering the fact that you're obviously a bright, astute person who spends much time in serious thought."

I smiled and spread some pimiento cheese onto my slice of pumpernickel and decided to eat it open-face. "Intellectual complacency is a right silly idea, isn't it, hon?"

"Hon," as you know, is one of those double-edged Southern niceties.

Judson ate his sandwich in a way that pleased me—like he was real hungry and believed eating to be pleasurable. I like to watch a man eat. Sometimes I invite C.I. and Dewey over just to see their big, steelworker hands at work buttering bread, carving a steak, indelicately using a napkin, unashamedly heaping second and third helpings of mashed potatoes onto their plates. Scotty never ate. He was, as I say, a tiny man, but his body was solid as a bedpost, right near inhuman in its rock-hard feel, as if he lived every moment with his muscles flexed to their breaking point. Those blue eyes carried the intensity of a man gone mad with passion. It was like Scotty was on a mission, but he had no idea what it was. I say he never ate. I can recollect one winter he decided he'd not drink. It lasted one week, best I recall. He wanted milkshakes. Lord, did I make the milkshakes. I beat up an egg, used heavy cream, cocoa, and globs of ice cream. I'd take the concoction to Scotty's bedside and bear the sensual pain of a lactating mother whose sick baby has finally decided to accept the breast—you know, that feeling when the milk finally lets down from its neglected, overextended source.

Anyway, Judson was indeed a hungry man, and I was heartened anew by his country-style table manners, his lack of hesitancy over eating. You know how some people timidly toy at their food as if it's foreign and a bit frightening.

"How old is Laramie?" I asked him.

"Mimi is thirty-two."

"You had her late in life."

"I was forty," he said, "when she came."

I did the arithmetic and saw that I was older than Judson, which was neither here nor there, of course.

"Your son?"

"Jackie is fifty-four."

Judson reached for another slice of pumpernickel and made himself an open-face with the pimiento cheese. He had, I noticed, separated the black olives from the rest of his salad and was now eating each one with his fingers as if they were a delicacy. "I love these things," he said. We ate in silence awhile, then Judson wiped his mouth with his napkin and finished his glass of ginger ale. He leaned back in his chair, stretched his arms, then crossed them in a relaxed fashion. He was studying me, and it caused me to want to get busy with something. The ambrosia!

"I think I'll wait a minute about the ambrosia," he said, and the fact that he'd read my mind caused me to believe he might have a mystical bone in his body. Or maybe lawyers just knew how to read minds, I reasoned.

We sat there. I turned my napkin over. Dinah's dinette tabletop was Formica with a nonsensical black-and-aqua design—curlicues, I suppose you might say.

"Christmas," Judson said.

I didn't say anything.

My hands were resting on Dinah's table. The veins were like the aqua curlicues on the Formica.

"Where do you live?" he asked.

"Down the road. Magnolia Lane, the horseshoe."

"You own your place?"

"I rent."

"Will you buy it now?"

I looked at him.

"Are you offended when people refer to your inheritance?" he asked.

"Yes."

"I'm sorry," he said, and I saw sincerity in his ice-colored eyes and sober face. He patted the pocket of his navy-and-tan flannel shirt, then chuckled. "I stopped smoking twenty years ago, but I still reach for that pack."

I smiled, nodded.

"I want to come over to your place sometime," Judson said.

"All right," I said. "Are there any foods you can't eat?"

"You don't have to cook."

"Don't be a fool," I said. "I'm *going* to cook."

Judson pushed his plate aside, crossed his arms, and propped his elbows on the table. "You're not a fundamentalist, are you?"

"I don't know what that means."

"You mean you're not going to answer the question."

"You need to read the Psalms," I told him.

His eyes took on that condescending mischief they'd carried earlier when we were discussing these kinds of matters.

"I've read the Psalms," he said.

"You need to read them again."

"Why's that?"

"Because they'll never be the same to you after today." I stared into his eyes, trying to shed some light, to transpire a seed of hope, but also to disarm him. It worked—the last part. Predictably, he looked away, spooked afresh, I knew, by my suggestion of the possibility that an angel might follow him home and change his eyesight, causing the meaning of Psalms to come up off the page and transform his intellect.

"Forget Revelation," I said.

"Beg your pardon?"

"Don't read Revelation."

"Who says I'm going to read any of it?"

I leaned forward. "Forget Psalms too," I decided. "Just read the first verse in Genesis. It's all there. If you can believe the first five words in the Bible, you've got it made," I said. "It's the seed." I reached across the table and laid my right hand near his. "Mustard seeds," I said.

"What?"

I patted his hand. "Nothing," I said.

He ran his finger along the veins in my hand, studying them

like a scientist or a physician in search of an irregularity that might suggest something. I didn't withdraw my hand, because why should I? It was Christmas, and all my family was dead, and Judson's presence was as odd and natural as an angel's. I sat there, trying to be as attentive as Mary was when Gabriel flew in to say she was pregnant with God's son, trying to view Judson's sudden appearance in Mama's kitchen as a likely event in the natural order of things, but I declare I felt perplexed as a pregnant virgin.

"Oh, Wash," I cried into the phone.

"Don't fret, Miss Shugart," he said.

"Please call me 'Honey,' " I pled as I'd pled with him before.

"I hope you're not frettin'," he said. "Miss Dinah *wanted* to go," he said.

"I know, I know."

"Mr. Winston was all she wanted," he continued.

"I know, Wash, I know. Listen. A lot has happened. Did you know the property has been rezoned?"

"No, I didn't rightly know."

"Well, it has. Neva Joy Cantrell and I own it now. They'll be putting a for-sale sign up next week. I wanted to ask you if you could keep doing the yard until it sells? That might be a long time," I added, hopefully.

"All right, Miss Shugart, all right. I'd be proud to work for you."

"I want to pay you six hundred dollars a month."

Wash didn't say anything.

"Wash?"

"That's too much," he said.

"No, it's not. It's five acres to keep up with."

"It's too much," he repeated.

"Consider it a raise," I said.

"I can't do it," he persisted.

"For God's sake, Wash. You got raises at the steel plant."

"Not a right many," he said.

"Well, this is one. How's Mary?" I asked. Mary is Wash's wife.

"Well and good," he said.

"Tell her Merry Christmas."

"All right," he said. "You want Monday to be my day? That's when Miss Dinah had me to come."

"That's fine, but don't consider it binding. You choose your days, OK?"

When we hung up, I collapsed onto my loveseat underneath the picture of the girl playing a harp. I was exhausted. Judson had left Dinah's at three o'clock after we'd eaten ambrosia. It was right good, the ambrosia, light on the coconut, heavy on oranges. I'd cleaned the kitchen and begun packing dishes. Then Carmen, having apparently noticed my car at Dinah's, had knocked on Dinah's door. Her face was all afret with worry over my state of mental health. Why didn't I just forget all this for today and join her and Paul Junior's family for turkey and cranberry relish? But when I told her Judson Carmichael had been there and we'd eaten ambrosia, she quickly lost all signs of distress and patted me all over like a mother might, saying, "That's good, Honey. I'm so happy you're willing to socialize."

"I socialize every day of the week," I'd reminded Carmen.

"But this is different, isn't it?"

"I'm not dating."

She smiled and gave me a kiss on the cheek. "I know, I know, Honey. I wasn't accusing you of that."

Carmen left, and I began sorting the linens. I went on and took some towels—some new, fleecy bluish ones—back to my apartment.

Now it was night. I was that kind of tired you feel when you've spent a day in a hospital while a loved one undergoes surgery and comes through all right, the loved one, of course, being myself, and Christmas being the surgical procedure. I simply sat there on the loveseat, hands folded demurely in lap. I studied my belongings—the small wooden table where I generally eat alone, the straight-back rattans, the brown ottoman, the framed photographs of Robin in various stages of growing up. Over and behind me, as I say, was the big oil painting, the girl playing a harp. I didn't have to face it in order to see it. I knew it by heart. The girl's peach-colored, bewildered face, the tentative fingers, her body parted and leaning forward in seeming obedience to the harp as if, in her desire to play, she's had to surrender all she has to her big gold instrument.

·

8

·

Neva Joy called three days later.

"We have a buyer!" she cried.

I was washing my breakfast dishes in the sink—a coffee cup and pot, one plate that'd held my cinnamon toast and cottage cheese, and a knife, fork, and spoon.

"Well," I said, quickly assimilating, as I'm a master at doing. "Well," I said, "that's right quick, isn't it? That's good news."

"Honey," she said, and I knew from the high pitch there was more to it than that. "It's a commercial outfit."

"Of course," I said. "It's zoned commercial—"

"From Louisiana," she continued.

I tucked the phone under my chin and dried my hands on a dish towel. From the window, I could see Sara Catherine's silhouette in her kitchen, prying open her own kitchen window, and I knew she was preparing to toss bread crust to the birds.

"It's a busing-tour line," Neva Joy explained.

"A what?"

"A bus company. They run tours. They want all of Dinah's

estate, plus C.I.'s, Dewey's, the McWaynes', Hollinses', Jernigans', and the horseshoe. They are loaded. They are offering six-digit figures."

"Well," I said. "That's great news for all, isn't it?"

Neva was silent.

"Neva?"

"Honey, they're black."

I smiled.

I saw Sara Catherine's little hands coming from under the pried window, then opening to release bread crumbs, her fingers flying apart like a covey of birds themselves, scattering to take flight. But after the task was complete—the crumbs released—Sara's hands were gone, back into her dark kitchen.

"Well, Neva, what's the next step?" I asked.

"I'm not sure. I need to talk to Clare."

"OK."

"Well?" she asked.

"Well what?"

"What do you think, Honey?"

I let the dishwater drain from the sink and sat on the stool I keep near the pantry.

"I guess it's a matter of wait-and-see, isn't it?"

"But what about this particular buyer?" Neva pressed.

"It sounds right interesting," I replied. "What kind of bus tours?"

"That we don't know," Neva said. She paused a minute. "But I can tell you we stand to net four hundred thousand on our property alone," she said, and I imagined her fluffing her light-brown French hairdo or brushing lint from her dress.

Throughout the whole ordeal, these figures were like marbles that rolled aimlessly over the surface of my brain, never finding a hole to rest in. Wealth, as I say, was just a stray cat who was staying temporarily on my porch until I could locate the right home for it.

"Clare will approach Dewey, C.I., and the others when the time comes, about selling."

"Where would they live?"

"Anywere they wanted," Neva cried. "Honey, we're talking six-digit figures."

"What do you mean?"

Neva Joy sighed, and I again imagined the words "old people" trailing facetiously across her mind. "I mean," she said evenly, "that they'll all have enough money to build new houses wherever they want. And *you too*," she added, her voice all pitched an octave high.

I didn't say anything.

"To tell you the truth," she said, her voice falling to a murmur, "I've considered using mine to build a lake house for myself next to the twins' lots." I imagined Neva now studying her nails. "Now, I haven't breathed a word of this to either of them," she went on in a murmur. "I didn't want to get their hopes up."

"No, no need to do that," I said.

"Anyway, I just wanted to let you know what's going on," Neva concluded, and I detected a trace of disappointment in her voice that I knew was the result of my lack of enthusiasm over the money.

"Well, I sure appreciate you calling, hon," I said.

"So, how was your Christmas?" Neva asked, and in my mind I saw her standing up, staring idly out her living-room window.

"Just fine. And yours?"

"It was all right. The twins gave me a new blender."

"That's nice."

"Well, I'll be in touch," Neva said.

"All right, sugar."

"Bye."

"Bye."

Now, it was Wednesday, and I must say I had no idea what was waiting for me at prayer meeting that evening. Naively, I spent a quiet afternoon at home, going through a box of Dinah's keepsakes that contained, among other things, a record of Winston's psychiatric visits which ended abruptly when he fell in love with Dinah. A copy of Winston's divorce decree from Neva Joy's mother was also there, along with some photographs of Neva when she was a baby. I saved all these things in a manila envelope to pass along to Neva. Then I made a squash casserole for covered-dish dinner and began getting ready for prayer meeting. I decided to wear the suit that Carmen bought me on my last birthday. It's tailored and neat, and it always gives me the confidence of a businesswoman, which was a good thing, as it turned out, because I'd no sooner driven into the parking lot than Carmen hailed me down. Here she came flying over the pavement in her teal-blue high heels as if she'd been waiting anxiously at the window of Fellowship Hall, her eyes peeled for my Plymouth. My first thought, of course, was that somebody had died, though death is so common an occurrence that I knew it wouldn't of sent Carmen flying across the parking lot like that. I clutched the squash-casserole dish and waited for her to get near enough to break the news—whatever it was.

"What is it?"

Carmen's hands fluttered about me, as they always do, touching my face, hair, and shoulders just the way your mother does to brush you up before you walk out the door.

"It's really nothing," she said and reached to adjust my lapel. "You do look good in ivory," she said. "Matches that complexion of yours."

"Carmen, what is it? Who died? Has somebody died?"

Carmen waved that away and took the squash casserole from me to carry herself, which was really a sweet but unnecessary gesture that only added to my growing anxiety over pending bad news. She walked fast, and I ran a bit to keep up. Carmen is a good six inches taller than me, and most of it's in her legs.

"It's just all this news about the property," she said. "The bus-tour line, is that it? Is it a busing company?"

I sighed deep and stopped dead in my tracks. "How do you know all that?"

"Neva Joy has told Dewey and C.I. and the McWaynes and the Hollinses and the Jernigans, and you know how news spreads on Wednesday night." I felt the armor rising in my legs and chest, my whole body. Having my business spread like fire is one of the most peculiarly uncomfortable things I can think of. I know it's got something to do with living with Scotty and keeping the windows closed at all costs, even risking August heat suffocation, but I swear I'd rather suffocate than hear my business discussed by others.

Carmen, sensing, I'm sure, my armor rising (she knows me like the back of her hand), gave the casserole back to me as if it were a weapon I needed, which it was—being food I'd prepared and was ready to dispense to hungry friends. No matter how up in arms they were, they'd still eat my casserole. It's no secret that I make the best squash casserole around, using last summer's frozen squash, peppers, heavy cream, and herbed-stuffing mix on top.

"Well," I said, regaining composure. "What camp are they congregating in? To sell or not to sell?"

"Honey, they're in the segregation camp."

"Oh," I said. "So it's the fact they're black that's causing—"

Carmen looked at me incredulously. "Well, of course that's the issue. What did you think?"

I shrugged. "It didn't seem to matter to Neva."

Carmen smiled, held up a palm, and drew a dollar mark in it. "That's why it doesn't matter to Neva."

"What does Dewey think? And C.I.? Do they want to sell?"

"Who knows?" Carmen said and opened the door to Fellowship Hall. "They're acting like they don't want to. They're into public relations at the moment, but you can tell they're right proud of the fact that their property's suddenly worth a couple hundred thousand dollars. C.I. is, anyway. By the way," Carmen said, "Judson Carmichael is here tonight."

Fellowship Hall is a large ordinary room with long tables for family-style suppers, a piano, and a lectern up front. The serving tables are by the kitchen, and this is where we line up to serve our plates in the manner of a buffet. The Hall was in its general uproarious state. There's nothing quite like a room full of sober, hungry Baptists who're half crazed with caffeine and gossip. I relaxed a bit because I realized all eyes were *not* suddenly on me, that it was the neighborhood, the issue, the *very idea*, that was the cause of the furor, not me. And, if anything, they were probably grateful for a reason to get agitated. However, as I deposited my squash casserole on the serving table, Kelsey Borden—who's Jackie's age, a handsome deacon who is on the School Board—grabbed my elbow. "Don't do it, Honey," he said.

"Don't do what, Kelsey?"

"Don't sell."

"All right, Kelsey."

He smiled, his face suddenly all bright with teeth and gratitude.

Thelma Nabors, our pianist, had begun a quiet medley of hymns, which meant it was time to serve our plates and get on with dinner. I saw that C.I. was leaning the folding chairs up against the table nearest the piano as he does every week, as if to say, "These seats are reserved." It's ridiculous, since all the church knows this is where Carmen, Dewey, C.I., and I sit every Wednesday, but he does it all the same. I spotted Judson, who wasn't wearing a tie. How refreshing, I thought—no tie; maybe he'll start a trend. Judson was listening to Kelsey Borden, who was clearly bending Judson's ear. Kelsey, who, as I said, is on the School Board, was karate-chopping the air to emphasize whatever point he was making, and Judson was staring at the floor, nodding politely, arms crossed.

Judson glanced up, caught my eye, smiled.

I held a plate up as if to say, "Join me?"

Carmen was behind me, chattering with friends. Kelsey Borden's daughter, a slight girl with caramel-colored hair, lightly touched my fingers in passing. "That was a pretty song you sang on Christmas," she said.

"Thank you, sweetie," I said.

"Oh, look," Carmen said to no one in particular. "Thelma made a sweet-potato casserole. Look at those pecans." She turned back to the women behind her and resumed the chatter.

Judson was ambling toward me, and Kelsey was at his heels, still making a point. Judson continued nodding, chin in hand, staring at the floor, as he made his way to the serving table. He caught my eye once more, and I indicated that he was to break in line in front of me. Kelsey looked up, from his argument, as if awakening from sleep. "Hello, Honey," he said, as if we'd not already spoken that evening. "Do you know Judson Carmichael?"

"Yes, I do."

Judson put a hand on my shoulder and let it rest there, natural-like, as if he were my husband, and I quickly loaded him with plate, napkin, and silverware.

"Are we breaking in line?" Kelsey asked.

"Looks that way," Judson said.

C.I. was over by the piano, guarding the table, and he held up two fingers questioningly, then pointed to two chairs at our table, asking silently if Kelsey and Judson were to be given the privilege of upturned, reserved chairs. I nodded yes, and smiled.

"What?" Judson asked of my smile.

"Do you know C.I. Foster?"

"No."

"Over by the piano. He's saving seats for us. He's one of my best friends."

"His house is involved with the property," he said.

"You've heard?"

"The second I walked in the door," he whispered.

"Do you know many people here?"

"Quite a few, actually. Just acquaintances from over the years."

Kelsey was out of earshot, heaping Thelma Nabors's sweet-potato casserole onto his plate. "How do you know Kelsey?" I asked quietly, surveying the food.

"Here and there," he said. "Most recently from the Zoning Board."

"He's not on the Board, is he?"

"Yes. He was absent the night of your hearing."

"He's on the School Board too," I noted.

Judson chuckled. "He's got a finger in everybody's pie."

Carmen leaned forward to pat Judson's arm, her gold bracelets knocking against one another. "Glad you're here tonight," she said to him. She was wearing a mallard-duck pendant, and I knew it was no accident her high heels were a teal-blue color.

"I'll do anything for a good meal," Judson told Carmen.

Kelsey turned to him. "Where do you belong?" he asked.

"Beg your pardon?"

"Where do you usually go? What church do you belong to?"

"I don't," Judson said.

Kelsey nodded, and as he spooned some of Carmen's cole slaw onto his plate I saw his ears were reddening.

"Which is yours?" Judson asked me.

"The squash casserole."

We served our plates. Judson's was nigh near overflowing, and I was heartened anew with his good appetite. Thelma Nabors concluded her medley with "Blessed Assurance." Then Brother Earl stood and returned thanks. I introduced Judson to Dewey and C.I., and Judson and Dewey allowed as how they believed they'd met once, and they finally nailed it down to the steel plant strike in 1961. Judson's firm was representing the company, and Dewey was, by then, part of management. Dewey delicately maneuvered the conversation elsewhere, since C.I. was a union man all his working life, and Dewey obviously didn't want to upset C.I. with memory of the '61 strike.

Somebody tapped me on the back. This is going to be Harold McWayne, I said to myself. The eyes in the back of my head told me so. I turned. "Hello, Harold." As I've said, the McWaynes, Hollinses, and Jernigans were all involved in the potential sell.

"We need to talk," he said. Harold is, by nature, the worrisome type. He has a flattop. It's gray.

"OK, Harold," I said.

His petulant face remarkably transformed itself to a smile. Oh, I thought, so he wants to sell. And before the meal was over, Rayburn Hollins and Sonny Jernigan tapped my shoulder, with "We need to talk." Rayburn's face was also bright with money. Sonny was, I felt, disturbed. Sonny is quiet, and so is Merle, his wife.

"Are you all right?" Judson asked and threw an arm over the back of my chair.

I sighed. "Makes me want to give my part to Neva Joy and be done with it."

Judson smiled.

Brother Earl stood. "We have several we want to remember in prayer," he said. "Adele Crumley remains at University Hospital in serious condition following her stroke last week. Brother Bill Harlan is resting at home, still recovering from hip replacement. Clara Ruth Sizemore's sister remains in critical condition in Selma."

Kelsey raised a hand. "Dothan," he corrected.

"Dothan," Brother Earl said.

"And then, of course, you'll see the regular prayer list for this week printed on the paper at your table." I reached for the mimeographed sheet.

"What's that?" Judson inquired.

"The chronic prayer list," I whispered.

Brother Earl held a hand up. "Do we have others?"

Rayburn Hollins stood. "Bessie Myron's daughter-in-law had her house broke into day before yesterday. They took her TV set and all her medication," Rayburn said.

"We'll want to remember her too, then," Brother Earl affirmed. "Others?"

Nobody said anything. "Then let us pray."

I didn't pray. I focused instead on the floral arrangement on the serving table, tonight's centerpiece, the only true testimony in the whole room that God was alive and well. There were roses, a daisy spray, and a spectacular bird of paradise. Where did that come from? I wondered. Didn't they grow in some other country? I let Sara Catherine come to my mind, and I visualized her tiny fingers splayed like five birds taking flight as she released the bread crust. Then I let my eyes travel upward to the stucco ceiling of Fellowship Hall, taking my mental picture of her up with me, beyond the bird of paradise, in the direction of heaven. This is how you lift someone up in prayer. You don't have to say a word.

After prayer, Brother Earl made an announcement that Carmen Dabbs would be speaking at next week's study club on "The Greenhouse Effect" and that we'd all want to be present for this timely presentation. Then he read Ecclesiastes 3, the "To everything there is a season" passage, but instead of speaking to, elaborating on, this splendid work of prose, he trailed off onto sin and its consequences, and I knew he was referring to the headline in the newspaper that morning regarding the demise of Birmingham's racetrack, which he'd denounced since its inception.

When it was over, Judson took me by the elbow and led me, fast-paced, like a bodyguard, from Fellowship Hall, across the parking lot, to my car.

"So, God is already speaking to you, I see," I said and held my chin up like Carmen does.

He smiled, that mischievous way he'd smiled early on, whenever God's name was mentioned. "I haven't heard a word from him," he said.

"Why else would you have come tonight? God told you I needed someone to lead me out of that mire."

"Aren't you perfectly able to lead yourself out of any mire? You certainly strike me as that kind of person."

"What kind?"

"Self-sufficient."

"Maybe so."

It was dusk. The night was unseasonably warm for December, with only a distant trace of wind. Only three days ago—Christmas—it had been freezing, blustery. The weather was behaving oddly. Judson was standing near me, leaning against my Plymouth, chin in hand, contemplatively posed, studying me in that invasive way. I'd had enough of it.

"Well?" I demanded.

"Well what?"

"What are you looking for?"

He began studying his hands, the way people do when they're suddenly disarmed, trying to find words.

"I'm glad you came tonight," I said.

He looked up, and I allowed myself a microscopic view into his ice-colored eyes. It was like viewing one of those photographs of the Arctic region—very foreign, exotic, clearly a place you've never dreamed of going.

9

I KNEW IT was snowing well before opening my eyes. There's that quiet you feel right near dawn, and since it only snows once a season, at best, in Alabama, the feeling is a sadly pleasurable sensation. When I finally rolled over, turning to the window, I saw that the flakes were big. My yard had only a dusting, though.

It was Friday, quilting day.

I called Carmen.

"Is it sticking?"

"The roads are clear," she said.

"Shall we go on?" I asked.

"I believe so, Honey." She paused. "Now, Buena and Ceil do live on that hill. They may not be risking getting on the roads." She paused again. "Oh, what the heck. Let's go on up there. I'll pick you up at eight."

I made some coffee and ate my usual cinnamon toast and cottage cheese, and at eight sharp Carmen's Mercedes pulled up in the driveway.

"C.I.'s putting chains on his car," she said as I slid into her blue plush front seat.

I smiled, affectionately picturing C.I. struggling to get the chains on the tires of his Oldsmobile. Of course, there was no reason for him to go to this trouble, no pressing appointments, nowhere to go. It's just that for forty years he'd been accustomed to making his way to the steel plant, come rain or shine, and I knew that to fail to put chains on his tires would be resignation, a full acknowledgment that he was *retired* and we cannot take that word to its final conclusion, because that would mean we're dead.

When we got to the Family Life Suite, it was clear no one else was there. Carmen has a key, and she opened the door. We're right proud of this new building. It was designed by a woman who teaches architecture at Auburn, and I'd go so far as to say it has a bit of grace—for a building of this sort. Essentially, it is one big room with a wall of arched windows, letting in light galore. The interior of the place is painted ivory, with a blue rug right near the same color as Carmen's Wednesday-night high heels, though that day she was, of course, wearing her fashionable boots.

"Shall I make coffee?" Carmen asked. She walked over to adjust the thermostat. "It's right chilly in here."

"I've already had a cup," I said.

"Have another." She went to the coffee maker, tore open the aluminum-foil package with her teeth, and poured the coffee into the machine.

We have what you'd call various "centers" within the big room, for various and sundry functions. The quilting area is a cozy corner near the door that leads you to the children's facilities, a gymnasium and whatnot. We have wicker furniture with rose-colored cushions "just for the ladies," as Brother Earl says. I stood by one of the arched windows, watching the big flakes float aimlessly to the good earth. It was very cold. There go the daffodils, I thought, and the forsythia too, and all the other confused plants that bloomed too early because the greenhouse effect told them it was spring and they believed it. Carmen walked over and joined me.

"Look," I said, and pointed to the bed of daffodils that Thelma Nabors had planted by the small rock garden that separates the sidewalk from the parking lot.

Carmen nodded. "It's serious, Honey."

I looked at her.

"It's as serious as anything we've run up against. It's as serious as the Movement was."

"Oh dear," I said.

She went over to the coffee maker. She'd taken off her boots and was in her stocking feet. The stockings were made of a thick material. Tights. Robin wears them all the time with long denim skirts.

Carmen and I sat in the wicker chairs and drank coffee, quietly beholding the snowfall. On the floor was the big quilt our group had been piecing for the fund-raising auction held in early spring to benefit the Baptist Children's Home.

"I'll be glad when that's done," Carmen said, eying the quilt with faint disdain, her chin up high. It was designed by Thelma Nabors and was a tribute to Alabama football, with a big crimson "A" in the center, a Roll Tide, and a print of Bear Bryant's face.

"It'll sell," I noted.

"Yes, it will sell," Carmen agreed.

Steam rose from our mugs. Carmen blew gently into hers. I was grateful for the solitude and hoped Buena, Ceil, Thelma, and the others wouldn't venture forth in the snow.

"What's Judson Carmichael like?" Carmen asked.

"I'm not sure."

"Hard to get to know?"

"I think he feels displaced."

"Hmm."

I stood up. The snow appeared to be sticking to the Family Life Suite parking lot. Carmen stood, too. Then we both sat back down. It didn't matter.

"Displaced because he moved back out here?" Carmen continued.

"Maybe so, but maybe just where he is in life." I cradled my mug with both hands and peered into the liquid. "He's not a believer."

"Is he looking?"

"He's having an argument with himself. I wonder if it's been going on for a long time."

"Probably so," Carmen said. "It's not the kind of dilemma that puts itself to rest unless it comes to rest on the believing side. Don't you think?"

I considered this.

"I mean," she continued, "that I've never known a tranquil atheist. Don't they always look like they just sat on a tack?"

"I don't know many of them," I said, trying to think whether I knew a single one, other than Judson.

"They're agitated," she went on, her chin up high, not in haughtiness, but in certainty of purpose. She brushed a tendril from her face with her sleeve. She was wearing a mint-green sweater.

"Is that one hundred percent wool?"

She glanced at her sweater as if it were a foreign object, and I knew she hadn't really heard me. "I don't think they sleep well at night," she went on, "and who wouldn't, there being no night-light, no lamp?"

"Now, see," I said, "Judson would say it's a psychological nightlight, an invention of the imagination. I made the mistake of mentioning angels to him," I confessed.

"Honey, no." She reached over to me. "Honey, you didn't."

"He was appalled," I said.

Carmen threw her head back in delight, then massaged her neck with her hand. "Oh, to have been a fly on the wall." Then she abruptly turned as if startled and soaked me up with her eyes. She didn't say a word, and I let her hold me captive because I knew something had hit her like a ton of bricks, and I was perfectly aware of what the something was. It was the idea that maybe Judson and I were courting. And it was as if I dared not believe this idea myself, but it was safe to see its reflection in Carmen's eyes. I had, naturally, known it at some distant level, but I didn't want to hold the idea in my hands. So, I just let Carmen hold it for me. She smiled, and her brown eyes were like chocolate as it begins to melt. Carmen has held ideas for me for a long time. Back when Scotty was beginning to wax passionate in his love for liquor, back before I started Alanon, she'd say, with flat nonchalance, "Honey, you're married to a drunk man, and you love him." And, hearing the truth spoken with such easiness was like listening to a translation—my own convoluted thoughts being the foreign language.

She didn't say anything, and neither did I. I allowed myself the risky contact with the idea as it swam a bit longer in her eyes, then I drained my coffee mug and set it on the blue carpet.

"So tell me," she pressed, letting the idea subside, "what did Judson say about your angels?"

"Well," I said, "it was in the context of angel-clouds."

"Oh, Honey, Honey," she howled.

"You remember how blustery it was Christmas Day," I reminded her.

"Yes. It was a bit windy."

"I was returning thanks for the food, and I just mentioned the angel-clouds."

"Well?" Carmen said. "So what did he say?"

"He just asked me what angel-clouds were. Then, best I recollect, he leaned forward and pronounced me not clinically crazy though it was up for debate."

Carmen leaned forward in her wicker chair, in the direction of the window. "Is that Neva Joy's van?" she asked, and rose.

I stood, too, and walked to the long arched window. I pressed my hand against the cold pane. "I believe so," I said.

Neva's big dark van was pulling into the Family Life Suite parking lot. She parked near the small rock garden where Thelma Nabors's bed of doomed daffodils were face down to the earth, sprinkled with snow.

"Has she come to quilt?" Carmen asked.

I shrugged.

"She's never quilted before," Carmen added.

We waited. Neva parked the van, but she didn't emerge from it. The big thing just sat there amidst the snowflakes, gathering a white dusting.

"Car trouble, you reckon?" Carmen said.

"Beats the life out of me," I replied.

"Trouble is, you can't see a thing inside, allowing as how those windows of hers are black. You ever ridden in it?" Carmen asked.

"To the Zoning Board hearing."

"Can you see *out* those things all right?"

"Best I recollect, you can."

"Come on," she said. "I reckon we ought to check on her."

We grabbed our coats, and Carmen slipped her stocking feet back into her fashionable boots. We had our red-and-white "Roll Tide" toboggans that Thelma Nabors had knitted us for Christmas. We'd worn them for her benefit only, thinking she'd be at quilting that morning.

The snow lightly brushed my face as we made our way to Neva's van.

Carmen rapped on the door, and the big thing slid open like a machine part. Neva Joy bent over from her high-up driver's seat so as to speak to us. A brown woolish scarf was wrapped turban-style all over her face, and sunglasses hid her eyes. A true incognito.

Mercy me, I thought.

"Well, forevermore," Carmen declared.

Neva was clutching a pair of binoculars. She waved downward as if to say, "Down, girls, down," like we were puppies trying to hop into her van.

"Neva," I said. "Whatever is the matter?"

She put a finger to her lips. "Shh."

"What's wrong?" I mouthed.

She motioned us to get in. We stepped up into the big van—Carmen and I are blessed with old-age agility. We sat in the backseat.

"His name is Antoine," Neva said and handed me the binoculars.

"Neva, honey, tell us what you're talking about," I said and held the binoculars in my lap.

She turned to us as if we'd just then suddenly appeared in her van. "Hello, Carmen. Hi, Honey."

"Neva," I pressed.

"Oh, I'm sorry." She fluffed her French curls with her gloved hand and removed her sunglasses. "The president of the busing-tour line is meeting with Clare Jenkins this morning to discuss the sell. I just wanted to get a look at him," she said and gestured toward Clare Jenkins's real-estate office directly across the street.

"Why don't you just go over and meet him in person?"

"Honey, buyers and sellers don't talk. It's illegal."

I made a mental note to consult Judson about that.

"But couldn't you just sit in Clare's waiting room and get a better look?"

"Lord, no."

"Why not?"

"Wouldn't that appear a little weird?"

I glanced at her brown turban-style scarf and tried to fight a smile. Carmen was staring out the side window. I knew she was disgusted. Carmen's got no use for crazy women.

"Why do you want to see him?"

"You can tell a lot about somebody from how they look."

"Well, have you seen him yet?"

"No. I saw a black man get out of a green pickup over at the service station, but it wasn't him. The license plate was an Alabama one, not Louisiana, and anyway he drove on after he filled up."

I looked through the binoculars, not in search of Antoine, but just to see if I might observe a snowflake up close. "Is Antoine his first name or his last?" I asked, scanning the sky.

"I'm not sure. Clare called him Antoine, and I didn't feel right pressing her."

"Isn't she your friend?"

"Well, yes, but friendship and business must be kept separate."

I had no idea what she meant, what that had to do with asking whether Antoine was a first or last name.

"How are the twins?" Carmen asked, pleasantly enough.

"Don's got the flu, and Ron's trying to catch it."

"I'm sorry to hear that. Have you had it?"

"No," Neva said.

I handed Neva her binoculars. "Well, we best be getting back to quilting," I said. "Let me know if there's any news."

Neva turned to me, her weak-tea-colored eyes all liquidy, her fretful lips set like a child. "We need to talk," she said.

"If anybody else says that to me, I'll snap," I told Carmen as we headed back to the Family Life Suite. "If they want to talk, why don't they just talk?"

"Don't you think we best head back home?" Carmen asked. "This snow's starting to stick."

We stopped at the grocery store and bought chili mixings. When it snows, you have to eat chili. The flakes were swarming against the windshield like mad insects, and as Carmen turned onto Magnolia Lane from Mineral Springs Road her Mercedes began to slide. For a brief moment, we were out of control. I felt that jellylike sensation, then the lightheadedness of adrenaline. When the car finally came to a halt, the rear was in my yard.

"Did I get the azaleas?" Carmen said, all afret.

"No, hon, I don't think so."

She opened her door and craned her neck around.

"They're not going to bloom anyway, are they?" I asked Carmen.

She looked at me.

"The greenhouse," I reminded her.

"It's not affecting everything," Carmen said. "Are those Pride of Mobiles?"

"No, they're gumpos."

Carmen waved it away. "That's right," she said. "No problem. Gumpos bloom late anyway, May, isn't it? It's these early-blooming things that're getting it."

When we got inside, Carmen unsacked the chili mixings, moving about my kitchen as if it were her own. She knew, of course, exactly where I kept the can opener, the soup pot, and the wooden spoon.

"Are you cooking?" I asked her.

"Yes. Call Dewey and C.I. See if they want to come for lunch."

I still had my coat on. "I'm going over to Dewey's," I said. "I want to see Sara Catherine."

Carmen emptied the ground beef into the hot skillet. It sizzled. She broke it up with the wooden spoon. "Dewey says she doesn't want company," Carmen warned.

Neither Carmen nor I had laid eyes on Sara Catherine for months on end—except for the dark silhouette I'd see every morning, tossing bread through the pried-open window. "I know what he said, and I'm not a meddler. But look," I said and held my arms to the kitchen window. My yard was a blanket of white. A chickadee was burying his beak into the snow by the gumpos. "This is too beautiful to miss. Surely she'll come out in the snow."

"Do whatever you want, Honey," Carmen said and brushed a tendril from her face. Snow had melted into her hair, and though the bun held firm, the loose strands, the tendrils, were curlier than ever.

"Can I wear your boots?"

Carmen looked at me. "Sure," she said, though a bit puzzled, I knew. It was unlike me to want to wear something belonging to someone else, and Carmen knew it.

She turned the eye down to simmer, sat down at my kitchen table, and slid her boots from her feet. They were a wine color. I put them on. They were quite roomy. Carmen is, as I say, a statuesque woman, and the various parts of her body are a mite larger than mine. Still, the boots felt good, warm and substantial. Carmen smiled at the sight of me, adjusted my collar up higher, situated my scarf, then kissed me on the forehead as a mother might. Who's to say what triggers a memory? All I can say is that when I stepped out my back door into the cold and felt Carmen's boots crunch into the frozen earth, I remembered with clarity that it had snowed in 1929, the year I met Scotty. I was fifteen. Mama kissed my forehead, and I stepped onto the porch of the old homestead, where Scotty stood, wearing a big—oversized, you might say—coat over his small, tight frame. He was like a robust bear cub. On his head was a tiny tam.

"Aren't your ears cold?" I asked.

He nailed me with those blue eyes, and I didn't say another word. There wasn't anywhere to go, so we just kept walking all over Papa's property, covering every square inch of the five acres,

Scotty's hands thrust into his pockets, mine probably clinging to each other inside the muff given me by one of Papa's brothers. We marched through the snow, silently, like devoted soldiers, only there was no tangible destination. The battlegrounds were beyond our developing imaginations, but we were in training, denying the fact that Scotty's ears might be frostbit, that the earth was frozen beneath our feet and hard to manuever, neglecting to behold the snowfall itself as we concentrated instead on covering ground. The fact it made no sense to tromp all over the place was irrelevant. All I knew was my blood was pumping and I had a growing sense of purpose and promise as if God meant me to wax strong with the cold, to face the season like a trooper while Dinah huddled close to Mama and Papa by the fire with her sweetheart bob, thin fingers stitching her sampler. I reached up, jerked my cap off, and threw it straight up so that my own ears could get frostbit, too, just like Scotty's. I had no idea where the cap landed, because right after I threw it Scotty grabbed me like an animal and kissed me, while his hands covered my body quickly as if searching for contraband. All this was my reward for doing something so cavalier as tossing my cap to the wind. I suppose some dog carried it away and gnawed Mama's knitting to bits. All I know is I never saw it again.

I knocked on Dewey and Sara Catherine's door.

"Honey," he said. "Come on in."

I went into their dark paneled den, and for a split second I caught a glimpse of Sara Catherine's body darting furtively into the hall. I heard a door close. My heart sank. I felt inexorably weighted with desire to see her. Dewey saw it in my face.

"I'm sorry," he said.

I waved it away. "I'm just sorry for *her*," I lamented. "And you," I added and put a hand to his sweet round face, the stoic face of a steelworker trying to hide his heart. I understood Dewey all too well. He was like a brother.

"Well," I said and allowed myself a tentative seat on the edge of his drab sofa bed. I had a mad urge to rip the heavy olive drapes from the valance to let some light in. "Well," I repeated, "Carmen's making chili at my place."

"You bet," he said without a moment's ado. He grabbed his coat and hat from the hall closet. Once we were out the door and in his snow-filled yard, I turned back around. There, at the kitchen window, was Sara Catherine's dark face. I raised my hand. "Sara," I mouthed, but she was gone in a flash.

When we got back to my place, C.I. was there, sitting at my kitchen table, wearing a bright-orange sweater over his big belly. He looked for the world like a pumpkin. His cigar perked up in greeting as Dewey and I made our way from porch to kitchen. Carmen was at my stove, stirring the chili. I took off her wine-colored boots.

"Y'all hungry?" she asked.

"Got that right," C.I. said and placed his cigar in the ashtray.

Carmen turned, kissed Dewey's stone face. "Hey, sweet," she said lightly. "How's Sara Catherine?"

Dewey didn't say anything, but glanced at me in deference.

"Not well," I said.

Carmen took off my apron—the one with turquoise ricrac—and reached up into the cabinet where I keep the phone book.

"Yellow pages," she muttered to herself and began thumbing through them. "I'm going to find the name of that therapist. Dearing," she said. "Marjorie Dearing." Carmen paused. "Ph.D.," she added and glanced up at Dewey, who had settled himself in a chair, where he sat solid and still as a statue. "Honey, you got a scratch pad and pencil?"

"Second drawer," I said.

"All right. Now, listen, Dewey. You call this woman and make an appointment for Sara Catherine. Her office is in Birmingham, but don't let that bother you. She understands country ways."

"She make house calls?" he asked, all monotone and deadpan as he's a way of doing.

Carmen put the pencil to her lips. She looked at me, then at the men, then out the window where that snow was still falling as glorious as angel song.

"It's a problem, isn't it?" she reflected. "Getting her to go."

Dewey crossed his arms and stared ahead, his eyes empty as a beggar's cup.

"Well," Carmen said and began busying herself with the food. "I'll go talk to Sara. We'll convince her, won't we, Honey?"

Dewey looked at me. I knew I was supposed to testify to the reality of the thing.

"I don't think she'll let us talk to her, Carmen," I said.

Carmen dipped some chili into one of the four bowls she'd set on the counter by the stove.

"She ran to the back when I came in awhile ago," I went on. "She doesn't want to see us."

"Don't you think it's time to face the music?" Carmen asked. "To force the issue?" She turned from the stove to face Dewey. She looked very, very tall. She brushed a tendril from her face. Her dark-chocolate eyes were unwavering. I inched toward Dewey. Carmen's face broke up a bit, and she returned to the chili, half smiling. She knows I don't like forcing issues, and she knew, at that point, I was feeling right sisterly toward Dewey.

When we sat down to eat, she handed Dewey the paper with Marjorie Dearing, Ph.D.'s, phone number.

"C.I., would you return thanks?" I asked.

C.I. scooted up to the table, as best he could with his pumpkin belly before him. We all took one another's hands as we've a way of doing. "O most gracious Heavenly Father," C.I. bellowed. C.I.'s always fancied himself a preacher. "We come to you with hungry hearts. We ache to see your face, and we seek you at every turn. We ask you to send a ray of light into the household of Dewey and Sara Catherine Lawler, 25 Mineral Springs Road." Carmen squeezed my hand, and I felt her silent laughter over the inclusion of the address. "Father, bless us all," he went on. "Forgive our shortcomings. Bless this food and the hands that prepared it."

All the men I know add that "hands that prepared it" line. They must know it's right complimentary, an incentive to keep the women cooking.

"Thanks for making the chili," I said to Carmen.

She patted my hand.

C.I. leaned forward, best he could, his cigar pointing upward. "One hundred fifty thousand dollars," he said.

We all looked at him.

"You heard me right," he said as if we'd argued otherwise. "One five aught."

Spoons clicked against bowls as Carmen, Dewey, and I began eating our chili. Both C.I.'s arms were flung forward on the table-top.

"Who gave you that figure, C.I.?" I asked.

"Miss Neva Joy."

"Does anybody need crackers?" Carmen asked.

"Your place is two hundred thousand," he said to Carmen. "Dewey's is one hundred twenty-five, aught aught aught."

"Crackers?" she repeated.

"No, thanks," I said.

"No," Dewey said.

"And we owe it all to you, Honey," C.I. went on. "If you hadn't rezoned, it wouldn't've happened."

"Nothing's happened yet, C.I."

"I just hope Miss Dinah can look down from heaven and see how her property has brought good fortune to this town." He put his cigar down in reverence.

"Eat, C.I.," Carmen said.

C.I. unfolded his napkin and took a sip of his milk. We were all drinking milk.

"What's that man's name?" Carmen asked me.

"Antoine."

"Do you reckon he's Cajun?"

I shrugged.

"What's that?" C.I. asked.

"The prospective buyer," Carmen said. "He's from Louisiana. Does it bother you that he's black, C.I.?"

C.I.'s face reddened. "I've always thought we needed some black businesses in the area," he lied. Carmen threw back her head in delight over the blatancy of the lie.

"Money, money," she sang.

I was getting right uncomfortable.

"I never had a maid," C.I. defended. "Back when all y'all had maids you paid three dollars a day, I never had a maid. Mina

Jean did all our ironing." Mina Jean was C.I.'s wife who died back in 1970.

I glanced over at Dewey. He was eating his chili silently. I passed the loaf of French bread to him. He tore a piece from it.

"Butter, hon?"

"No, thank you," he said and bit into the bread.

I kept staring at him. When he finally looked at me, the ghost of a smile—that's all you'll ever see from Dewey—crossed his face.

"Well, what do you think, Dewey, about all this?"

He dipped the bread into his chili. "I think it's serious business," he said. "I think it's serious business when a neighborhood breaks up."

"Ah, Dewey," C.I. said. He had a mustache of milk over his lips. I reached over and dabbed it with my napkin. "We can all move to the same place," he went on. "There's that new development over in Laurel Wood, or, shoot, we could all go to St. Francis in the Pine." He was speaking of the retirement home between here and Birmingham.

"It's a serious matter," Dewey said again, to me.

"I know it is, Dewey."

"I think it's all a moot point," Carmen said.

"What?" C.I. asked.

"It's the most farfetched thing I ever heard in my life," Carmen said and put her spoon down. She brushed a tendril from her eyes. "Nobody's talked directly to Clare Jenkins, have they? Aren't all these figures coming from Neva Joy? Why on earth would somebody want to house a busing company here? Why do they need all this space?"

"They've got to park all those buses," C.I. said.

"But they got five acres in Honey's property alone. Why do they need mine and yours and Dewey's and everybody else's?"

"Don't look a gift horse in the mouth," C.I. said.

We all stared at him.

"Harold McWayne told me it's strictly a package deal," Dewey noted. "We all got to agree to sell or there's no deal."

"Sonny Jernigan's going to be a problem," C.I. declared. He

picked up his cigar and pushed his bowl aside, real serious-like. "Sonny believes this Antoine fellow is being planted here by the NAACP to see if we will refuse to sell to a black business. He says that's why the figures are so high," C.I. said. "Mark my word," he said, using his cigar as a pointer for emphasis, "Sonny Jernigan will be a problem."

"Harold McWayne is hiring a private investigator," Dewey said, to me.

I threw my hands up, then covered my ears. "I can't deal with this! This is out of hand."

All eyes were on me. It's not like me to get all afret. But I couldn't help it. I was beside myself.

Carmen sighed and shook her head. She pushed the sleeves of her mint-green sweater up, placed her bowl aside, and leaned forward, drumming her painted nails—they were a mauve color—on my tabletop. "It *is* rather insipid, isn't it, Honey?"

C.I. looked at me for the translation.

"Dull," I said to him.

"There's nothing dull about money," he argued. "Now, you and Paul always had some," he said to Carmen. "He never went into a mine." Most of the men here worked the mines, as their fathers had, before going to the steel plant. It remained a source of embarrassed pride.

"Well, what do *you* think, Dewey?" I asked.

"It's a serious matter," he said.

"Everything's serious to you, Dewey," C.I. said.

Carmen took the hands of both men, and held tight. "Let's stay together on this," she said.

When they all left, I sat on my loveseat underneath the girl playing a harp. I propped my legs on the brown ottoman. I didn't want to think. The radio was on a classical station. Violins. The snow was falling.

At nightfall, Judson called.

10

"HAVE YOU VENTURED out?" he asked.

"Carmen and I went to quilt this morning, only nobody showed up."

"Still coming down at your place?" he asked.

I pulled the cord and resituated myself on the loveseat so as to have a view of the streetlight where the meager flakes were illuminated.

"Yes. A bit. The flakes are real tiny, like dry baby cereal."

"I don't recall ever having seen dry baby cereal."

We didn't say anything. I looked at my feet propped on the brown ottoman. I was wearing the bedroom slippers Robin gave me last year on my birthday. They were a pale orange, size five. I have small feet.

"So what have you done all day?" I asked.

"I drove into Birmingham."

"Didn't you have trouble on the roads?"

"I have a Jeep. It's four-wheel drive."

"You have two cars?"

"Yes," he said.

"Mercy."

He chuckled.

"Why do you need two cars?" I went on.

"I use the Jeep when it snows," he said.

"It only snows once a year at best."

He chuckled again. "I use it for other purposes too."

"Like what?"

"I have some land in north Alabama. You need four-wheel drive to get to it. It's in some backwoods."

"You go there much?"

"Almost every weekend."

"Hmm."

I looked at my slippers. I was taken aback with how little I knew about Judson. It wasn't an entirely pleasant feeling. It's the way you feel over an unplowed garden, when it's still grass, a part of your yard, and you're wondering if it's worth disturbing. Who's to say the soil will be suitable? Getting your hands dirty day by day, all an act of faith, because who's to say what will grow and what won't? All the hoeing, raking, handling, loving.

"I want to come see you," he said.

"All right. When do you want to come?"

"Now."

I was a bit jarred. I stood up. There wasn't a thing to eat. Carmen, Dewey, C.I., and I had polished off the chili. I stretched the cord to the kitchen and opened the pantry. Only ordinary staples—crackers, tuna, mayonnaise, sugar, flour, you know the picture. I knew there was some cottage cheese and raw vegetables in the refrigerator and plenty of frozen squash in the freezer, but there wasn't enough time to make a casserole and anyway I didn't have a bell pepper and what's a squash casserole without a pepper? There was some ice cream in the freezer, and, oh! the rest of the butterscotch pound cake I'd baked two days ago. Dessert, at least.

"Honey?"

"Yes," I said. "I'm here."

"I've already eaten," he said.

I sat on my kitchen stool and felt a lighthearted relief. "Now, how did you know what I was thinking?"

"It's the only thing about you that's transparent. I'll be there in half an hour or so."

"But that hill! Nectar Hill is so steep."

"The Jeep," he reminded.

When we hung up, I stood in my parlor, suddenly bewildered. I realized how easy it'd been to entertain Judson at the homestead, because it wasn't really my home and therefore I wasn't exactly myself. Having him here was a different matter. See, my parlor is all there is to this place. It's a smallish room, and there's only the loveseat, ottoman, rattans, the oil painting of the girl playing a harp, and an old buffet given me by Scotty's parents. Then there's the kitchen, bathroom, and bedroom. I'm no packrat. I don't believe in whatnots, collectibles, or keepsakes. My simplicity, in fact, defies reason in some regards. I can't quite shake the transient lifestyle I led with Scotty. We were forever moving from one rented place to another, and I still assume I'm on a long camping trip and must keep my surroundings spare for who knows when some old ramshack pickup will appear on the front lawn to haul my belongings someplace else.

Where would we sit? The rocker in the bedroom! I went in, and, turning it on its side, this way, then that, I was able to maneuver it through the door and into the parlor. I situated it where I'd be on the loveseat and Judson in the rocker, but when he got there he went straight to the kitchen and sat on the red stool just like he was a husband or son or somebody who lived there. He said, "Burrr," and removed his giant-sized gloves and big overcoat, which he tossed over the tabletop. His tanned face, reacting to the cold, was a deep-ocher color, making his skin like that of an Indian.

"Did you have any trouble on the road?"

"Not a bit. I'll bet I-59 will be closed in the morning."

I glanced to the table where he'd thrown his coat. He'd also tossed some rolled-up papers there.

"What're those?"

"My maps."

I looked at him.

"Topo maps," he clarified.

I nodded, though I had no idea he'd bring topo maps here.

"I want to show you where my place is, the one in north Alabama."

"Oh, all right."

"It's in the Bankhead National Forest."

"I've never been there."

"Well, I want to take you."

"Coffee? Tea?"

He considered, hand on cheek.

"Wait," I said. "Hot chocolate. Let's have hot chocolate."

He sat on my stool, kind of straddling it like a cowboy. He was wearing the same navy-and-tan plaid flannel shirt he'd worn on Christmas. It was then I noticed his boots.

"Are you a hunter?"

"Guns are despicable," he said.

"Yes, they are."

"No, I don't hunt. I don't understand a hunter's mind."

"But you do fish."

"Yes. I'll take you sometime."

I held the saucepan over the eye, rocking it to and fro so as to not scald the milk. "There's some cocoa in that cabinet right above you. Could you get it, please?"

Judson reached up and got the cocoa, handed it to me, then sat down on the stool again, inching closer to the stove. Steam was beginning to rise from the milk.

"Scotty was a hunter," I said and poured the milk into our mugs.

"Game or fowl?"

"Fowl." I pointed to the stuffed pheasant on the windowsill. "You know, that's the only thing of Scotty's I have." I paused, considering whether or not to ask what I wanted to ask. "Do you have anything of your wife's?"

Judson put a hand on his cheek in thought. "A piece of sculpture," he said. "It's called 'Jacob's Ladder.' It's a strange little piece, quite unlike her."

"How so?"

"For one thing, she's a painter, not a sculptor. A realist, not an abstractionist. This thing is abstruse."

"Jacob's ladder is abstract, anyway, don't you think?" I asked. He smiled, shrugged.

"Well, it was just a dream Jacob had. All those Old Testament symbols are a mite peculiar to me."

"Symbols! You're *not* a fundamentalist!" he exclaimed and slapped my countertop, his face all aglow with crazy light. I recalled Carmen's words about atheists looking like they just sat on a tack.

"Shall we go into the parlor?" I asked.

Judson chuckled. "Parlor," he said. "That's quaint." His face was still lit up and ruddy like a drunk man, and the thought crossed my mind that he might be a trifle insane. "I'm so happy we're over that hurdle," he said.

"What hurdle?"

"The fundamentalist one."

"You've been in Birmingham too long," I said, standing under him. I say "under him" because that's what it felt like. I wasn't yet used to Judson's tall body. Frosty hairs were sprouting from his chest, right where his shirt parted near the neck.

"How's that?" he asked.

"All those Birmingham churches battling over whether a whale really swallowed Jonah."

"Well, did it?"

"Don't be silly," I said.

I maneuvered Judson to the rocker and sat myself on the loveseat.

"This is nice," he said of the hot chocolate. I watched his eyes discreetly scan the room. I knew he was trying to size me up according to my belongings, as we've all a way of doing when we enter someone's home for the first time, but I knew my belongings revealed nothing. His eyes fell, finally, on me.

"Well?" I asked.

He smiled. He knew what I was asking.

"I'd call you a minimalist," he said.

"I like spare rooms. *Things* make me nervous."

"Where did you get that painting?"

I glanced up over my head to the girl playing a harp. "Jackie's ex-wife, Ellen, gave it to me."

"People don't paint that way anymore, do they?"

I shrugged.

Judson stared at the painting.

"Where's your wife now?" I asked.

"She's in Tennessee."

"What's she doing there?"

"I have no idea."

"But, I mean, why Tennessee?"

"Oh, she's married again. I think this fellow was from there, or his people were."

"That must be something, to get a divorce."

"It's a bleak ordeal."

"I mean to have a choice in the matter. I can't imagine. Death is a bleak ordeal, too."

"So you loved Scotty very much?"

"Yes. What was your wife's name?"

"Lanier."

"Lanier," I repeated.

"Yes. Family name. She was from Montgomery."

"Oh."

"Wealthy people," he added.

"Why did you divorce?"

"We didn't love each other."

"Not at all?" I asked.

"I'm afraid not."

"That's awful."

Judson chuckled and leaned forward in the rocker, cradling his mug. "It *is* sad," he agreed.

"Why did you save 'Jacob's Ladder'?"

"I like it."

"But does it remind you of her?"

"No. It's her work, but it's got a life of its own."

I set my empty mug on the floor. I don't believe in coffee tables. Too many people trip over them. Judson set his mug beside mine. "Thanks for making that," he said.

I got up, walked to the window. "I believe it has stopped snowing," I said. "Would you like some butterscotch pound cake?"

"You bet."

"Ice cream too?"

"Why not."

He followed me into the kitchen, carrying our empty mugs He put them in the sink and ran water over them. Then he studied the stuffed pheasant with somewhat detached curiosity.

"Touch it," I said. "It feels nice."

Judson ran a finger along the colorful feathers.

"Was Scotty a Christian?" he asked.

"Heavens, no."

He moved nearer to where I was cutting the cake.

"Didn't that bother you?" he asked.

I looked into his ice-colored eyes. He just had no earthly idea. "That was the least of my problems," I said. I studied his face, searching for a trace of camaraderie, but I just *knew*, I simply could tell, that Judson hadn't been down any back roads. I visualized him with his Montgomery wife, Lanier, in a finely decorated Birmingham home, traipsing down to the art museum or dining in naive elegance at one of those old renovated hotels.

I walked over to the refrigerator and got the ice cream from the freezer. He followed me like a pet. "Didn't you even urge him to become one?"

I set the ice cream—it was a good ice cream, Breyer's—on the countertop. I shook my head and smiled in what was certainly an oblique way. "He was a drunk, Judson."

"I know. You told me that."

"He was in another world most of the time."

"Did he believe any of it?"

"Any of what?"

"Any of the Judeo-Christian tradition."

"What an odd way to put it." I spooned ice cream onto the pound-cake slices. "I don't know what he believed. He wasn't the type to ponder."

"So do you believe he's in hell?"

"No. I believe he's right out there." I pointed to the window. Judson shuddered, and his eyes quickly averted themselves from the window. I held his arms, then ran my hands over the flannel material. "What I meant, hon, is that his spirit probably comes on certain days, to that big open field over behind Carmen's where the Birmingham young people keep their horses. It would be like him to hover near animals to recapture what it was like being human. He probably has many missions in his angelhood. Despite his shortcomings, he was a real go-getter."

Judson put a finger under my chin.

"You are an interesting woman," he said.

I nodded. I felt very strange. I looked down at our feet. I still had on my pale-orange bedroom slippers. Judson let his finger fall from my chin, but we didn't move. We stood there for a spell. We were less than an arm's length from embracing, but let me tell you, old age bears the mark of overembracing. You embrace so many people and ideas along the way in order to seek an understanding of who you are in the universe, to grasp a tangible object that will give definition and substance to your flesh and soul, desperately hoping the mystery will be suddenly a light of clarity, but you arrive at this place—your own tiny kitchen—with yet another butterscotch pound cake and a new stranger, and you just don't want to embrace. You're a mite weary of embracing. I had no idea how Judson's mind worked, but I knew he was feeling something kin to what I was, because his arms were as limp as mine.

"Are you afraid of dying?" he asked.

"No, I am not afraid."

I peered into his eyes and detected a paper-thin crack in the ice. "Are you?"

Judson ran his hand through his thick frosty hair and smiled halfheartedly. "This angel business of yours is very sweet," he said.

I held a finger up. "Angels aren't necessarily sweet. They're on missions, you know. They don't have time for niceties."

"I just mean it's a sweet part of you—the belief in them."

I looked up at him. "You need to eat some cake," I said and kissed his cheek.

I handed him a plate of cake and ice cream and took the other myself. We sat at the kitchen table and ate the sweet stuff.

"Carmen says you were into the Movement," I said.

"Which one?"

"Which *one*?"

Judson put his spoon down and enumerated, using his fingers. "Civil rights, ecology, the women's movement, nuclear disarmament." He paused. "Prohibition." He laughed.

I smiled. "I meant civil rights."

Judson picked his spoon up again. "I knew what you meant. And, yes, I was involved." He licked his spoon. "Not as intimately as I could have been or should have been. You?"

"I rode in the back of the bus, in deliberate disobedience, to Alanon meetings in Birmingham in 1957. I'm afraid that's all I can rightfully claim, but my heart was there, every step of the way."

Judson looked at me. "What about your church?"

"What about it?"

"Wasn't it an issue there?"

"Judson," I said, leaning forward. "This isn't Birmingham. It was never even brought to the surface here. It still hasn't been. There are no black neighbors in this town, in case you haven't noticed. Wash lives down in Riley Springs. That's the closest you'll come. Now this whole business with the property is probably going to bring something or another to a head." I shook my head, then put my chin in hand. "Do you understand how distasteful all this is to me?"

He ran his finger through the remaining liquidy ice cream and licked it. "You mean all the neighbors being involved?"

"That, and also just the whole business of money."

Judson pushed his plate aside, rolled his flannel sleeves up a cuff, then crossed his arms, real businesslike. He leaned forward like a serious lawyer. "You know I was concerned from the beginning. You remember me questioning you the night of the hearing."

"I was right uncomfortable when you did that."

"I could tell."

"I mean, you were acting like you already knew me, and you didn't."

"I wanted to."

I looked at the veins in my hands. "Why?"

"I liked your name. I liked your grace. You seemed classy."

I laughed. "Oh, spare me."

"What?"

I patted his hand. "Thank you. That's a nice compliment. It's just an odd idea."

"Why is it odd?"

"It's a city notion—class."

Judson looked at the floor, then at me, then to the side as he's a way of doing when lost in an idea. "So what's going to happen if this thing comes through? What will you do?"

"I can't consider all that just yet."

"Do you want to sell?"

I picked up my napkin and turned it over. "I am amused by this busing-tour company. I would like to see the neighborhood integrated. I would like to see the issue forced." It was then I first realized this might upset Papa. I put my hand to my mouth.

"What?" Judson asked.

"Papa's not going to like this."

"Papa's in his grave," he said.

I looked at Judson's face. Oh, the absence of imagination, of a creative faith. "Papa is *not* in a grave," I corrected.

Judson smiled and raised his eyebrows in mock disbelief. "He's not?"

"No. He's in China."

Judson's married eyes narrowed a bit so as to survey my words. "China," he repeated.

I knew I was about to carry things too far, but something about Judson's concrete mind made me want to. "Papa, in his early manhood, wanted to be a missionary to China. I believe God probably has stationed him there in his angelhood."

"Permanently?"

I shrugged. "How can I know that?"

Judson backed away from the table, where he'd been leaning forward with legal intensity. "I don't know when to take you seriously," he said. "I really don't," he added with the earnestness of a boy.

"Carmen told me I oughtn't talk to you about angels."

"You tell Carmen about our conversations?"

"Bits and pieces."

"Does she think you're crazy?" he asked.

"Absolutely not." I reconsidered. "Well, she thinks it's crazy to discuss angelhood with an atheist."

"Who says I'm an atheist?" he demanded.

"You do."

"I've never identified myself as such."

"Y'all never do," I said.

"Y'all who?"

"You atheists. I bet you say 'agnostic,' don't you?" I pressed.

"No, I don't. I think that's a pseudo-intellectual jellybean of a word."

I reached over the table and tried to grab his hands, though they were in his lap, well beyond my grasp. "Good for you!" I praised.

He sat like a stone in his chair, arms folded over his chest all stoic and serious—just like Dewey. "It's just that I don't know if you believe all you say."

"It's just the angels, isn't it?" I asked.

"Maybe so. How do you visualize God?"

"It's not visual. *He's* not. You know him by his work, for one thing, and that part is visual, I suppose, isn't it? The sky, moon, stars, and trees, all those exotic colors you're apt to see in birds' feathers." I glanced over at Scotty's pheasant. "When you look at a painting, you don't try to visualize the artist, do you?" I leaned forward. "But you know somebody painted it or it wouldn't be there."

He smiled. "That's very nice."

"It's very true."

He put an elbow on the table and held an accusatory finger to me. "You've never *seen* an angel, have you?"

"Yes."

He raised an eyebrow.

"Carmen is one," I said.

He waved that away. "I mean a dead one," he said.

I raised an eyebrow.

"Oh, all right. A *live* dead one. A transparent one."

"I don't know what you mean."

"Yes, you do know what I mean," he insisted.

Judson's ice-colored eyes began to storm. I felt a tingling sensation crawl my spine, and I knew it was something from way back—a dormant excitement, watching the passion of anger rise in a sober man. "You know, the kind that fly in white robes?" he pressed on.

"Do they really wear robes? Do you think so?"

Judson's face grew red. "The kind that fly in with good and bad news," he continued.

"You *have* read the Bible," I declared.

"Well, have you seen one of those?" he demanded.

I moved to the chair nearer to Judson. "No, hon, I haven't. I have never seen an angel in a white robe who could fly and tell good news from bad."

"All right, then," he said loudly as if he'd just made a big point, won an argument.

I fought the impulse to cradle and kiss his hands. I knew I was in fertile soil. I decided to get up and clear the table. I took our dishes to the sink and ran water over them. I covered the rest of the butterscotch pound cake. I wiped my hands on my slacks. I was wearing the royal-blue ones given to me by Dinah when her weight dropped under a hundred pounds after Winston died. These slacks are size eight. Can you imagine anyone wearing less than a size eight? Dinah was skin-and-bones.

When I turned back to Judson, he was unrolling his maps. "Sit down," he said and pulled the chair out that was nearest to him. "I want to show you my property."

"Let me get my reading glasses," I said.

I walked to the cabinet. I keep them beside my spices. Occasionally, they'll get specked with cinnamon or paprika, but that's neither here nor there.

"Are you familiar with topo maps?" Judson asked.

"No, I'm not."

He rolled his navy-and-tan sleeves up to his elbows. The hair on his forearms was dark, but the ones on his chest and neck were, as I've said, a frosty color just like that atop his head. I touched the dark ones on his arms, curiously. He patted my hand distractedly but kept searching the maps with his finger. Three maps were connected. "All this pink in Walker County is strip-mining," he said. "We're trying our best to stop it."

"We who?"

"The Conservancy."

"Miners got to make a living, too," I said.

"The white part is pastureland, or clearing in general," he went on. "Was Scotty a miner?"

"Before he went out to the steel plant, he was."

"This is the Bankhead National Forest," he said. "All this," he said and ran his hand in a circular motion over almost the entire third map. "You familiar with the Sipsey Wilderness?"

"No."

"We, the Conservancy, worked on this for years. It's been expanded—the boundaries of the wilderness have. It's virgin forest. It will take your breath away."

He looked at me. I peered into his ice-blue eyes. "This is the Sipsey River," he went on. "As you see, it runs through the wilderness. This is the Bee Branch of the river. There's a tulip poplar there that's twenty-two feet in circumference. We believe it's five hundred years old. All right, you follow this creek—it's called Sugar Creek—and you'll come to my place, which is right here. I own these eighty acres." Judson had penciled in a rectangle to show his property.

"How do you get in?"

"There's a dirt road coming in from this way. It crosses a field, then winds a bit into the beginnings of the forest. I hike the rest. My cabin is right in this bend of the creek. It's deep into the woods. There are some old hemlocks."

"I didn't know hemlocks grew in Alabama."

"Only in Winston County. Actually, this spot is quite tropical-looking—defying the fact of the hemlocks' survival. It's damn near exotic. You'll see."

"You take your Jeep, then, along the dirt road to the cabin?"

"Right," he said.

"You go alone?"

"Yes."

"You like being alone?" I asked.

"Yes, don't you?"

"The only way to live," I said.

Judson rolled his maps up and looked at his watch. "You think it's all over?" he asked, meaning the snow, of course. We stepped out onto the back porch. "I wish I was up there right now," he said, "in the woods." We stood still in the cold, surveying my snow-filled yard. I glanced up. The sky remained saturated with those particularly heavy clouds that hold a promise of more.

"Carmen is going to talk about the greenhouse effect at study club up at the church next month."

Judson turned. "Does she belong to the Conservancy?"

"Not that I know of."

"I want to come hear her," he said.

"Good. We have lunch at eleven-thirty, then the program begins at noon. Mark your calendar. Third Wednesday in February."

"I'll be there."

Judson opened the screen door and held it that way for me, as if we'd agreed to a walk in the snow. We didn't have coats on, of course. It didn't matter. I knew instinctively that Judson was tough-skinned as me, that we could've gone barefoot if we'd taken a notion to. It wasn't until we were in his wilderness woods that I discovered he was, like me, of Cherokee Indian lineage, but I'll get to all that later. The pressing problem at that moment was that there was no pressing problem. I felt alive and free from the gravitational pull of ordinariness and predictability. I knew the road had veered, and because I'd lived so long without *things*, I was unencumbered and free to travel. The old pickup had finally arrived to take my spare belongings elsewhere, and I stood in my yard in the snow with Judson. I could see that his Jeep wasn't like his Chevy. It was new, of another generation—a vehicle meant to take modern men to virgin woods.

11

NEVA JOY WANTED to take me to lunch the following Monday. I knew this meant she wanted to discuss business, and the prospects of doing so pained me to the point of considering an alibi. I had none. No use feigning illness, as everyone knows I'm healthy as a horse, and I'd sung a solo in church the preceding Sunday, chipper as a robin in spring. There was no way out, and anyway, if there's one thing I learned in Alanon, it's that you got to face the music because it just grows louder when you ignore it.

"All right, Neva," I said into the phone. "Where shall we go?"

"The DQ?" she suggested.

We have a new Dairy Queen up where Mineral Springs Road meets the interstate. Many of my friends consider this significant, a testimony to our growth. Carmen and I find it a source of mild irritation, especially the way they've constructed the greenhouse section of the establishment. "It's like a California fern bar," Carmen says. I've never been to California, of course, and I've never been to a bar, modern or roadside, but I've got a feel for what she's saying all the same.

"Pick you up at eleven-thirty," Neva said. "You might want

to bring your sunglasses," she added, and that's when I knew there was trouble.

I dressed warmly, wearing the royal-blue slacks of Dinah's and a heavy wool pullover that's got a reindeer design woven into the material. Carmen, naturally, gave me this sweater. I'd never spend this kind of money on attire. Carmen keeps me fashionable, and I keep her fed and spiritual.

I stood at the window, in my parlor, watching for Neva's big dark van. The snow was all gone, of course. It had melted the day after it fell. January was moving on, and I knew February would herald the beginning of spring. Winter ends suddenly in Alabama, with no warning. Just one morning you wake up and the world has gone green.

Neva arrived right at eleven-thirty sharp. Neva is the punctual type.

"I don't own any sunglasses," I apologized as I climbed up into the big van. The machine-part door slid closed.

Neva was wearing her sunglasses, of course, and once more I was reminded of the mystery photos where the eyes are blacked out, leaving me with Neva's tiny nose and rose-petal lips. Her hair was gathered into a spray of caramel-colored curls, like a fancy ponytail. Neva, when wearing a smile, looks like one of those former Miss America contestants who's grown up to be a business leader. Trouble is, she won't smile. Even the winners who grow up to be stars with some terribly peculiar cause still know how to smile.

Anyway, Neva said not to worry, she had an extra pair of sunglasses in her purse.

"I didn't want to say anything over the phone," she said, "but Antoine is meeting with Clare Jenkins again this morning."

"Why didn't you want to say anything to me about it over the phone?"

Neva put the van in reverse and began backing out of my gravel drive. "Because you never know."

"Never know what, Neva?"

Neva rubbed the tip of her nose with her black-gloved hand. "Who might be listening," she said.

"Neva, that's ridiculous. Now, hon, you're going off the deep end with this thing. You're getting paranoid and acting like a crazy woman, and I know good and well you're not crazy." I learned how to be up front like this in Alanon, to call a spade a spade before things get out of hand.

Neva smiled. We were at the red-light intersection of Magnolia and Mineral Springs.

"You ought to smile more, Neva, honey. It's so lovely, and it's bound to be good for your nerves. Did you know that petting a puppy makes your blood pressure go down?"

"I've read that," Neva said, "or heard it on TV or something. Isn't that why they're putting pets in jails?"

Neva took a right rather than a left onto Mineral Springs Road, which headed us toward the church rather than the Dairy Queen.

"Neva?"

"I know, Honey. The DQ is the other way. I just thought we might drive by Clare Jenkins's office, chancing a glance at Antoine."

"Don't park in the Family Life Suite parking lot," I said.

"But that's the best view," she argued.

"Why don't you just park in Clare's lot?" I suggested. "Let's go inside her office."

"Honey, no!"

"Why not?"

"Sellers don't talk to buyers. I've told you that."

I recalled I had forgotten to consult Judson about the legal ins and outs of all this.

"Can't sellers *look* at buyers?" I pressed.

"Antoine might get the feeling we're checking him out."

"Well?"

"He might think it's racial."

"Well?"

Neva pulled into the Family Life Suite parking lot and stopped the van.

"It's not racial, Honey. I mean in a way it's not. I just want to see if he's a desirable type. There are, you know, two kinds of . . ."

I covered my ears. I didn't want to hear it.

Neva took my hands from my ears, cradling them in her black-gloved hands. "I think you ought to know that Harold Mc-Wayne has hired a private investigator," she said.

"Did he really do that?" I asked, appalled.

"Honey, it's reasonable. We wouldn't want the NAACP infiltrating the neighborhood. Harold's of the belief this is all a ploy to see if we'll sell to blacks. Now, you wouldn't want Clare wasting all her time striking a deal only to see Antoine back out at the last minute because it's all been a game, would you? What a waste!"

Neva peered out the van window, searching the Jenkins and Major Real Estate parking lot. "Oh, my God," she cried and fumbled through her glove compartment, retrieving her binoculars. She grabbed the caps from the lenses and tossed them in the air. One landed in my lap, the other on the floorboard. "There he is," she said. "That's got to be him." She handed me the binoculars. "Look, Honey, look."

I took the binoculars because what else could I do, and looked. They weren't focused right, though, and I couldn't make out much except he was a right handsome black man who carried himself well.

"He's right cute, Neva," I said.

Her face fell, and she gave me a look.

She took the binoculars. "He's wearing jeans," she said.

I squinted. "New jeans, don't you think?"

"Jeans all the same."

"Men wear jeans, Neva. Some of Kelsey Borden's peers wear them to prayer meeting. They look right nice with a white shirt and tie. Carmen says you pay nigh near fifty dollars for a good pair of jeans."

Neva's eyes were glued to the binoculars, and she was studying, with the intensity of a young fool in love, Antoine's finely framed body as he crossed the parking lot. "His shirt is a pale lemon," she said. "Open neck," she added significantly. "Collar isn't button-down. His shoes look expensive, maybe a burgundy loafer."

Antoine disappeared through the door of the realty office. Neva put the binoculars down, took off her sunglasses and her black gloves, then faced me squarely. "Clare says they're getting down to the nitty-gritty. She's going to need to talk with us soon, and with the others too, of course. Is everybody in agreement to sell? Is Carmen Dabbs going to be a problem?"

I shrugged.

"Because if she is," Neva went on, "Clare says we can probably work around her property, since it's in the horseshoe, and the horseshoe isn't really necessary. It's just an aside." By "the horseshoe" she meant, of course, our side street, Magnolia Lane, off the main road. "I think they were interested in the house itself. It being brick and all, they might've envisioned it an office building. I feel sure they'll tear down Dinah's place, since it just sets there in the midst of all that fine cleared land. I think they'll park their buses there."

I felt myself growing ill at heart, that vague hole of anxiety you feel yourself falling into when you've lost something, even something insignificant like your keys or earbobs, if you wear earbobs. I have one pair of clip-ons Carmen gave me—pink hearts I wear once a year to the Valentine banquet at the church, but that's neither here nor there. At that moment, I was falling, and the thought of a Dairy Queen cheeseburger didn't help a bit. Naturally, Neva didn't know a thing was wrong, because all of us Alanons have Academy Award–winning performances up our sleeves whenever the moment demands it, and you'll rarely see me overtly vulnerable though my heart may be turning ten shades of purple.

"Well," I said, brushing invisible lint from my royal-blue slacks just like Neva does. "Shall we go get some lunch now?"

Neva cranked up the big van, and we left the Family Life Suite parking lot and headed down Mineral Springs Road to the Dairy Queen. Neva, of course, insisted we sit in the greenhouse-looking, fern-filled part with the multicolored Tiffany lamps hanging so low as to brush your hair as you seat yourself. I ordered a cheeseburger and lemonade. Neva got the chicken-finger combo.

"Don't you want some slaw or something?" she asked.

"No, hon."

"A bag of chips? They have sour-cream-and-chive."

"I'm fine, hon."

Neva set her gloves aside, folded her hands demurely, and looked at me. Her weak-tea-colored eyes were sweet with sunlight that flooded the greenhouse section of the establishment where we sat—co-heirs, sharing the legacy of a homestead, two women as different as daylight and dark. It dawned on me that Neva was enjoying all this. Since she'd become an heir, she'd worn business suits. That day she was wearing a navy one with white collar and gold trim, making her look as spiffy and reliable as a military officer. Only her beauty-pageant ponytail curls gave it away.

"Your hair looks nice, hon. It's in a different style, isn't it?"

"Yes. Gerard felt I needed softening. A light cascade is how he described it."

"Well, it's right becoming," I said.

"Thanks. The twins said I looked like a girl from *Grease*."

It always puzzled me to hear her say, "The twins said this" or "The twins said that." I imagined them speaking in unison as if programmed to do so.

Our food arrived.

"Most DQs don't have waitresses, you know," Neva said. "They are serve-yourself."

I took a bite of my cheeseburger.

"Oh? This is the only one I've ever been in."

"Birmingham has lots of them. Daddy used to take me to the one over by the Continental Gin on Highway 78 when he worked there." Neva's face clouded over, and her eyes grew liquidy. She picked up a chicken finger and ran it back and forth through the sweet-and-sour sauce distractedly. "Daddy was sweet," she said.

"Yes, Winston was a gentle man."

"Dinah saved his life," she said.

Saved him from the untimely death of psychiatrist bills, I thought. "Well, Dinah loved him," I said.

"Mama didn't love him, I don't think," Neva said. "Not really."

I'd only met Neva's mother once—at Winston's funeral. Even when Neva was growing up and would spend holidays with Winston and Dinah, I never met her. She was a mystery woman. "A strange bird" is what Dinah called her. Neva herself is a tad eccentric, but I'd not classify her a strange bird.

"I don't rightly know your mama," I commented.

"Who does?" Neva said and took a bite of the chicken finger. "Mama's very distant. She keeps you at arm's length." Neva squeezed some lemon into her tea, then stirred it contemplatively. "It's hard to explain, Honey, but it has something to do with gender."

"How so, hon?"

"Well, she always said things to Daddy like 'If you were *man enough* to do something about this or that, then maybe we'd be better off.' And to me she'd say, 'If you'd just be more of a *lady*, you might get better treatment in the world.' Now, that's not right, is it, Honey?"

"No, it's not."

"I mean, these extremes of gender—a *real* man, a *real* woman. It makes you feel sexless, like a lukewarm kind of person. It sent Daddy to a shrink."

"By the way, I found some of your daddy's belongings among Dinah's things."

"What?"

"Some photographs of you and his psychiatrist visit records that, I noticed, ended abruptly about the time he met Dinah."

"Dinah was such a dear," Neva said. "You want some of these fries?" She slid her plate toward me.

"No, thanks, hon."

"I'll never eat all these. I guess I'll get a doggy-bag and take my leftovers to the twins." Neva ate a fry or two, and I worked on my cheeseburger. It was really better than I'd anticipated—cooked on a grill, I reckoned.

"Did Dinah and Daddy try to have children together?"

"Well, yes," I answered. "Did they not tell you that? Dinah wasn't able to conceive. Of course, she was almost forty when they married. Something wasn't right with her system. She had an emergency hysterectomy when she was forty-something. I mean she was really bleeding to death for some reason. It was necessary. Hysterectomies weren't in vogue then. You only got them when you needed them. I'm surprised you didn't know about that, that Dinah didn't tell you."

Neva leaned forward. "Well, Dinah was very private. You and Dinah are quite different. Did you know that?"

"How so?" I asked, but I knew what she was going to say, because I'd heard it before.

"Dinah was more proper. Is that the right word? Mannered, maybe? But, at the same time, more fragile. You're the Rock of Gibraltar."

I smiled.

"More earthy. It's nice, Honey."

"I suppose."

"Were you and Dinah different like that when you were children?"

"Oh, maybe so," I said and leaned back with my lemonade in hand. "I was the older. Dinah was six years younger, you know. She was the kind to hide in Mama's skirts, real feminine and sweet. It wasn't like I was a boy, but I must say I had a streak of something."

"A streak of what?" Neva was eating heartily now, and it gave me that relaxed feeling, watching a nervous type of person settle into the pleasure of food, even though I hadn't prepared it.

"Oh, maybe a streak of rebellion," I said. I paused, reconsidering. "Perhaps not rebellion, but just this call to battle, like the trumpet had sounded, and I was off to war."

Neva laughed. "What war?"

"Well, when I was little, I suppose it was the war against sewing by the fire or wearing shoes when I'd go outside or whatever the general expectations were. Then I made up my own wars, you know, hon, like me against the elements, trying to capture an elusive lizard or redirect the path of a whole colony of ants or make a pile of leaves stay in one place on a particularly windy day."

Neva doused her fries with ketchup and licked her fingers. "That's wonderful, Honey," she said.

"Then I met Scotty, and I was off to the real races."

"He was an alcoholic, wasn't he?"

"Yes, he was."

"Hmm. That must have been awful," she said.

"It was."

"Real challenging, I bet," Neva said, and her enlightenment on the subject was cause for pause.

"Was your husband a drunk?" I asked with all indelicateness.

Neva laughed. "No. But he was a con artist."

"Oh."

"The twins are like me, thank goodness. I've often thought how blessed it is they are identical rather than fraternal, because if they'd been fraternal, one might have carried more of his father's gene pool, and it might have been hard to love that one equally."

"Yes," I agreed. "It's a blessing."

"Are you dating Judson Carmichael?"

Naturally, I was taken aback, but I regrouped instantly, as I'm a master at doing. "Dating," I said so as to survey the meaning of the word. "Dating," I repeated.

"Courting?" Neva said, and I wondered if the words "old people" might again be trailing sympathetically across her mind.

"Where did you hear that? Or did you hear it?"

Neva put a hand on mine. "Honey, I swear this is the truth: I didn't hear it anywhere. I just felt it was in the cards the night of the Zoning Board hearing. That man was all over you."

"All over me?" I tried to recall.

"Not literally. I just mean his eyes were all over you. He was all over you in a figurative sense."

I considered this. It was a nice thought.

"Well, I have seen him since then. He's an interesting man."

Neva ate her last chicken finger. "No doggy-bag for the twins, I guess," she said. "I didn't realize I was so hungry."

I picked up Neva's check and mine. "On me," I said.

Neva tried to take hers back. "I can't let you do that, Honey."

"I'm three-quarters richer than you," I said, and when I said it I felt, for the first time, a natural kind of delight or maybe just a sense of easiness over having money, like the way it is when you realize that new shoes aren't hurting your feet anymore. It's not that they feel good; it's just that they're not so blatantly foreign and ill-fitted. Still, the problem with the old homestead sat heavy on me, and I couldn't bear the image of its absence amidst a collection of buses parked on Papa's land. No matter how pleasing the thought of a "forced issue," that is, an integrated neighborhood, I didn't want to see the place torn down. Being a rebel isn't necessarily a gift. Indeed, it's more of an uncontrollable passion like the love of liquor perhaps. It causes you to go against your own heart and home simply for the sake of bending the wind.

I looked at Neva, then cast my eyes about the interior of the Dairy Queen. Ferns were threatening to eat me alive, and Tiffany lamps were hanging precariously overhead. The sun was too bright. I was reminded afresh of my disdain for spring—the feeling of heating up. But it was still late winter, and the greenhouse effect of this restaurant was only an illusion. It was cold in reality outside, still time. It was at that moment I knew I was going to track down Antoine and meet the man face to face. No binoculars and dark glasses for me. I was going to sit down with him and ask him with all candor and warmth, "Are you for real?" I wasn't going to sell the old homestead without meeting the man who was going to buy it. I didn't care if it was legal or not for sellers to talk to buyers. I felt all the angels hovering near me, and I wasn't sure why they were flying in. To protect, warn, encourage, comfort? That's the thing about angels—they don't talk out loud. After Gabriel flew in to tell Mary she was pregnant with God's son, there just wasn't any way an angel could ever speak aloud again. I mean, what more was there for angels to say? Who could top that? It'd be almost a sacrilege for one of Gabriel's descendants to come to visit me at the Dairy Queen and say aloud, "Don't sell your papa's land to Antoine," or "Do sell your papa's land to Antoine." I kept thinking of that proverb that says, "He who troubles his own house shall inherit the wind." I'd never understood that exactly, and I still didn't. Was it an omen or a promise of flight?

12

I MADE MYSELF wait a week before calling Clare Jenkins. I tried to get busy with people. I obtained the chronic prayer list from the church and prayed for people I didn't know. You could tell by their names what generation they represented and therefore their approximate age. There were the Ellas, Beulahs, and Adeles from my group. Then the Mary Beths, Carolyns, and Franklins from Jackie's peers. Then the Christophers, Jennifers, and Kimberlys from Robin's generation. I prayed while I baked. I prayed while quilting on Friday and during bingo. Carmen knew I was preoccupied, but she didn't pry. I knew I ought to tell her I was going to meet Antoine, but I was afraid she'd cause me to reconsider. Judson had gone up to north Alabama to his place in Winston County, his virgin woods. It was probably for the best, as I'd surely have called him, just to escape my problems, and I might have confided my plans, and he might've advised against meeting Antoine.

Tuesday morning, I woke at dawn. I made myself a cup of hot tea and went to the front porch, where I had a dim view of Mineral Springs Road. It was still that thin, smoky color of presunrise. A few cars, headlights still on, were traveling east to Birmingham, or perhaps beyond. Atlanta, maybe. I felt these early risers were embarking on business trips, and I knew it was the day I'd make one myself. The early-morning air was subtly flavored with warmth, and I knew spring was coming. I prefer making decisions in winter when the earth isn't green, causing an obscuring of the lay of the land and the patterns of tree branches.

At nine, I called.

"Clare Jenkins, please," I said into the receiver. I'd gotten my reading glasses from the spice cabinet and had the phone book on my kitchen table. I was standing up, trying to feel businesslike.

"One moment, please."

I looked at the veins in my hand. I surveyed my fingers, considering the fact I might start wearing Mama's opal ring.

"Clare Jenkins," Clare said.

"Hello, Clare. Honey Shugart here."

"I was just this morning thinking we needed to talk. Hold a minute, Honey."

I heard her close her door.

"OK," she said. "I trust Neva Joy has been keeping you abreast."

"Yes."

"Antoine is going to make an offer by Friday."

I felt my knees hedge a bit as if they weren't particularly up to supporting my body. But I made myself keep standing.

"Is that his last name or first?" I said with all casualness.

"His last."

"Oh?" I tucked the phone under my chin and poured myself another cup of tea. "What's his first, Clare?"

"Michael."

"Michael Antoine," I said, gaining strength with the acquisition of information. "And what's the name of his outfit?"

"Southern Trails."

"What do they do exactly?"

"They charter buses to churches, businesses, hobby groups, that sort of thing. It's quite a nice organization."

"I'm sure."

"Michael Antoine is a jewel."

"Hmm."

"This is all on the up-and-up, Honey."

"That's good to hear."

"I guess you know about Harold McWayne hiring a private eye," she offered.

"I heard."

"Doesn't that beat all?" she said. I was trying to picture Clare in my mind, which wasn't altogether easy as I'd only met her once, at the Zoning Board hearing. I recalled her height, the peach-tinted, monogrammed glasses—"CJ," her immaculate business suit.

"This company is from Louisiana?" I asked.

"Yes. Baton Rouge."

"Why're they wanting to move here?"

"It's a more strategic location. Alabama is the Heart of Dixie!" she exclaimed.

"Yes, seems I've heard that."

Clare laughed, and I heard the jostling of ice as she apparently sipped something.

"Did you see that article in *Newsweek* where Birmingham is listed as one of the ten most desirable places in the nation to live?"

"No, I didn't."

"Part of the reason is the low cost of living. And, see, out here it's even better because there's all this land, all this space, but we're close enough to the city to attract new businesses like Antoine's. Exciting things are about to happen here."

If you're a real-estate agent, I thought, but didn't say.

"I don't know why everybody's so shocked with the figures Mr. Antoine—Michael—is tossing about. This land is worth it! Your and Neva's place is a goldmine what with the interstate only two miles down the road and all. By the way, Honey, we can work around the horseshoe if you and Carmen Dabbs don't want to move. Lawrence Bunting, your landlord, says he'd love to sell for this kind of money, but he's concerned about you."

Clare paused.

"He's an old hunting buddy of my former husband's," I said. "I've known him a long time."

"It's none of my business," Clare said, "but have you ever considered *buying* it from him?"

"No, I have never considered that."

"Uh huh," Clare said. "Uh *huh*," she repeated. "Well."

"Is Michael Antoine here in Birmingham or is he back home in Louisiana?"

"Oh, he's here. As I say, he's making an offer Friday if not sooner. He's staying over at that new Quality Inn by the interstate."

I jotted this down and looked to the ceiling in gratitude. That was all I needed to know.

"Well, Clare, I appreciate all you've done and are doing on Neva's and my behalf. You just let us know when the offer's made."

"All right, Honey. You take care."

I didn't waste a second. A mission is a highly motivating force. I selected the ivory tailored suit that Carmen finds "stunning" on me and put on the charcoal-colored high heels, reserved in general for funerals and fifty-year-wedding-anniversary parties. I stood in front of my old, filmy beveled-glass mirror and brushed my natural curls. I felt defined, perfect as a fresh acorn.

"All right," I said to my reflection. "Now."

The Plymouth cranked without hesitation, and I headed down Mineral Springs Road toward the Quality Inn by the interstate. I'd been there once, to the restaurant part, for a luncheon with the senior citizens' choir. I parked beside an old white oak. How charitable, I thought, that a motel chain would think to save a tree. How odd that they'd give a damn. I knew that something was cooking in me. I wasn't angry with Michael Antoine for wanting to buy the land—he was, after all, just being a good American entrepreneur. I wasn't exactly mad at Clare Jenkins for believing that the demise of my family's homestead was "something exciting about to happen." Nobody was at fault, really. I knew, too, that my situation wasn't unique, that sooner or later everybody watches their family home get demolished one way or another. It's just that I felt a growing sense of purpose. It's the way I felt boarding that bus to Alanon meetings in 1957—like there's no such thing as pre-destination. If you turn your vehicle sideways in the road, the other drivers *will* stop to avoid a wreck and, at the least, will have to ask what the hell your problem is.

The lobby was spacious and well lit. Beside the front desk was a baby-blue parakeet. I smiled at it. Caged birds make me anxious.

"Hello," I said to the boy behind the desk. He looked seventeen and had one of those stylish mohawks. A gold ball pierced his left ear.

"Yes'm," he said. "Help you?"

"I'm meeting a Michael Antoine here, and I've lost his room number. Could you give it to me?"

"Antoine," he said and punched it into a computer. He studied the screen. "Room 214. It's on the other side of the courtyard"—he gestured with his hand—"right over beyond the pool."

"Could I call his room from here, please?"

"Certainly," the youngster said. "That's an in-house phone by the entrance to the restaurant."

"I like your earbob," I said.

"Earbob," he repeated, laughed, then reached to lightly touch the gold ball.

"Earring," I corrected.

"Thanks," he said. "Just dial the room number to call in-house."

I walked over to the phone. My charcoal high heels sank a bit into the plush beige carpet. I dialed 214. There was no answer. I ambled over to the other side of the lobby. An ornamental ceiling fan was overhead. Planters of wandering Jew hung near the wall of windows that faced the pool and courtyard. I sat in one of the easy chairs and considered my next move. I felt quite capable in my tailored ivory suit, and I wondered why dressing up had always been so troublesome to me. I began pondering what it'd be like to have a real job—the kind like Carmen had in that exclusive clothing store in Birmingham where you dress up and carry yourself with pride. When I waitressed after Scotty died, I wore a yellow cotton dress and apron.

I decided to go into the motel restaurant. My sixth sense told me to do so. The place was a bit dark, the color scheme a mite garish for my taste—red, gold, and black. A few late breakfasters were polishing off remnants of toast and coffee. Then I spotted Michael Antoine. I recognized his handsome face based on the binoculars view I'd gotten from Neva's van. He was reading a newspaper, dressed very spiffy, neat, and fashionable like one of those models you see in the men's-department clearance-sale leaflets you get in the mail. Setting my shoulders squarely, I went straight to him.

"Excuse me," I said.

He glanced up from his paper, then rose in appropriate genteel etiquette—a Southern man, I knew immediately.

He smiled, almost wistfully, as if to say, "How quaint of you to call."

I extended my hand. "I'm Honey Shugart. I own the Dinah Bluet estate."

He shook my hand, then held a finger up and frowned. "Cantrell?" he asked.

"No. Neva Cantrell is my co-heir. She owns a quarter of the estate."

Gradually, his eyes lost their confusion and a smile eased back over his ebony face. "Ah," he said. "Right. Ms. Jenkins mentioned your name. I'm aware of the situation, the division of the property. Have a seat, Ms. Shugart." He held out a chair.

"Call me Honey," I said.

"Beg your pardon?"

"Honey is my name."

"Oh, I see. All right. Honey. Would you like a cup of coffee?" he asked.

"Thank you. That'd be nice."

Instead of flagging a waitress, he picked up the empty overturned cup by the unused place setting, walked over to the tea cart that held the coffeepot and poured me a cup.

"How did you find me?" he asked and studied me with honest curiosity. I liked his nature. His face wasn't forested with murkiness. Rather, his eyes were bright and wide open.

"I asked Clare Jenkins," I said and tore open a packet of sugar.

He folded his newspaper, set it aside, and put an arm around the back of my chair. He was sitting in the one right next to mine rather than the one directly across from me. I found the close proximity of his body reassuring rather than disquieting, much the way it feels when Jackie is near—as if Michael Antoine was intent on treating me with the respect granted mothers and old people.

"It's a lovely piece of land," he commented.

I stirred the sugar into my coffee and cast my eyes about for some cream. Michael Antoine was up in a flash, and returned with a tiny chilled pitcher of milk.

"Thank you, hon."

"I was passing through here on my way to Chattanooga right after the holiday season—you know, up I-59 through Meridian and Tuscaloosa—and I took this very exit." He gestured toward the interstate, which was visible through the restaurant window. "I drove around town and saw the for-sale sign on your property."

"My family homestead," I said.

"Ah."

Michael Antoine sat quietly. I felt his eyes on me, and he held his arm solidly on the back of my chair. I realized that his nearness was all part of business tactics. People engaged in business meetings do hover close around tables, don't they? Studying documents, negotiating, coming to terms?

"Where are you from originally?"

"New Orleans."

"Hmm."

"You ever been there?"

"No, I don't travel."

"You stay put."

"Um hmm."

I blew gently into my cup. Steam rose and dissipated. "Your mama and daddy both still living?"

"Yes'm. They are strong folk. Good stock. My daddy's a chef. My mother is a schoolteacher."

"Close family?"

"Yes, ma'am. I see them often. I have two little boys. They love their maw-maw and paw-paw."

"I bet Maw-maw and Paw-paw love them, too." I looked into Michael Antoine's brown eyes.

He smiled. "You have grandchildren?" he asked.

"One. Her name is Robin. She's a social worker."

He nodded.

"My son Jackie's a preacher."

"I'm a lay minister," he said.

Very good, I thought. Easy to sway.

"I pastor a small congregation right outside Baton Rouge. I share the responsibility with a fellow minister, so when I have to leave on business, he preaches."

"How long have you owned Southern Trails?"

Michael Antoine looked up. "Going on seven years now."

"I like buses," I said.

He leaned back and crossed his arms. He put a hand to his cheek and shook his head, pensively, in distant amusement. "Why do you like buses?" he asked.

"They are a vital force in Southern history, don't you think?"

His married face grew a bit serious. "I suppose."

I realized he was quite young, full of the blessings of naiveté.

"And, too, buses were my only means of transportation for years on end. I didn't own a car until '71."

He raised his eyebrows and nodded.

"My sister died three months ago. She was living in the old homestead." I picked up a napkin and turned it over. "What are your plans for that part of the property?"

"The frame house?"

"Yes. But shall we just refer to it as my homestead?"

His brown eyes narrowed. I knew he was a bright, perceptive young man. I knew he was beginning to understand. He leaned forward, got a fountain pen from his pocket—he was wearing what appeared to be the same light-yellow shirt that Neva had pointed out from the van—and began drawing shapes on his napkin. "To be honest, we haven't gotten very far with specifics. Our immediate venture is simply to secure the land."

I touched his lemon-colored sleeve. "I want you to understand that I personally would welcome you heartily to the neighborhood. Do you understand?" I looked squarely at him. I wasn't sure he did understand this part. I felt he might be too young, that Birmingham to him was just a growing metropolis, a discovery, a great place to move a small business. "I just am having a hard time, though, letting go of my family . . ." I felt the armor rising in my throat that would prevent my voice from cracking. "Do you understand?" I knew he did understand this part, or at least he was enough of a lay minister to have taught his eyes to be pools of understanding.

"What do you want me to do?" he asked, evenly.

I sighed. I kicked my charcoal high heels off, under the table, and looked out the restaurant window to the parking lot. I saw a piece of the saved oak and the interstate beyond. Sunshine darted like electricity off the cars, causing that awful blinding light you're apt to experience in the hell of Alabama summers. I knew it was technically still winter, but I was aroused into a hot seasonal delusion.

"I don't know what I want you to do," I said with all honesty.

"If I make an offer, you can always turn it down," he said.

I smiled. "This is a ridiculous conversation for a buyer and seller to be having, isn't it?"

"Well, it is a rather serious undertaking for both of us, isn't it? For very different reasons, of course."

"Neva Joy Cantrell tells me it's illegal for buyers and sellers to talk. I'm dating a lawyer," I added and felt myself waxing strong in my tailored ivory suit.

"As long as we aren't making any deals," he said.

I searched his handsome ebony face. I wondered if he believed this—that we weren't making deals.

"Turning down your offer isn't all so simple," I said. "There are others involved, you know. The other neighbors."

He nodded.

"The others *want* to sell. My property is essential, isn't it, to the overall sale?"

"Yes," he said. "Unfortunately—why do I say 'unfortunately'—" he asked himself and paused—"your land and homestead is in the heart of the endeavor. We need that big yard."

"To park your buses."

"Yes."

"My mama grew strawberries there," I snapped.

He smiled, shook his head, and closed in on me, so close I could smell his breath—fresh and sweet with something kin to spearmint. "Listen, Ms. Shugart, Honey, are you here to ask me to forget this property? To not make an offer?"

"I'm not sure why I'm here," I said.

"Because I too have associates just like you have your neighbors, and I'm in too deep to just pull out without making an offer. I have partners." He took my hand. "I hope you understand that."

I put my free hand atop his so as to sandwich his hand in mine. "I do understand."

He put his free hand on the very top, completing the pyramid. "This thing must get played out." He paused. "But, business aside, you just remember that you *can* turn down the offer. Your neighbors might hate you a day or two, but it is in your hands." He gave them a squeeze.

I broke away. "I know, Michael." I looked at his watch.

"More coffee?" he asked.

"Yes, thank you."

He walked over to the tea cart, poured us each a cup of coffee, and returned.

"What denomination is your son?" he asked.

"Interfaith."

He frowned.

"I don't know what it means, either," I said.

"Is that the same as Unity?"

I shrugged. "He's got all kinds of people."

"I'm AME," he said.

I turned my high heels on their sides with my feet, under the table, and smiled over to Michael Antoine. "This property sale is causing quite a stir in the neighborhood."

He tore a packet of Sweet'n Low into his coffee.

"How so?"

I hesitated. Oh, why not? I thought. "There was a rumor that one of the neighbors was going to hire a private investigator to see if you were associated with the NAACP."

"What does that stand for?"

I tried to get a close look at his eyes to see if, surely, he was joking, but his eyes were downcast to his coffee which he was stirring. Finally, he looked up and saw my questioning face. He smiled. "I'm serious. I know vaguely what they do, but I never knew exactly what the letters stood for. Always embarrassed to ask. The N is for National. I know the CP. It's the two A's."

"Association. Advancement."

"Ah," he said.

I wanted to ask him his age, but it wasn't the appropriate moment to do so.

"How many partners do you have?"

"Two. I'm the people man. I handle business that requires meeting and negotiating."

"Well, I understand why. You are a real gentleman."

"My partners are from up there." He pointed up. "Michigan. Ohio."

"Oh."

"They'd not make it one minute with Clare Jenkins," he said.

I laughed. "I understand, hon."

"Southerners got a business language all their own. Manners and subleties come into play."

"They sure do."

"It's a languid game of bridge," he said.

"When are you making an offer to Clare?"

"I told her Friday. I'd ask you if you'd like me to wait till next week, but I guess that would be stepping off into illegality. We'd be negotiating independent of the agent."

"That's right, hon."

But I gave him a mannered, languid message with my eyes, and I knew he wouldn't be making an offer on Friday. I knew he'd wait as long as possible, as long as his partners would allow, so as to buy me time to think. We really didn't say much more, because the angels of silence began to hover nearby, and we knew we'd reached the limits of sublety. We'd danced gracefully.

13

WHEN CARMEN PICKED me up the following Wednesday to take me to study club at the church, I was seriously considering telling her about my meeting with Antoine. But she was preoccupied with the talk she was going to give that morning on the greenhouse effect.

"I hope this won't be boring," she said and glanced at her face in the rearview mirror. Her gray tendrils were especially fresh and rambunctious as if they—like Carmen—had a mind of their own. She was wearing a scarlet dress, and earrings that reminded me of stained glass—quite colorful. I reached to touch them.

"Are these the ones from Guatemala?"

"Costa Rica," she said.

"When is Paul Junior going back?"

"Probably in June. To Panama."

I stared out the window. We passed C.I.'s, the Jernigans', the McWaynes', Dewey's and the old homestead. I felt a growing sense of betrayal, and I wondered how on earth I'd be able to move through what lay ahead. If only Michael Antoine would leave town, abandon his plans, tell his partners that the land was problematic. Naturally, I knew better. I knew that pain doesn't vanish but waits patiently like a hungry beast as you approach it.

"Well, you look lovely, Carmen," I said. "I'm looking forward to what you have to say."

"Honey," she said when we pulled into the church parking lot. "What's eating at you?"

"Nothing, hon," I lied.

"I know it's related to the property. I just wish you'd say what."

She stopped her Mercedes and turned to face me, throwing her arm over the back of the seat so as to gently touch my shoulder. The sun was all over her face, making her radiant as a star sapphire.

"I met Michael Antoine."

"Who?"

"The fellow who owns the busing-tour company."

"Oh, this is news," she said. "This is news."

"Not to be spoken," I said.

"Of course not."

"It's illegal for buyers and sellers to talk."

"Who told you that?"

"Neva Joy."

Carmen waved it away. "Have you asked Judson about that?"

"No. He doesn't know any of this. He's been out of town."

"Isn't that his Chevy over there?"

I turned. Yes, there was Judson's Chevy parked by Thelma Nabors's daffodil-and-rock garden, near the Family Life Suite lot.

"I told him you were speaking today. He's interested. He's a member of the Conservancy."

She brightened. "That's wonderful! I just joined."

"He has some virgin woods."

"Oh?"

"In Winston County."

"The Free State of Winston!" Carmen said.

"What?"

"Get Judson to tell you about it. They've got quite a history up in those parts." She looked at her thin gold watch. "Better get on in," she said. She leaned over and gave me an angel kiss on the forehead, then adjusted my collar in motherly fashion.

"That's quite a punchy shade of aqua," she said of the shirt I was wearing.

"Jackie sent it from Florida."

We got out of the car.

"I know he gave his art historian, Celia, one just like it," I continued, "because she's wearing it in the most recent photos I got. She's standing on a pier beside their sailboat."

We walked toward Fellowship Hall.

"Do you think he'll marry her?" Carmen asked, holding the door open for me. A manila envelope was tucked under her arm— her notes, I supposed.

"I reckon he might marry her," I said. "But you know how they are in Florida."

"How are they in Florida?"

"They take their precious time."

Fellowship Hall was right crowded—for study club. Generally, there's only a handful of retired people for this monthly luncheon, but it was clear that a lot of the younger generation were interested in hearing Carmen.

"Would you look at this?" I said.

"Quite a flock," Carmen agreed.

"It's because of you, hon."

Carmen waved that away. "It's just the topic. Remember last month?"

Last month featured a representative from Blue Cross coming to expound on the value of carrying C-Plus on your health-care coverage. The month before was a fireman speaking on safety in the home.

Naturally, I'd had my eyes on Judson from the moment we walked in. He was standing beside the piano, admiring, with Thelma Nabors, the arrangement of purple iris that somebody had placed near the lectern. He was predictably tanned, and I wondered just how all that sunlight, in his virgin woods, had filtered itself through the hemlock grove he'd described. He was undeniably handsome, and, I knew, a warmhearted soul, despite his stubbornness in admitting God's handiwork. But his stubbornness was, I understood, part of the reason I was drawn near. A man caught in a struggle—even a spiritual one—is something to behold as long as you just study and desire it from a distance.

When he finally caught my eye, he smiled and walked toward me.

"Honey," he said, and I appreciated his restraint—the fact he didn't lay a hand on me publicly.

"How was your trip?"

"Magnificent. The dogwoods are already in bud. Everything's early this year. In a coupla weeks all heaven's gonna break loose."

I raised an eyebrow. "Heaven? Have you seen the light?"

He put a finger to my lips as if to say, Not another word along those lines.

"All right," I said. "In all seriousness, what's going to happen in a couple of weeks?"

"The wildflowers."

"Oh."

We went through the cafeteria line in the church kitchen and picked up our sandwiches, fruit salad, and iced tea. Only a few tables were set, as this was study club lunch, not prayer meeting. However, as I said, the crowd was big—a tribute to Carmen. I spotted Dewey and C.I. over at the table nearest the lectern. "Come on," I said to Judson. C.I. was busy turning chairs up to the table. I noticed that he'd turned up three rather than the usual two for Carmen and me. "Looks like you've been accepted into C.I.'s fold," I said to Judson.

He chuckled and popped a cherry, from his fruit salad, into his mouth. "Do we sing and pray at this thing?" he asked as we walked toward the table.

"No, we just eat and listen."

"Good."

I glanced around to see if Harold McWayne and Sonny Jernigan were there. I was relieved by their absence, feeling I'd be spared any discussion of the property. However, when I sat down the first words out of C.I.'s mouth were "Honey, we getting close to a sale?"

I picked up my sandwich and took a bite. Chicken salad, too light on the mayonnaise.

Carmen put a hand over C.I.'s. Her rings sparkled with color and magical power. "Please, hon," she said to C.I. "Let's not get into all that now."

C.I. looked to me for intervention, his brown eyes flat. He looked sad and lost without his cigar. In the old days, he smoked freely in Fellowship Hall, but with all the secondhand-smoke consciousness he'd been forced to leave his habits at home or in the homes of tolerant friends like myself.

Carmen kept her jeweled hand on C.I.'s while she toyed with her fruit salad. I looked over at Dewey, who was, naturally, stone-faced, partaking of his chicken-salad sandwich as if it were as serious as the Last Supper.

"How are you, hon?" I asked him.

He nodded, meaning "I'm the same as always."

The room was noisy with chatter, laughter, and the occasional distinctive cough of emphysema. Thelma, Ceil, and Buena had their needlepoint with them, and they were admiring each other's work while they ate. Brother Earl tapped his iced-tea glass with his spoon, requesting silence. He made a few announcements which I didn't absorb, since my mind was racing with Michael Antoine, the idiocy of Harold McWayne hiring a private investigator, the idea of my family homestead becoming a bus terminal, and Judson's presence at my side. I wanted to crawl up in some part of him—not his arms, but his aura, that part of him that reminded me of snow.

Brother Earl concluded his announcements and started to pray. "Sorry," I whispered to Judson. "We generally don't pray at Study Club." He didn't smile. Neither did he grimace. He just held me with his icy eyes—steady, unwavering, with the freedom allowed an old man. I matched his gaze. I didn't pray. Brother Earl went on, referring to the church in feminine terms like it was a country or a ship. "Bless her, guide her, hold her." Judson and I didn't *search* each other's eyes, like you're apt to do when you're younger. It was more like an otoscopic light that pierces right to the heart of the matter.

When the prayer was over, Carmen turned to Judson.

"Honey tells me you own land in the Free State of Winston," she said to him.

He smiled broadly. "You know about the Free State," he said. "Not many people do."

"Well they ought to," she said. "You in the Bankhead Forest?"

"Right. Near the Sipsey Wilderness."

"Well, bless my soul," she said.

Judson finished off his chicken-salad sandwich in one giant bite.

"That's the most precious land in the Southeast," she continued. "Well, in my informed, opinionated opinion it is."

"What's that?" C.I. asked.

"Virgin land," she said.

C.I. looked to me for translation.

"Never been cut, right?" I deferred to Judson.

"I'm taking Honey up there real soon," he said to Carmen.

Carmen raised her hand to Kelsey Borden, who was walking around with a pot of coffee, pouring it up for the old ladies. "I'll take some, Kelsey," she said. He poured. "Thank you, hon," she said.

"So what is the Free State of Winston?" I asked Judson.

He rubbed his hands together, and his eyes were bright. "When the South seceded from the Union, Winston County seceded from the South," he said.

Dewey looked up from his plate. A flicker of interest crossed his stoic face. "I got people there," he said.

"Who are they?"

"Name's Lawler, just like mine. We was from east Tennessee originally, best I recall."

Judson nodded and leaned forward, moving his plate aside. "I know some Lawlers up near the Lawrence County line. They own a hundred acres of the prettiest hardwood you'll ever see."

Dewey nodded. "That's us. That's my brother's family."

Judson tried to flag Kelsey Borden, then thought better of it. "Guess I ought to get my own," he said and walked toward the kitchen, cup in hand. Dewey got up with his cup and followed.

Seeing Dewey interested in something was heartening. Sara Catherine's illness had taken its toll.

Carmen began sorting through her notes.

"You nervous, hon?" I asked her.

"Nah," she said.

When the men returned, Judson settled himself beside me and blew into his coffee to cool it. "Winston County was full of independent Appalachian hill people during the Civil War," he told me.

"We're still that way," Dewey said and almost smiled.

Judson nodded to him. It was clear they liked something about each other. "Correct me if I'm wrong," he said to Dewey, "but wasn't Winston County originally Hancock County?"

"That's right," Dewey said and spooned an ample amount of sugar into his coffee. "Changed to Winston about 1858 in honor of Alabama Governor John Winston."

"Why did they secede?" I asked Judson. "Was that legal?"

He chuckled. "About as legal as the South seceding."

"They was sympathetic with their neighbors," Dewey said, "but being as they was dirt poor, they didn't have much use for the plantation owners to the south. They didn't want to fire on the flag to protect the interests of a bunch of rich folk."

"Mostly, they were just rebels, weren't they?" Judson asked.

"They—we, I should say—got a mind of our own," Dewey declared.

I could tell Dewey was feeling right proud of his heritage.

Judson turned to me. "About your question—their logic was that if a state could secede from the Union, then a county could secede from a state. Who could argue with them?"

"My daddy used to tell us they met at a place called Looney's Tavern, just north of Addison, and adopted their resolution. When it was reached, somebody stood up and yelled, 'Winston secedes! The Free State of Winston!' "

I hadn't seen Dewey this animated in years.

Brother Earl was clinking his iced-tea glass again with his spoon. "Folks, as you all know, we got a special treat today. Our own Carmen Dabbs is here to speak to us today about . . ." He searched his pocket for his spectacles and glanced down at his notes, reading the words as if they were a foreign language. "The greenhouse effect." He paused. "Carmen needs no introduction, but she did want me to tell y'all," he glanced at his notes, "that she's a new member of the Alabama Conservancy and that anybody can join who wants to." He looked at Carmen. "I believe they'll get a bumper sticker if they do, right?"

Carmen didn't answer that. She rose and stood behind the lectern in her scarlet dress—radiant, fashionable, tall and secure as a church steeple. "We all know what a greenhouse is," she began. I listened carefully because that's about all I did know regarding the topic. She went on to say that last summer was the warning sign of a worldwide climate crisis known as the greenhouse effect. Temperatures were at record highs, rainfall at record lows, and America's heartland was scorched, crops damaged. The greenhouse theory, she said, is that the world is getting hotter. Increased levels of carbon dioxide in the atmosphere were the cause. "It works like this," she said. "When sunlight strikes the earth, it radiates heat as infrared rays. Carbon dioxide in the atmosphere acts as a blanket, trapping some of the heat that would otherwise escape. Without the carbon dioxide to hold in heat, the globe's average temperature would be in the forties rather than the comfortable fifty-nine degrees."

I glanced over at Dewey and C.I., who were all ears. So were the others in the room, mainly because Carmen is an icon of wisdom in our community, having been married to a Yankee and all, plus having gone to college and having worked in the clothing store in Birmingham. Naturally, Judson was nodding at every word she said. Speaking of environmental issues to Judson was like preaching to the choir.

"In recent years," she went on, "levels of CO^2 in the atmosphere have increased. This concerns greenhouse theorists. This concerns me." She paused, folded her arms, and moved away from the lectern. "The world is getting hotter," she said. "The culprit is excess CO^2 which traps heat inside the earth's atmosphere."

She moved back to the lectern. She was wearing a pair of high heels I'd never seen before. They were turquoise with a red design that looked for the world like a bird, near the heel. Only Carmen could get away with wearing something so odd, but on her they looked the height of fashion, and, no doubt, they were.

"The sun's radiance has dropped. We *should* be cooler, but we aren't. We are emitting things into the atmosphere. Of course, the Industrial Revolution is responsible for a lot—power stations, factories, homes, cars. Burning fossil fuels makes CO_2. But there are other things too. You wouldn't think something so benign as agriculture would contribute, but it does. Bacteria generated during rice growing can contribute. Cattle generate methane as they digest. Then there's the well-known fact of chlorofluorocarbons—spray propellants and Styrofoam products."

She paused, considering. I knew what she was about to say. "We still use Styrofoam plates for Meals-on-Wheels. We might want to explore other ways to transport food."

I looked at Judson's hands—the tanned skin that almost hid the aging veins. It was hard to imagine him kneeling to touch a wildflower. Did he actually hail their arrival?

"So," Carmen said, "the prediction of atmospheric scientists is that as CO_2 levels continue to rise, so will temperatures. By the year 2050, it may be three to nine degrees warmer. Of course, we will all be well into angelhood by that year," Carmen said. Everybody chuckled good-naturedly. "But our grandbabies will be our age—still, God willing, alive on this earth. Now, what scientists *can't* predict is exactly what geographical regions will be affected. The warming won't be evenly distributed. It may, in fact, be beneficial to Canada or the Soviet Union. Britain and most of northern Europe will get more rain. The Mediterranean will be drier, and so will North Africa and southern California, according to some predicters. But, now listen to this: the American Midwest, the world's safety net against starvation, may well suffer as much as or more than anybody. In a warmer world, winter snow will melt early. An early spring. Did you see it this year? Did your forsythia start blooming in December? But the longer growing season will be marked by drought. The summer soil will be drier."

Carmen looked at her notes, then at her watch. "You may be thinking, But crops grow faster in greenhouses. True, they do, but everything is controlled in an artificial greenhouse. Experimental greenhouse labs show that *weeds* grow fast, too, much faster than the crops. There will be more pest damage in a hotter world." Carmen stepped away from the lectern again. "Down in Tuskegee," she said. She looked over toward the far-left table. "Nettie Saucer has a son who teaches there." Nettie smiled in appropriate pride. Nettie's got a bowl-shaped hairdo. "Anyway," Carmen continued, "the Tuskegee health nutritionists have shown that sweet potatoes grown at high CO_2 levels have less protein, are less nutritious. Now, we can't have that, can we, Thelma?"

Thelma, as I've said, makes an extraordinary sweet-potato casserole.

"Plants *can* adjust, but can they adjust to a greenhouse world?" Carmen leaned forward, over the lectern. "So what can we do?" She paused. "Are there alternatives to fossil-fuel plants? Is nuclear power an alternative? Some of my new friends at the Conservancy may cringe at this idea, but we can't afford a knee-jerk attitude against nuclear power." I glanced over at C.I.'s sweet flat brown eyes. I wondered if he was still following. "One thing we can do is recreate the carbon cycle by planting forests to absorb CO_2 again. Our tropical rain forests are being destroyed. Not only are we destroying the trees which could save us, but the process, the fact that the land is being cleared by burning, further contributes to CO_2 levels in the air. Developing countries must avoid getting hooked on fossil-fuel dependency, but then, that's easy for us to say, isn't it? Let me close by saying that the research being done—the knowledge of science—must be transferred to policy-makers. The Alabama Conservancy which I very recently joined is working to educate us about the use of Styrofoam products. We are trying to save trees and to protect valuable land. We'd like to see you at our next meeting. Thank you."

Now, of course, Carmen received a standing ovation, and I gave her jeweled hand a big squeeze. "That was real good," I told her.

Judson shook her hand. He was beaming with approval for what she'd said. He turned to me. "Got your car here?"

"No, I'm with Carmen."

He hesitated.

"You coming back to prayer meeting tonight?" I asked him.

He ran his hand through his frosty curls. "Well," he sighed. "Almost too much church in one day. Goes against my grain," he said.

"Oh, come on. You liked this, didn't you?"

"Well, sure, but this wasn't church. This was truth."

I shook my head. "Aren't we standing in a church?"

"I mean the content. It wasn't propaganda."

I put a finger in his face. "I bet it was to some people here. I bet it was to Kelsey Borden. He belongs to the National Rifle Association and the Republican Party and all those strange groups. I bet he thought this was nonsense, except for the nuclear-power considerations."

Judson chuckled.

I shook my finger. "But that's the good thing about this place. You don't have to agree. Now, you go into those suburban Birmingham churches and you might find intolerance, but not here. Not on either side. If Kelsey wants to carry a gun to prayer meeting, I still love him, because he's part of the family."

Judson backed up, hands in front of his body, in mock retreat. "Forgive my ignorance," he said.

I smiled and touched my palms to his. "When are you taking me to the Free State of Winston?"

His icy eyes melted somewhat. "When do you want to go?"

"When the wildflowers come, I guess. Isn't that what you want me to see?"

Carmen lightly touched my elbow. "You ready to go?"

"Yes."

"Tonight. See you tonight," Judson said.

When we pulled into my driveway, Neva's dark van was situated in the gravel drive—a big, foreboding thing. On seeing Carmen's car, Neva leaped from the driver's seat. She was wearing jeans. This was odd, I'd never seen her in jeans.

"We have an offer!" She grabbed me like an attacking animal. "We have a grand offer! Antoine has made an offer!"

14

I WASN'T EXPECTING Michael Antoine to *not* make an offer, nor did I feel that this offer now was premature. After all, he'd waited five days past his original target date. I knew the ball was headed for my court. I simply wasn't prepared for the velocity of it all. The ball caught me off guard. Maybe I'd been staring too pensively into the light of Carmen's greenhouse words or Judson's physical presence. I just know I felt suddenly old, weary, feeble-spirited—so much so that I didn't even invite Neva in. I thanked her, there in my small yard, for bringing me the news, and I went inside, saying I'd call Clare Jenkins directly.

I changed into my favorite things—Dinah's royal-blue slacks and a ragged old sweater the color of oatmeal. I decided I wanted some fresh-squeezed orange juice, because I knew fructose to be a pick-me-up. Jackie had brought me a big burlap bag of citrus fruits when he flew up for Dinah's funeral. I cut three oranges in half and squeezed them into an iced-tea glass. I took my drink to the backyard and settled myself in the hammock. I had a view of Dewey's yard. I suddenly desired to see Sara Catherine—not that she was ever a best friend or confidante; it's just that I felt unspeakable curiosity over her, and I wanted the advice of a woman who had existed in a dark place for the past several months. She'd hibernated. She knew, I supposed, nothing of the pending sale, of Michael Antoine, the neighbors' frivolity over growing rich, the fact I was seeing Judson. I stared at her window, hoping for a glimpse of her dark silhouette. She didn't appear. I kept waiting in my hammock, orange juice in hand, for the sight of an agoraphobic woman or some other kind of angel. It was no use.

My despair was heightened by the fact that the redbud trees were beginning to bloom, and the quince that lines the pasture-land fence where the horses stay was profusely flowering. Spring was here. There's never adequate warning, and what with this greenhouse-effect business, soon we'd have no winter at all. The seasons were bleeding over into one another—summer heat crawling into November, spring tiptoeing backwards into February. I and my personal season, winter, were moving into extinction. There was no place to hide from the creeping ivy, the kudzu, the vines of summer. I like to be cold. I like to see the patterns of tree branches, the truth about the lay of the land, a dormant garden, a stiff wind. Who wants to relax in a hammock with a mint julep or a glass of orange juice with apple blossoms overhead? What am I and who am I unless braced, cold, on a mission with wind in my face? I was thinking those things. I believed those things at that moment. I was missing Scotty.

I went inside and got my reading glasses from the spice cabinet. They were behind the vanilla extract. I called Clare's number and sat at my kitchen table.

"Clare Jenkins, please."

"Yes. Hold."

"Clare Jenkins," Clare said.

"Clare, this is Honey."

"Three hundred forty thousand!" she exclaimed.

I looked at my hands. I let them do a light dance on the wooden table.

"Can you believe that, Honey?"

"No, I can't," I said, all flat. It was hard to muster any delight.

"It's true," she said. "Now, of course that's just for the Dinah Bluet estate. I haven't contacted the others yet, because I'll need first to see if you and Neva will accept. As we've discussed, the enterprise must include your property."

"Um hmm."

"Now, Honey, this is, of course, up to you and Neva Joy. I realize the property's original estimated value was three hundred fifty thousand, and this is ten thousand short, but believe me, you will *never* do better than this. But," she sang, "it's your decision."

"All right, Clare." I drew a rectangle around the figure 340,000 on the back of my yellow-pages directory. I took my glasses off. "When do I have to let you know?"

"Well, as soon as you want to." She paused, and I heard the jostling of ice. "I've already spoken with Neva Joy, as you know. She's given me the green light, but the final word is yours." Clare paused again. "I wouldn't counter with the full three fifty. That's asking for trouble."

"All right, Clare."

I hung up.

I went to the refrigerator, opened it, and stared at the milk, cranberry juice, cottage cheese, and vegetables. I closed it. I went to the pantry, but I simply could not interest myself in baking. I didn't want to prepare a covered dish for prayer meeting. I didn't want to go. I was reasonably certain that Neva had probably already informed C.I., Dewey, Sonny Jernigan, and Harold McWayne of the offer. I did not want to see Harold McWayne's gray flattop and hear his report on the private investigator's findings regarding the NAACP. I didn't want to pray or sing. I wanted to see Judson. I looked his number up in the directory and dialed. He answered on the first ring, and I looked to the ceiling in gratitude.

"This is Honey."

"I knew it was going to be you."

"Ah!" I said. "More mystical by the minute are you becoming, Judson."

"What's up?"

"An offer."

"Oh, Honey, I'm sorry," he said quietly.

I felt the armor rising—I was so touched he knew to be sorry rather than happy and interested in figures.

"Meet me at the old homestead," I said.

"I'll be there in half an hour. I need to walk the dogs, then I'll come."

"I didn't know you had dogs."

"Black Labs. Gretchen and Lincoln."

"Bring them with you."

"They might destroy the place."

"Better them than a bulldozer. Bring them."

I don't know why I wanted to see the dogs. Scotty had hunting dogs. I liked those dogs. They were more reliable, certainly more predictable, than Scotty. After he died, they lived on with me for a spell until one of Scotty's buddies asked to take over their care, and I acquiesced.

I kept the ragged oatmeal-colored sweater on and dabbed my lips with peach lip gloss Carmen had given me. I brushed my curls vigorously, shook my head to let them establish their own destiny, got my keys, and left.

When I pulled into Dinah's driveway, I saw that Wash had indeed been taking his job seriously. The lawn was raked, new pine straw was in the beds, and, bless his heart, Wash had planted some pansies. I felt heartened as I went inside.

I pulled Dinah's ornate drapes open, making room for all possible light. I dusted the piano, grandfather clock, secretary, and tables. I made a pot of tea and wished I'd brought the frozen sweet rolls from my place. I realized, despite my resistance to it, that spring was here and I best open all the windows, because the old home was a mite stuffy. In the dining room, the breeze caught the ivory sheers by surprise and blew them forward in one grand billow. Something in me rose, too, then subsided as the wind let go.

Judson didn't knock. He merely appeared in Dinah's kitchen, toting a box of donuts.

"We are on the same track," I said. "I was wanting something sweet." I heard scratching, and I realized the dogs were on the sleeping porch. "Let them in," I said. Judson looked at me incredulously.

"Are you sure?" he asked. "They are wild. Especially Lincoln. He's discovered he's a boy, and he's hell-bent on claiming the world."

"I can handle him."

Judson opened the back door, and the dogs bounded through the kitchen like euphoric maniacs. A new place.

"Let them be," I said. "They'll soon see there's nothing very interesting here."

"Don't be so sure. They've never seen angels before."

I smiled and gestured for him to have a seat at Dinah's table. "Wait," I said. "Let's go to the dining room." Judson stopped, as he had his first time in the house, to admire the secretary and the china cabinet. He peered in and studied the intricately designed stemware.

"What are you going to do with all this? Where are you going to put it?"

"I haven't decided." I felt myself sinking a bit. "I haven't decided anything. Here," I said. "Have a seat. Tea?"

"Yes."

Judson took off his beige jacket with plaid lining. His snowy hair was windblown, his icy eyes a tad more blue than I'd recalled. "Get some of those good plates for the donuts," I instructed him, nodding toward the china cabinet.

I brought in the tea. I peeked into Dinah's bedroom. The dogs were lying on her hooked rug, panting.

"The kids are settling down," I told him. "How old are they?"

"Ten months."

"Just pups," I said.

"Yes." He sipped his tea. "I got them when I retired last summer."

We both took bites of our donuts. The wind blew the ivory drapes once again. They rose in full. Judson stopped chewing and stared at them in wonder. Our eyes met.

I sighed. "The first thing I need to tell you about myself is that I've never liked spring."

Judson smiled. "Should I take notes? Is this a deposition?"

I ran my hand over Dinah's damask tablecloth. I glanced over to the drapes. "I'm beginning to reconsider. I never knew a breeze could be so heartening."

"You'll see," he said.

"See what?"

"You'll see when you get to the woods. Spring in the city *is* depressing. Those pink contrived azaleas. It's like globs of bubble gum all over the place. You need to see some trillium and blood-root."

I drank my tea and stared at the big lawn, Papa's hickory trees, the great expanse of cleared land. "Judson," I said and leaned forward, "I do not want to sell."

"Then don't."

"It's too late."

"No it's not."

"I should never have rezoned."

He got a pocketknife from his jacket and began doing something to his nails.

I set my plate aside. "I don't care about money. I don't like money. I have no use for money."

Judson was silent. He held his big hand out, examining his fingers.

"If only Neva weren't involved. If only the whole neighborhood weren't involved. It couldn't be worse."

"Yes it could."

"How?"

"If you weren't the kind of woman who ultimately gets what she wants."

I looked at him. He wouldn't look at me. He was acting preoccupied with his hands. He was being a lawyer.

"What do you mean by that?"

He shrugged. "I mean that, in the end, you'll make a good decision."

"I don't know what to do!" I cried.

"What are your options?"

"I don't know."

"Yes you do."

"What?"

"There are only two, aren't there?"

"What?"

"Either yes or no. Yes, I accept. No, I don't. Well, three actually, if you're considering a counter."

"Clare says don't counter."

"Good. Then you're back down to two."

"If I say no, the others will never forgive me."

"Have you ever given a damn what the neighbors thought?"

"Yes," I said and felt the armor rising.

"When?"

When I was married to a drunk man who screamed all night! I wanted to shout, but whenever I thought of me and Scotty in Judson's presence I conjured up the picture of him and his rich Montgomery artist wife traipsing down to the art museum in finery and fashion. This made the making of any disclosures about my back-alley past existence out of the question.

"Who are you most concerned about?" he asked.

"Neva."

"Why?"

"It'd break her heart to forfeit all this money."

"What's she planning to do with it?"

"Build a lake house next to the lots she bought her twins."

Judson chuckled. He crossed his tanned arms and leaned over the table a bit. "What about that fellow with the flattop?"

"Harold McWayne. He's the one who hired the private eye."

"You care what he thinks?"

"Not especially."

"Who's the other fellow, the one I met at prayer meeting who's got the nervous wife?"

"Sonny Jernigan."

"Care about him?"

"About like Harold, I guess."

"Then that leaves Carmen."

I smiled. I knew Carmen didn't care one way or another. I knew she was waiting for me to decide. I knew she probably didn't want to move but was willing to do whatever I chose. "Carmen's no problem," I said.

"She doesn't care about the money?"

"Lord, no."

"Well?" he said.

"So what if I say no to this? There'll be other offers down the road, probably real soon. Clare says this is hot property."

Judson nodded. "That may be true."

"If only I hadn't rezoned." I stared at Dinah's secretary. "Hey," I said. "Can I have this zoned back residential?"

Judson leaned back and studied his hands again. "I guess you could make the request."

"Do people ever do that?"

"It's not come up since I've been on the Board. There would be some big questions asked—about your reasons, motives, etcetera. It might not be pleasant. Those neighbors might make a scene."

I felt myself growing weary. There was no good end in sight.

"You know," he said, but would not make eye contact with me, "you could just leave it commercial, jack the price sky-high, lean back and forget it awhile." He then looked at me. "Are you wanting to live here?"

"No."

"You just don't want to see it commercialized."

"I don't want to see it torn down!"

"And you assume they would tear it down?"

"I know this Antoine fellow would."

"How do you know?"

"He told me so."

"You talked to him?"

I hadn't meant to disclose this. "Is that illegal?" I asked him, my breath catching. "Did I break the law?"

Judson waved it away. "Don't worry about it. You didn't talk money, did you?"

"No."

Judson's ice-blue eyes narrowed. "Where did you meet him?"

"At the Quality Inn."

He raised an eyebrow.

I started laughing, and once I started, I couldn't stop. I laughed until my side hurt, then I felt myself trembling, and a light vertigo overtook my armor until it was beyond my grasp and I was crying.

15

I USED TO imagine scenarios so devastating, so horrid, as to make me cry. But unceasing deaths hadn't done it. Losing my home-stead, or the possibility of such, to a busing-tour line hadn't done it. Of course I'd never considered the idea of laughter, something so simple as merriment. Anyway, Judson, of course, hardly no-ticed the tears. I knew that he'd probably seen a lot of women cry—in his office, during the Movement, in his own household. Maybe his wife cried as she signed the divorce papers, though Jackie told me that this act is generally done in the most stoic manner. The experience left me feeling a mite queasy; indeed, the entire past several months had transpired like a dream in which you see yourself moving in familiar surroundings yet you feel displaced, a stranger to your own skin.

So when Judson suggested that we go up to his virgin woods, that it seemed a good time to go since I faced a great decision, I wasn't taken aback or hesitant.

"The wildflowers won't all be out," he said and took an-other donut from the bag.

"Will we go in the Jeep?" I didn't know what else to ask.

"Of course."

"When are we going?" I looked at my watch. "Prayer meeting starts in an hour."

"We can go in the morning if you'd like or wait to Monday if you'd rather."

I cast my eyes about. The sun was playing in my water glass, making a dancing pool of light on the ceiling. Dinah's house was quiet. Mineral Springs Road hadn't yet filled with rush-hour traffic. It was deep afternoon when shadows begin to grow, light becomes gold, and you realize that this particular day has reached its destiny. Like old age, it's not yet over, but there's no denying the time of day.

"I'm not going to prayer meeting tonight," I said. "I don't want to pray about this."

Judson chuckled and reached over to pat my hand. "It's really nothing to pray over," he said.

"I need to tell somebody I'm not going."

Judson nodded.

"I'll tell Carmen."

"All right."

But already, in my mind, I was feeling I ought to call Jackie. I needed *permission*.

When I did get home, with plans for Judson to pick me up the next morning at seven, I called Carmen.

"This is Honey."

"You ready, love?"

"I'm not going tonight."

"Are you ill?" she asked. I never miss prayer meeting.

"No, I'm not ill, Carmen. I'm going to Winston County with Judson tomorrow."

"Oh, that's great, Honey. You'll love it. Get him to show you Bee Branch."

"What?"

"That's where that big tulip poplar is."

"Oh, yes, he mentioned a big tree one time."

"Call me when you get home," she said.

"I'm going up there in order to make a decision about the

offer." I paused. "You don't care, do you, one way or the other about the offer?"

"No, Honey. I don't care. Whatever you want is what I want."

"You'll stand beside me?"

"Of course, hon."

I felt my eyes tearing up. It was miraculous—twice in one day.

I made myself a cup of chamomile and called Jackie.

"Hello, Mother," he said, his voice all deep and calm.

"I cried two times today," I blurted.

Jackie didn't say anything. Then he made a strange noise—like he was clearing his throat. Finally he said, "What's the matter? What happened?"

"Oh nothing, hon."

"Mother, are you all right?"

"I'm fine."

"Why did you cry?"

"I was laughing so hard I cried."

"Well, what was funny?"

I started laughing. "The idea of me rendezvousing with a black man at a Quality Inn."

Jackie said, "Just a minute, Mother," covered the phone with his hand, and I heard muffled mumblings, and I visualized him turning to Celia, his art historian, with something like "Mother's gone off the deep end," with the word Alzheimer's crossing his mind.

"Jackie," I said. "Jackie?"

"Yes, I'm here."

"I'm sorry, hon. It's a long story." I sat on my red stool. "It's the longest story in the world. What's happened is that a man named Michael Antoine who owns a busing-tour company has made an offer on Dinah's property. He's also trying to buy up all the land on Mineral Springs Road including the horseshoe here—my place and Carmen's house. He's made an offer, and I've got to make a decision. I met this man, Michael Antoine—he's black—at the Quality Inn just so I'd know him personally, and I've been dating a retired lawyer named Judson Carmichael who was involved in the Civil-Rights Movement, you'd approve of him, and he wants to take me to Winston County—they call it the Free State of Winston—to show me his virgin woods so I can make a decision."

Jackie was silent.

"Hon?"

Jackie cleared his throat. "I'm here," he said.

"Well, what do you think?"

"Well, Mother," he said in his most pastoral of voices. "How do you feel about all this?"

"How do I *feel*?" I sighed. Oh, Jackie's got a peculiar way of surveying a situation.

"Jackie, I'm going to the woods with a lawyer."

He started laughing. It was heartening to hear Jackie laugh in such an obviously deep way. Preachers have to take life so seriously.

"Hon?" I said. "Is it a funny idea? Do you think it odd?"

He tried to stop laughing. "No, Mother," he laughed. "It's not odd. People go to the woods all the time, don't they?"

"But with a retired lawyer?"

"What's his name?"

"Judson Carmichael. He was on the Zoning Board. That's how I met him."

"Well, are you involved with him?"

I sipped my tea, then reached up to get my reading glasses from the spice cabinet. I didn't have anything to read, but I felt the situation called for glasses. "Am I involved with him?" I repeated. "Well, yes, I suppose I am involved. He's giving me advice." This wasn't true.

"So he's acting as your attorney?"

"No, he's just a friend. Listen, Jackie, hon, I just wanted you to know that I'm going, and I also wanted to let you know that I accept Celia, and I think art history is a legitimate calling in life, and I'm glad she cares for you, and I have accepted your and Ellen's divorce."

I didn't intend to say all that. I didn't even know it was on

my mind until I said it, but once the words were out I realized
I believed it and never had until that moment.

"Well," Jackie said. "That means a lot to me, Mother."

"Jackie," I said and stood up so as to feel an accurate sense
of myself. "My life is changing."

"I can see that," he said.

"Angels are nearby."

"Well, give them my best," he said. "I'm serious."

I knew he meant this.

Judson arrived the next morning at seven sharp with some
sausage biscuits and coffee from the Dairy Queen. I was waiting
on the porch. Carmen had come over at six-thirty to bring me
something to wear. "It's for spring," she said when she handed
me the ivory-colored sweatsuit. "It's lightweight." She said she'd
bought it for herself and it might be a tad big on me, but it didn't
matter. "You look so fresh in ivory," she said, fluffing my curls
and examining my lips, which meant, Be sure to wear lip gloss.

I got into Judson's white Jeep. I'd never ridden in a Jeep
before. I felt uneasy but willing to try to blend in with the am-
bience of a vehicle meant to blaze trails.

"Here," Judson said and gave me a sausage biscuit. He
showed me where to put my coffee cup—in a special device that
was an appendage to the dashboard. Judson had on jeans and his
beige jacket with the plaid lining. He was also wearing a safari-
style hat.

"Sleep well last night?" he asked.

"Yes."

"Good."

I took a sip of coffee. "I called Jackie, my son, to tell him
where I was going."

Judson was devouring his biscuit like a hungry animal.

"I felt I ought to tell him where I was going," I went on.

Judson nodded, then pulled some sunglasses from his pocket.

"Do you ever call your daughter to tell her your plans? Do
you ever feel you ought to let her know?"

Judson wadded up his sausage-biscuit wrapper, tossed it in
the sack, and turned briefly to me so that I had one quick glimpse

into the blue ice of his eyes. He smiled. "Usually, when I call her, she's chasing her boys or preparing lectures or harboring aliens."

"Is she interested in your life?"

"In a way," he said. "But she doesn't fret over me. Why? Does Jackie?"

"No. Maybe it's different with a son, though. I sometimes feel I'm obliged to get his, ah, *permission?*"

Judson stopped at the red light by the interstate ramp and turned to me again. "This is something out of the ordinary, going up here with me?"

"Well, certainly."

Judson got a map from the glove compartment. "I know where we're going, but I thought you might want to follow on the map. You like maps?"

"I never need them."

"No?"

"My life is stationary, Judson. There are many things you don't understand about me."

The light changed to green. Judson headed up the interstate ramp.

"Where are we going?" I asked and looked at the map.

Keeping a loose eye on the road, Judson traced his finger along the map. "Up Highway 78 here, through Jasper and on up to Double Springs. That's the county seat of Winston County." He took my hand. "Tell me what I don't understand about your life," he said and held my hand hard. "I want to know." He gave me a piece of his eyes. "It excites me to know."

I found this an odd yet pleasurable thing for him to say. "It's *not* exciting," I said. "That's the point."

"But the ordinariness of it is part of the excitement," he said. "You intrigue me. You know, a diamond in the rough, that kind of thing." Color rose in his handsome face. "I'm serious," he said.

I sighed. "Well, for one thing, I've never been anywhere. This map is like trying to read a foreign language. Sure, I understand where things are. I have a good sense of geography. It's just that I have not traveled these roads. I stay put."

"But you're not heavily anchored, I take it."

"What do you mean?"

"You seem up for anything. You're not weighted by your existence."

I smiled. "You referring to my spare belongings? My 'minimalism'?"

"Well, I guess so. But also, you're free-spirited."

I considered this. I took a bite of my sausage biscuit.

"Judson," I said. "When I tell you I was married to a drunk man, do you understand?"

"Probably not. I've never been married to a drunk man."

"But I guess it's more than that. We didn't live in the city, you know. We moved here and there. We had a gas station—just one pump. I kept it most all the time, especially when Scotty was hunting or drinking. I wore slacks long before they were fashionable. Scotty didn't want my petticoats showing when I pumped gas into pickups."

He smiled and kept his eyes on the road. "A nice thought," he said.

"What?"

"You operating a gas station."

"Just one pump," I reminded him.

"Well, is that all? Is that what I need to understand about you?"

To be honest, I wasn't sure what I felt so constricted over. It was a subtle, amorphous memory of myself sweating demurely on that loveseat in Alabama summers, mad with passion and outrage over this man I adored with the encumbrance generally reserved for motherhood—that blind, instinctive love that enslaves, thrills, and rakes the surface of your soul's skin until there's hardly a thing left but the *object* of your affection, and not the affection itself. Trying to explain this to Judson was a seemingly insurmountable task and, at the moment, I still felt I had to. I hadn't yet realized that it wasn't necessary because I hadn't yet been transformed into something new. Once a butterfly becomes a creature of flight, he hardly, I suppose, frets over his days as a caterpillar.

The land had become barren and, in places, grotesque. Strip-mining had been, until now, only a mental concept—one that caused me to want to defend miners. Now I saw the source of Judson and Carmen's anguish. The earth was blown to bits, barren, gray.

"It's like being on another planet," I commented.

"Yes," he said. "A horror movie, maybe? Seeing it from a distance," he said and pointed to a bald spot in the hill up ahead, "is different from seeing it up close like this." He gestured out the window to the granite-colored land.

We drove up through the mining communities. The old pick-ups, row houses, one-pump gas stations, and brawny people were, for me, symbols of nostalgia and stoic survival. All Papa's family were once miners. We stopped at a traffic light by a general store, and I studied a woman who was sweeping gravel from the concrete stoop by the screened door. She was barefoot and wore a trucker's cap. A miner's wife. She knew secrets dark as coal.

"Now watch what happens when we leave Walker County and enter Winston," Judson said when the light turned green and we headed on up the road.

"What's that?"

"The economy is forest-based rather than mineral-based. Some agriculture too."

He was right. Fields of horses donned the landscape. A sign read, "Quarter Horses, Broke and Trained." The earth was green rather than gray. Purple thrift bloomed against big rocks. Cherry trees and wild crabapple cast a pink spell upon farmhomes. Fences, painted snow-white, framed vast pastures. "Welcome to Poplar Springs," the sign said. Judson told me we were in the Bankhead National Forest. "All over there to the right is a big sea of forest. It'll always be there." Judson shifted gears, and the jeep coughed a bit, then sprang forward, carrying us deeper into tree shadows. Occasionally, the land opened up to fields, but then it'd narrow once again to a tunnel of hardwoods.

"Look," I said. It was a big dilapidated log building with THE FREE STATE OF WINSTON lettered across one side.

Judson smiled. "We're almost to Double Springs," he said.

The town was small and, unlike my own hometown, apparently hadn't lost its flavor to progress. The county courthouse reminded me of a fort—strong and manly. There was a diner. A few flattop stores were open, but the streets were empty and carried a windswept aura. "Something about this place gives me a Wild West–frontier kind of feeling," I commented.

"I understand," Judson said.

We drove on, and once free from the town, we began making a series of turns that carried us into the shadows of trees, and I knew we were probably getting close to our destination. Judson stopped the car at a fence, unlocked a gate, and we drove right through a meadow where a few fawn-colored cows grazed languidly. Almost abruptly then we were once more taken into a heavy forest, and the reality of where life had carried me—into virgin woods with a man I desired—caused me to call on my armor, but it wasn't there anymore and I knew it.

The cabin came into view. Judson stopped under a canopy of water oaks, and I realized we'd never left the road because we hadn't *been* on a road for quite some time. We'd merely been traversing a broad path in the woods. Judson parked the jeep and got an ice chest from the back. "Lunch," he said and heaved it up over the seat. I got out, stood still, and listened. All was quiet, save for a light trickle of water. "The creek," Judson said and gestured past the cabin. I'd never been so deep into forest. Overhead was an umbrella of green, causing an eclipse of the sky. The air was moist. It was all very exotic, like the tropical rain forests Carmen described in her talk. I shook my head. Judson put the ice chest on the ground and took my hand. He led me to the hemlock-lined creek.

"I've never seen hemlocks before," I told him.

"There aren't many in the Southeast," he said. "These are rare. A blessing."

I looked at him and smiled, mouthing the word "blessing" questioningly, as if to say, Who do you think sends blessings? But he put a finger to my lips and shook his head. "No church in the woods," he said.

"I didn't say a thing."

He leaned against a poplar and studied me. "You look different out here."

"*You* look like that poplar," I said.

He glanced up into its high branches.

"Tall, sturdy. Those tulips bloom in the sky. They aren't there for show, are they?"

I looked at the stream. We were standing in an obtuse triangle of land where the moving water made a slight yet distinct turn. Ferns were growing like crazy, and this season's fronds were sprouting up amidst last year's green that hadn't even died yet. Judson took my hand once again and led me over mossy rocks until we'd crossed the stream and were headed into the woods, away from the cabin.

"If we followed this a mile, we'd be in the wilderness," he said, "but we'll save that for next time. I just want you to get a feel for it today."

A host of tiny blue butterflies swept past us. Judson stopped and, not letting go of my hand, pulled me down to a kneeling position with him. "Trillium," he said. A bold maroon bloom cast itself up from the three whorled leaves. We stayed there a bit as if in prayer, then got up and proceeded. He pointed out the phlox, sorrel, and wild ginger. I recalled the ginger—the little jugs at the base of the plant—from my girlhood. "Ah," he said and extended an arm as if to prevent me from moving forward. For a moment, I thought maybe he'd seen a snake. "There it is," he said. Reverently, he knelt and touched a single leaf that was growing up from the earth by itself. "Do you know what this is?" he asked and looked up at me.

"No."

"It's bloodroot."

I knelt beside him.

"What I'm about to do is a sin," he said. "A sin against *nature*," he clarified.

"God and nature are one and the same," I said.

He peered into my eyes, and I knew he was considering a new angle, a possibility. "Maybe," he said. "I'll give that one some thought."

He snapped the bloodroot at its base. "It's so rare; that's why it's a sin to pick it, but I wanted to show you." His fingers were already stained with the red juice that bled from the stem. "The Creeks and Cherokees used this as dye and face paint."

"I have Cherokee blood," I said.

"So do I."

We explored each other's face anew, then smiled. "No, neither of us looks it," he agreed.

"On the inside, maybe?" I asked.

He took my hand, and we walked back to the cabin. It was just that, a cabin—one big room with a wood-burning stove, a table, and a quilt-covered mattress on the floor. Judson took some bread, cheese, and grapes from the cooler. He handed me a thermos of tea and two plastic cups. I poured. He spread a cloth over the table, and we sat down to eat. The grapes were ripe and sweet. We tore bread from the loaf, and he cut the block of cheese into two big pieces.

"You still haven't told me what it is I don't know about you," he said. "You were going to tell me something in the car."

I shrugged and picked grapes from the stem. "I don't even know what it was, exactly."

"The past is another country," he said.

We didn't say anything else. After we'd eaten all the grapes and most of the cheese, we drank our tea. A hint of sun crept over the table, casting a gold light on certain objects—the thermos, Judson's keys, our hands, which had, in response to our verbal silence, begun to acquire a language of their own. Judson clasped and unclasped his as if handling a ball of clay. I studied the veins on the backs of mine, drew shapes on the table, pressed my thumbs against the wood. Judson took my hands and held on hard until I was forced to meet his eyes and fathom the blue ice. There was nothing more to say, because words, in the end, can't take you the final stretch. That abstruse, elusive thing I needed to tell him about myself was, in actuality, nothing more than the fact I'd once loved a man. Liquor, premature death, and the light of old age had caused the animal's shadow to become larger than the animal itself, but it was just love, that simple—that part of me who loved a man, and who, I now understand, desires a complicated man caught in a struggle of passion with himself.

The quilt was fresh, clean, like baby skin. I knew Judson had surely placed it there the last time he was here, in preparation for me. It wasn't musty and damp like the rest of the cabin, and the fact he'd planned this—the thought of him planting the quilt here, alone—caused me to begin the soar. Once we were into it, I began to remember. I remembered that I always cried when I made love, not because it hurt but because it is what it is—no more, no less. A man, a woman, trying to escape their bodies and become angels. It's like a suicide attempt, you know— a repeated act of merciless abandon, something that Scotty and I took seriously. It wasn't sweet or kind, nor did we want it to be. We wanted to die of love, and I knew that Judson was this sort of human being, too—unsentimental and quite forthright in his desire to be solitary. I knew by his clenched fists, the way he let his hands be themselves rather than mold distractedly to fit my body. He was at his own helm, and I was at mine. His body was my horse, and mine his. But the ride you ultimately take alone.

16

I KNEW WHAT I was going to do.

I called Carmen, C.I., Dewey, and Neva Joy over for lunch the next day. I didn't see any need to involve Sonny Jernigan or Harold McWayne, the truth being I hardly cared anymore what they thought.

I rose early in the morning, fueled with readiness to act, quite capable, I now knew after my afternoon with Judson, of inheriting the wind. I baked a hen, made a broccoli casserole, and mixed a batch of homemade biscuits.

Neva Joy arrived first, chipper as a songbird, her freckled hands fluttering with anxious merriment over my pending decision. She squeezed my hands in hers as we stood in my parlor. "Oh, Honey," she said. "Isn't this all like a dream?" I smiled at her and lightly touched her caramel-colored curls. She was just a girl, in my eyes. The dream she fancied was only a fragment of a larger vision she'd not yet beheld—the grander scheme of her life. One of the most painfully poignant things about old age is watching the younger ones pass through moments of great joy or anguish and see them perceive the situation as wildly significant when in actuality it's only a small piece of it all. Isolated events don't stand on their own and can't be seen in context until way on into life when the tapestry nears completion.

Anyway, I led Neva into the kitchen and put her to work on a fruit salad—recalling the one she made with gusto the day of Dinah's funeral. She's the type you want to set to work chopping food because it channels her energy.

"Have you talked to Clare?" she asked.

"Once," I said. "Just to get the offer. I was out of town all day yesterday."

Neva wiped her hands on the apron I'd tied around her skinny waist.

"Oh?" she said. "Where'd you go?"

"To the woods with Judson Carmichael."

Neva's hands froze, and she turned to me, her mouth in a tiny O. I patted her hand. "I've fallen in love, Neva."

I felt the new sense of myself beginning to flower—the fact I'd be so bold in so intimate a revelation. Neva, on the other hand, was obviously confused and nigh near frightened. She gathered herself together, however, and began mixing the fruit into the light-green bowl I'd inherited from Dinah's kitchen. "Well, Honey," she said. "This is certainly news, isn't it?"

I chuckled.

I knew it would be broadcast news by the end of the day, and this troubled me about like a pending rainstorm on a hot summer day. The fact was, this news might diffuse the other news regarding my decision over the sale of the land.

Carmen arrived with a lemon icebox pie in hand.

"Oh, hon," I said.

She kissed my forehead, set the pie on the table, and busied herself with putting ice into the tea glasses. Carmen moves in my kitchen like it's her own, and it practically is. "Hello, Neva Joy," she said. "You doing all right?"

Predictably, Neva responded, "Have you heard the news?"

Carmen got another ice tray from the freezer. "What's that?"

"Honey's in love."

Carmen gave me a knowing expression meaning, Neva Joy and her gossip!

"Well, that's not news, is it?" she said to Neva.

Neva turned and untied her apron. "It is to me. I had no earthly idea."

Carmen sliced some lemons for the tea.

Dewey and C.I. came in together. C.I. was wearing his navy pants and red suspenders, signifying his belief that this was an "occasion," not just an ordinary meal. Dewey was wearing his general attire—nondescript, earth-colored clothes, and a stoic moon face.

"Hello, boys," Carmen greeted.

Neva, still seemingly shaken by the news of the day, tentatively held a hand up to the men. "Hi," she said quietly. The news had apparently been like a tranquilizer on her, numbing her anxiety. This was desirable, because a nervous person can spoil a good meal.

I took the hen from the oven and basted it with honey mustard. The men took their places at my table, and there was momentary awkward confusion over having a fifth person, as we were accustomed to only the four of us. Carmen gracefully took Neva's hand and led her to the place next to her.

C.I. extended his hands, and we all clasped hands as is our custom. "O Heavenly Father who art host of the universal gathering of hungry spirits at the one communal table of love," he began. Heavenly days, I thought. Where did he come up with this salutation? "Bless this meal, and make our bodies strong, our hearts eager to open afresh to new truths, foreign ideas, and forgotten people. Take this family of friends and make us one in purpose so that we may venture from this table as soldiers. Bless the tie that binds us. And, now, Father, bless this food and the hands that prepared it."

"Thank you, hon," I said.

I passed the hen to Dewey for slicing.

Carmen started the broccoli casserole.

"Neva made the fruit salad," I commented.

"Thank you, Miss Neva," C.I. said. "It's right colorful." His big belly was pressed against the table, and I noticed his cigar was missing. I felt this might be a gesture of courtesy to Neva, since she was a newcomer to our group and might not share our tolerance for secondhand smoke.

"The biscuits!" I said and rose to get them from the oven.

I made certain that small talk prevailed through the meal itself. Announcements are best kept intact until stomachs are satisfied. News settles easier when blood sugar is stable, which presented the problem of whether to tell them before or after the lemon icebox pie. I decided on the moment when Carmen was handing out plates with slices. Everybody already had fresh coffee, so as they absorbed the news they could at the same time be filling up with sugar and caffeine, causing a momentary surge of well-being.

I drew my breath in.

"I wanted to get you all together," I said, "to let you know what I have decided to do about the offer." I felt my voice begin to crack, and I feared I might once again cry. "I hope you will understand my reasons for wanting to preserve the dignity of my homestead. I intend to turn down Michael Antoine's offer. I will not make a counteroffer. I do not intend to sell—not now, perhaps not ever, but certainly not now."

Carmen took my hand, squeezed it, then began eating her pie.

C.I. picked up his coffee cup and stared inquisitively into the liquid as if strange objects were floating there.

Dewey, of course, remained unchanged, and I was grateful, at that moment, for his lack of emotion. He simply moved on with eating his pie as if nothing had occurred.

Neva, as I knew would be the case, had turned ashen and forlorn. She stared at me like I was a scary ghost. Then she put her hands to her face, and color rose in her cheeks, causing the freckles to come alive. I noticed she was wearing a black choker around her neck.

"Oh, God, Honey!" she exclaimed, and tears welled in her eyes.

C.I. frowned into his coffee and moved the cup back and forth as if the strange floating objects were multiplying.

"I knew you'd be mightily disappointed, Neva," I said.

191

"*Why* are you doing this?" she demanded.

I sighed. "I can't begin to explain this all to you, hon. It's just too early for me to sell. I probably shouldn't have rezoned in the first place, not this soon after Dinah's passing on."

"You'd never have met Judson if you hadn't rezoned," Carmen commented and ate her pie easily as if this were all not so serious.

"*He's* the reason, isn't he?" Neva cried. "He advised you not to sell, didn't he?"

"He had nothing to do with the decision, hon."

"The twins," she said. "The twins will be so disappointed."

"Neva," I said. "You need to let me finish. I may consider trying to reverse the zoning back to residential."

"Honey," she cried and rose from the table. Her nose was pink. Her face appeared on the brink of a tiny explosion.

"Sit down, hon," Carmen urged.

"Listen to me, Neva," I said. "What I want to do is go ahead and buy you out at the commercial rate. I have the money to do so. Dinah had all those accounts, as you know. You will be getting just what you would if the sale had gone through."

Neva eased back into her chair and studied me curiously. "Are you serious?"

"Yes."

Neva's face bent into a coy pose. She picked up her fork and began toying with her lemon icebox pie. "Oh, Honey, I couldn't let you do that," she said.

"Don't give me that hogwash, hon. Of course you can, and of course you will."

"Oh, Honey."

I took her hand and stared squarely into her young eyes. "Don't think it all so benevolent, though it is. I want control of the land."

Her eyes wavered, and she cast them down to her hand that held the fork that held the bite of pie.

"And I want to be fair to you," I went on.

"I appreciate that, Honey."

I looked over at C.I. and Dewey. "I hope you understand, old friends," I said.

"Of course we do," C.I. said.

Dewey shrugged and finished up his pie. "Real good," he said flatly, speaking of the pie.

"Thank you," Carmen said. "Glad you enjoyed it."

"I was wondering where we'd all move anyway," C.I. said.

"And trying to stay together was going to be a big problem," Carmen added.

"We would've had to of had our house moved on wheels," Dewey said. "With Sara Catherine in it."

I started laughing and felt myself begin to lose control. I didn't want to cry. I got up and walked to the window. I stared at the trees in my yard, the hammock, the magnolias that lined Mineral Springs Road. I tried hard to see inside Dewey's kitchen window. My desire to see Sara Catherine wasn't waning a bit over time.

I turned back to the table.

"Does she look the same?" I asked Dewey.

He glanced up from his coffee. My overhead light caused his bald head to shine like the moon.

"Pretty much," he said.

"Is she thin?"

He nodded. "She's lost some weight."

"What does she wear?"

"Dresses."

"Dresses?"

"She wears a dress—pretty ones—every morning while she sits in the rocker."

"Does she do her hair?" Carmen asked.

"She looks real good," Dewey said. "You'd be surprised. She reads."

"Oh, how marvelous," Carmen exclaimed.

"What are y'all talking about?" Neva asked. She'd gotten a compact from her purse and was powdering her tiny nose, examining it in the mirror as it turned a salmon color.

"Sara Catherine is agoraphobic," Carmen said.

"Oh? I have a friend who's anorexic."

"Hmm," Carmen said.

"All she'll eat is raisins. Those gold ones. What're they called?"

"Anybody want more pie?" Carmen asked.

When they'd all gone home, I called Wash. His wife, Mary, answered. She told me Wash wasn't there. I asked her if he was still using Monday for his lawn day at Dinah's. She said he was, and she thanked me for the hefty check I'd been mailing them on the first of each month. I told her that I hadn't seen Wash because I was always busy on Mondays, but that I wanted to thank him for planting the pansies and laying new pine straw. I also told her I'd plan to meet him up at Dinah's next Monday to reimburse him for the pansies and pine straw.

After the phone call, I began tidying up the place. I emptied the leftover fruit salad into a Tupperware container and washed the light-green bowl I'd inherited from Dinah. It's a special one—old-fashioned, with raised birds and clusters of berries. I knew I hadn't sensed Dinah's presence since she'd died, which wasn't entirely settling. Generally, when somebody dies, her angel-form hovers nearby for a spell. Driving in your car alone, you scream in grief at the innocent blue sky and immediately your voice is absorbed rather than cynically echoing back, and you're comforted. This absorption that you sense is the angel hearing your plea, which is usually, "Dinah, where *are* you?" or "I love you, Mama," or *"Speak to me,* Scotty." Or, maybe—this happened to Carmen after she lost her brother—you're standing there washing dishes, crying perhaps, and suddenly a halo lights your hands and a sweet glow dances all over your body. This is a creative kind of angel (Carmen's brother was a writer) coming to you when you're engaged in a simple, domestic task—so as not to scare you.

On many occasions, Papa has come to me in dreams with special messages about Jesus—still trying, I suppose, to make my spiritual side more in keeping with traditional Christian belief. I listen, naturally, because Jesus is an angel, too, and I'm sure Papa has talked with him extensively about all those miracles he performed and his reaction to all the rumors regarding Mary Magdalene who happens to be my favorite character in the Bible—all that passion, devotion, and suffering. She was troubled. Now, I treasure Paul—not Carmen's Paul, but the Damascus Paul—because he was troubled, too. Some women find him disgusting, but you can be sure I would've been drawn to him like a moth to lamplight because he was so perpetually tormented.

So, anyhow, angels do come in various forms. Kelsey Borden's deceased father appeared to him once in the middle of the night and, according to church gossip, Kelsey tried to shoot him with a pistol. Naturally, it didn't work, since angels are immune to all weapons, including the abstract ones like hate. Kelsey's father ought to have known better. Kelsey, though a devout believer, is much too concrete to handle the sight of an angel, especially after midnight. A more appropriate thing, for instance, might have been this: Kelsey and his family are at the breakfast table on a cool spring morning. It's the anniversary of Kelsey's father's death, and Kelsey glances over at his daughter who, I understand, looks for all the world like Kelsey's father, and suddenly Kelsey beholds a gold aura all over that sweet face of hers. He knows it's a mystical moment, and he wouldn't dare fire at his daughter. Still, the point is that angels generally appear to people who accept mystical happenings, who believe in angels as easily as they believe the sun will rise.

I washed all the dishes. It's actually a rhythmical, soothing act, don't you think? Haven't dishwashers robbed us of something— the sight of our hands at work? Machines disturb me.

Pollen was especially heavy this year. Blessed with freedom from allergy, I got my broom and went to the porch, where I began sweeping the yellow dust up with gusto. It rose a bit, scattering itself into the yard. I surveyed the blue hydrangea, inspecting it for bloom, knowing it was too early, but what with the greenhouse effect and all, you never know. I bent to spade a dandelion from the grass, and just as I was standing back up and tossing it aside, I saw the figure. Inwardly, I jumped a bit. I shielded my eyes from the strong afternoon sun and tried to readjust my vision by squinting, as I do have a mild astigmatism. No, there was no denying the reality of Sara Catherine's body, just as pretty as you please, sweeping her porch stoop. I didn't move. I feared she'd vanish if I spoke. She cast her broom side to side like a man with a swing-blade. There was grace and easiness in her task as if she were lighthearted as a robin, happy to be a woman alive with a chore at hand. I imagined her humming a song and tossing her worries to the wind. Well forevermore, I thought. I wanted some answers. I was seized with curiosity, yet I dared not approach her to ask why she was out or what it'd been like for her inside the dark, paneled rooms of her home. Did she stare at the drab olive curtains, grateful for their heaviness, their utility in obstructing the light of day? Perhaps her own fingers had made those drapes years ago. Deliberately, she'd chosen a weighty fabric free from ornament or design, pragmatically considering the fact that some-day the world might grow too bright and invasive. Privacy is right sacred, you know—a civilized need. Did she handle the objects in her bedroom, the plaster-of-paris ballerinas, the tortoiseshell combs, the tiny music box with movable parts—the boy and girl lovers whose hands draw near but never touch? Did she prepare for her-self modest and unencumbered meals? Soda crackers and juice? A solitary piece of fruit, an orange gently sectioned, all hers. A hand-ful of nuts. Something special—milk from a coconut, sliced with an imaginary machete by a man of color from a region she'd never known because of life's linear nature, the absence of a tricky in-tersection that might have led her to a more exotic state of mind.

"Sara!" I called, unable to contain myself.

She glanced up. In her apron, she looked solid as a farm-woman. She raised a hand tentatively like you do when greeting a semi-stranger.

"Honey," she called back.

"Good to see you!" I hollered.

She held her palms up, shook her head, then let her hands fall to her apron pockets, as if to say, Don't ask me where I've been or why.

I blew her a kiss, meaning, Don't worry, I've been there my-self.

17

I DROVE UP to Dinah's on Monday. My feelings regarding spring hadn't changed, but I must concede the morning was swarming with angels. I suppose the day was free from humidity, because the sky was arched overhead like a big blue dome rather than the muted low ceiling we're apt to get as the season wears on. The hickory trees in Dinah's yard cast dark elongated shadows onto the green lawn. I turned into the driveway and paused before getting out of the car. Wash was trimming the hedge. His muscled brown arms were fine as bronze sculpture. He's strong as an ox, yet his body moved in labor with ballerina grace. I don't know how old Wash is, but I'm certain he's past seventy. This sight, Wash trimming the hedge, was as familiar as morning coffee, and I loved the man not only for himself but for his place in my memory of Dinah, for the way his hands preserved the homestead.

"Wash!" I hailed.

He turned, and a smile spread like good news over his ebony face. I moved to embrace him, and he gathered me up.

"You all right, Miss Honey?"

"The pansies are gorgeous, Wash. And this bed of pine was

much needed." I began fumbling through my purse for the money I owed him.

He put his big hand on my wrist. "Don't pay me. You overpay me enough already."

"No," I said and kept searching for my change purse that held the folded bills. "Here," I said, tucking some tens into his palm. Wash wouldn't have it, though, and finally I gave up.

"You got anything to drink?" I asked him.

"Sure 'nough do," he said and led me around the corner to his pickup. He heaved a big jug from the back. "Lemonade," he said. "Mary made it this morning. I only got one drinking cup, though."

"Never mind that. I'll go in and get myself a glass. You want to come in or shall we sit out?"

"Too pretty to be inside," Wash said.

I stepped onto the sleeping porch and then into the kitchen. It was all so quiet, and that peculiarly strong light—gold as heavy syrup—caused all the objects to come alive. I ran my hands over the toaster, the mosaic-tile rooster, trivets, cabinets—all spared relics who had, like me, barely escaped the bulldozer.

Wash was waiting on the front porch, lemonade in hand. I sat beside him. He took the glass from me and filled it with lemonade from the big jug.

"Mary outdid herself," I said. "That's a lot of juice. I bet she squeezed two dozen lemons."

Wash chuckled. "Could be," he said. "She's an awfully righteous woman."

"I'm not selling the place, Wash."

He turned to me. The white of his eyes was stained yellow, and a road map of red lines led to their brown heart. Wash wasn't jaundiced or drunk. He was just old. No matter how muscled and fit was his body, the eyes knew the grave was coming.

"I thought that bus company already gone and bought it," he said.

I shook my head. "I turned down the offer."

Wash picked up a piece of pine straw. "You moving in, Honey?"

I looked up into the hickory leaves. "No, not now. Maybe someday, but not now."

"You just leaving it vacant?"

"For now."

"Moving furniture out?"

"No," I said. "I just want everything to stay as is for a spell. I've been through too much since Dinah died. I want all those things—the grandfather clock, the piano, the secretary—to stay like Dinah and Mama left them."

"Miss Dinah was a fine soul," he said. "I miss her mightily."

"So do I, Wash."

He drained his cup, rose, and picked up his hedge clippers.

"How's Twila?" I asked him, meaning his grandbaby.

"You oughta see her," he said. "She's . . ." He raised his hand up over his head.

"Tall, huh."

"Never known a woman that tall. And pretty as a evening star."

"I remember her chasing butterflies along that hedge," I said.

Wash smiled and started trimming, handling the big clippers like they were light as a pair of scissors.

"You ever considered getting electric ones?" I asked him.

"Naw. That's how otherwise smart men lose an arm—at least a few fingers."

"Where's Twila now?"

"Movin' back, matter of fact. She been in Atlanta modeling. Got a new baby. A girl."

"Oh, Wash, that's news! A great-grandbaby. Is Mary just proud as punch?"

"Yeah." He smiled. "Twila's got her a good man, too. He's studying to be a preacher up in Chicago. I forget the name of the place. He's going to be an Episcopalian. Not AME; I mean the white kind of Episcopal. Now, he's black, don't get me wrong. He just going to be a white preacher."

I smiled and sipped my lemonade.

"Twila and the baby are coming down here until he finishes up at the end of summer," Wash went on.

"They moving in with you and Mary?"

"We don't rightly have the space. Twila's looking for a place to rent." Wash stopped clipping, and I stopped sipping, and we looked at each other. I glanced around to catch a glimpse of whatever angel was hovering nearby, then I realized the angel was myself. "Tell her to call me," I said.

"Were you planning to rent the place?"

"Not until just this second."

Wash put the clippers down and cast his eyes to Mineral Springs Road, then to the McWaynes', the Jernigans', and beyond, searching, I knew, for the black neighbors that didn't exist.

I waved it away. "Don't worry, Wash. Just yesterday, a whole black busing-tour company was moving in. What's Twila and her baby compared to that?"

"You think they—those neighbors up the road—might resent you for it?"

"Wash, have I *ever* cared?" I stood up. He held his big palms in front of him, as if to say, Sorry I even mentioned it.

I stooped to get a closer look at the velvety pansies.

"Anyway," I said. "They're already probably giving me down the country for turning down the offer. Race is just an aside from the real issue."

"What's that?"

"Money."

Wash wiped his hands on his jeans, then got a handkerchief from his pocket and mopped his brow. "Twila's gonna be thrilled," he said.

"Good, good."

"She spent many a day here."

"I know, I remember. Those wiry, fine legs running amongst the hickory trees, that butterfly net."

I rose from the pansies and went inside to call Judson.

18

I'VE HEARD PEOPLE say, when searching for a new home, that they know the moment they walk into a certain place that they'll be living there. Naturally, I've never experienced this because, as I say, I've never owned a home or even looked for one. When you're moving from one rented apartment to another, you hardly have any such mystical moment or realization.

Judson's home is brick and sturdy as poplar trees. We drove up in the white Jeep and parked inside the garrison of fence that surrounds the estate. I'd driven *over* Nectar Hill thousands of times, but I'd never stood still to behold the pastures and the land beyond. I had no idea where it all led—those foothills, valleys, and fields of fresh corn. I only knew that this was a high place, especially for a woman who hadn't even been to Lookout Mountain, much less all those grand ranges out West that Carmen has seen. Judson took my hand and led me over the land. Pecan and apple orchards, old as sin itself, were getting ready to bear their seasonal fruit. Judson told me he'd not planted a garden this year because it was his first spring back here. The house had been rented to assorted kinfolk ever since his parents passed on, and he just had too much to do on the interior of the place to fret over a plow. "Maybe we'll plant one next year," he said. I told him I knew how to operate a tiller.

The front porch had a tile floor. I touched the ocher brick facade of the house and considered the desirable life of a mason—knowing your work will stand for years upon years. Judson opened the door. I suppose I'd anticipated my idea of a masculine motif—dark paneling perhaps, a brown carpet, and heavy oak furniture. Instead, the hardwood floors were polished honey, the walls were ivory—my favorite color—and maidenhair ferns grew from delicately painted containers. There wasn't much furniture—a blue sofa, a Martha Washington chair, and a rocker.

"You are a minimalist, too," I said.

Judson said he'd only become one during the past couple of months as I'd opened his eyes to the comfort of spare belongings.

"Want some orange juice?" he asked.

"Yes. That would be nice."

"Look around if you like."

"I'll save that," I told him, feeling I ought to absorb one room at a time. If Ecclesiastes is true, and there's a season for everything, then this was the time to savor. I sat on the sofa and ran my fingers over the blue material.

The orange juice Judson brought me was over ice and decorated with a sprig of mint.

"Is this how y'all drink it in the city?" I asked.

"Yes, it is," he said and pinched my arm.

"Well, it's right pretty this way."

Judson sat beside me and threw an arm over the back of the sofa. "Don't think I'm going to try to civilize you," he said.

I patted his leg. "I know you won't, hon."

I shook my glass a bit. "Look at this ice. The pieces are tiny as sugar cubes. How'd you do that?"

"I have ice trays that make little cubes."

"Well, I declare." I studied them.

"Do you like music?" he asked.

"I prefer the Broadman hymnal, but the Baptist hymnal will do."

Judson smiled. "I have some classical tapes if you ever want to hear any."

"OK, hon."

"I love to hear you sing," he said.

I nodded. "Yes, I'm blessed with voice."

"Have you always liked doing it?"

"I suppose."

Judson rolled up the sleeves of his flannel shirt. "I'm proud of you for the decision," he said.

"The land?"

"Yes."

"I'm going to rent the place to Wash's granddaughter."

Judson chuckled. "That ought to send that fellow with the flattop to his linen closet."

"What do you mean?"

"To get his sheets out."

I waved that away. "We are beyond that, hon. Even Harold McWayne's cleaned that closet."

Judson raised a frosty eyebrow. "You never know," he said. "You heard about that Klansman from Louisiana being elected to Congress last year."

"Yes," I said. "Carmen mentioned that to me."

Judson rose and walked to the door leading to the hallway. He put a hand on the doorjamb and held his mint-sprigged orange juice in the other. He took a sip and studied me with surgical precision.

"What is it?" I asked. It still shook my insides when he dissected me with those icy eyes. I wondered if it would always be that way. He went over to the one small table by the Martha Washington chair and picked up his newspaper.

"Do you subscribe to any magazines?" he asked with a serious expression.

"No," I said. "Should I?"

His face almost broke into a smile, but didn't. "No," he said. He bent his fingers against the doorjamb until his knuckles popped. He paced a bit. He was wearing old jeans and fishing boots. I liked this. Still, he looked for all the world like a lawyer—the way he was pacing all serious-like, a hand on his cheek in contemplation.

"What time do you get up in the mornings?"

"Dawn. Or earlier."

He nodded and took a sip of juice.

"You?" I asked, only because I felt it was the appropriate thing to do, to ask him, too.

"Six," he said. "You have an alarm clock?"

I laughed. "Lord, no. Why would I need one?"

He sat on the edge of the Martha Washington chair, put his juice glass on the floor, and clasped his hands together. "I want you to know I like your friends," he said.

I nodded.

"They're quite refreshing," he added.

"They're good folks," I agreed.

He popped his knuckles, then ran a hand through his lustrous snowflake hair. "Honey, there's only one thing we got to get cleared up," he said.

"All right. What?"

"It's this angel business."

"Ah." I smiled inwardly, feeling the little mischievous sprites begin to dance lightly all over my body.

He laughed a broken laugh. "It *bothers* me that I've fallen in love with a woman who sees angels."

"I've told you, Judson, I don't *see* them."

"Well, all right, you *sense* them. Is that how we will phrase it?"

"Phrase it to whom?"

He sighed and put his head in his hands as if suddenly fatigued beyond all belief. "All right," he said, color rising in his face. Anger—ah, the sweet desire of it.

"My daughter, for one," he said.

"Laramie," I clarified.

"Mimi," he said.

"Yes, Mimi."

"Well?" he demanded.

"Well what?"

"Dammit, Honey, we're old! When people talk about angels at our age, there's reason to be suspicious."

"Are you suspicious?"

His face almost broke into a smile again. "What if *I* start see-ing them!"

"Ah," I said.

He got up in my face. "When you live with someone, as you well know, you begin taking on their habits, their ways rub off on you, you even start *looking* like them."

I stood up. "Oh, and God forbid," I yelled, "that this attorney at law should see an angel! Lord, what next? Why, before you know it, he'd be believing in God and not have to be scared of dying anymore and sleep better at night and know he'd get to see his mama and daddy again someday and be like one of his wildflow-ers! Oh, the wretched idea of such!"

He turned and walked away. I heard him in the kitchen, loosening ice tray upon ice tray as if a dozen people had suddenly ordered orange juice with a sprig of mint. A door slammed. I assumed it was the backdoor. I set my glass on the small table and noticed that the coasters were all adorned with various birds—a robin, a goldfinch, a warbler, a bluebird.

I went into the kitchen. Obviously it had been remodeled during the fifties, because all the appliances were that aquamarine color you were apt to see during that time. I resisted the urge to glance into his cabinets, just to see what the plates looked like. And the pantry. What did he store? And the refrigerator too. Did he keep raw vegetables? Skim milk or two percent or perhaps buttermilk? All to come in time. All to learn. All his desires, idio-syncracies, fears, secrets, sins, visions, and scars.

I opened the door.

Judson sat on the back stoop, staring into the distance—to the pecan orchards, the cornfields beyond, the foothills, valleys, the unpaved road that connected his land to the rest of the world. I was born right below Nectar Hill. If I strained hard enough, could I see—from here—myself, in the distant past, redirecting a a colony of ants or chasing butterflies or riding that mule-drawn wagon that Papa's brother drove on his way to repair company houses when they all worked the mines? Or the day Papa coerced his buddy to swap shifts so he could plant some fruit trees in our yard? Dinah and me on our knees watching Papa dig big holes in the earth, Papa's face when he heard the explosion, knowing that his buddy would be charred black when found, Papa's guilt, my gratitude over his spared life, the fruit trees of mercy, the miner's wife left widowed, Papa poisoning the trees in order to absolve himself. Scotty leaping from a car—the first one I ever saw—wearing a bright cap, so dapper, wanting to teach me to drive, me behind the wheel, moving on along the chert surface, feeling what it was like to steer, down Mineral Springs Road, over the railroad tracks, in the shadow of Nectar Hill, the oak canopy overhead, branches breaking the sun into patterns and making the road ahead light, then dark, then light. The wheels of Alabama buses that took Rosa Parks to town, me to Alanon meetings, Carmen to work, Dr. King to jail. The one-pump gas station that carried me through the Depression and caused me to first shed my petticoats. Mama's rose garden. Papa's leg lost in the mines. Papa's wheelchair, Wallace's wheelchair, Lurleen's election, Lurleen's death, Kennedy's death, Robin's birth. The steel plant, flat meringues, squash casseroles, nursing, waitressing, polishing the silver armor, burying husbands, baking cakes, tending to wills, singing God's praise, making love with the windows open.

I sat down on the back steps, next to Judson. He turned to me, and I looked into the solid ice of his eyes, knowing that even if it never melted, I, at least, knew how to skate on it.

"Marry me," he said.

I will.

VOICES OF THE SOUTH

Hamilton Basso
The View from Pompey's Head
Richard Bausch
Take Me Back
Doris Betts
The Astronomer and Other Stories
The Gentle Insurrection
Sheila Bosworth
Almost Innocent
Slow Poison
David Bottoms
Easter Weekend
Erskine Caldwell
Poor Fool
Fred Chappell
The Gaudy Place
The Inkling
It Is Time, Lord
Kelly Cherry
Augusta Played
Vicki Covington
Bird of Paradise
Ellen Douglas
A Family's Affairs
A Lifetime Burning
The Rock Cried Out
Percival Everett
Suder
Peter Feibleman
The Daughters of Necessity
A Place Without Twilight
George Garrett
Do, Lord, Remember Me
An Evening Performance
Marianne Gingher
Bobby Rex's Greatest Hit
Shirley Ann Grau
The House on Coliseum Street
The Keepers of the House
Barry Hannah
The Tennis Handsome

Donald Hays
The Dixie Association
William Humphrey
Home from the Hill
The Ordways
Mac Hyman
No Time For Sergeants
Madison Jones
A Cry of Absence
Nancy Lemann
Lives of the Saints
Willie Morris
The Last of the Southern Girls
Louis D. Rubin, Jr.
The Golden Weather
Evelyn Scott
The Wave
Lee Smith
The Last Day the Dogbushes Bloomed
Elizabeth Spencer
The Salt Line
The Voice at the Back Door
Max Steele
Debby
Allen Tate
The Fathers
Peter Taylor
The Widows of Thornton
Robert Penn Warren
Band of Angels
Brother to Dragons
Walter White
Flight
Joan Williams
The Morning and the Evening
The Wintering
Thomas Wolfe
The Web and the Rock